THE KILKIVAN HORSE RIDE

Karin Marchen

Copyright © Karin Marchen 2023

Edited by Carrie Jones

Proofread by Rebecca Sutherland

Cover by The Illustrators

Cover design concept by Lachlan Bullock

ISBN 978-0-6481555-6-0

Callistemon Publishing

To my friend and muse. You believed in me.

Last Day of School

There is one at every high school. That boy, you know the one. The boy with that smile; the smile that makes all the girls go weak at the knees. The boy who is on the sports teams, gets awesome grades and looks lithe and comfortable in whatever he wears. At Wattlewood Grammar, Javier Evans was that boy.

In movies that boy always has a girlfriend and it's invariably the most beautiful and popular girl at school. But Javier Evans was different, he didn't have a girlfriend. As far as anyone could remember he never had a girlfriend. There was speculation that he was gay. After all, the most gorgeous guys always seemed to be gay these days. But he never showed signs of having a boyfriend either. He spent recess hanging out with a handful of his Year Eleven friends at a table in the shade of a lone tibouchina tree at the edge of the main quadrangle. The purple petals scattered about the table and lent this group an air of royalty. Lunchtime and rainy days found them in the school coffee shop at the second-best table. The best table was claimed by a hallowed group of Year Twelve students. Yet Javier Evans' group was the envy of all other students.

Each friendship group had their own outdoor zone at recess, when the students were excluded from the school buildings. The Nerd Herd occupied a secluded nook beneath a set of stairs. The Ruggers (rugby players) and their fans lazed under the jacaranda trees that arched around the main oval. The HB Mob played handball on the paving of the quadrangle except when it was pouring rain or when it was so hot and humid that their sweat made them look as if they had been standing in a storm.

Olivia McKinnon sat with the Year-Ten Drifters at tables shaded by an overhead walkway, except when she drifted off to the library, or the art rooms. Like every other girl in the school, Olivia was resigned to being invisible to Javier.

The summer air was so humid it was thick in her nostrils and lungs and she was barely able to focus on the book in her lap. She repeatedly checked her watch, counting the minutes until the bell, not because she enjoyed schoolwork, but because it signalled access to the air-conditioned classrooms where she would feel more like a human and less like a melting waxwork figure.

Olivia looked up from her book and saw her best friend fixated on Javier as he casually conversed with his buddies in the distance. "There's no point gazing at him, Mel. He's unattainable you know."

"I know." Mel sighed without taking her brown, almond-shaped eyes off him. "But wouldn't it be amazing though? I mean, imagine how awesome it would be to be his girlfriend."

"Awesome but impossible Mel." Olivia placed a bookmark and closed the book. "Keep it real, or you'll just end up breaking your own heart."

Mel slumped her shoulders, her gaze still fixed on Javier. "I suppose so."

Olivia chuckled to see her friend sit totally mesmerised. She had no problem with imagination; sometimes hers was so vivid she thought she could almost make it real. So, she let her mind wander. She imagined writing a note to Javier.

Hi Javier
I think you are perfect!
Do you like sushi?
Olivia

Olivia looked up at Javier and imagined sending the note to him, hopeful of a reply.

Then it happened! Javier turned away from his conversation, raised an eyebrow and looked right at her. As his gaze met hers, a harsh pang twisted in her stomach. His face spread into a warm, gentle, knowing smile and Olivia's insides totally melted. She gripped the bench seat to steady herself. If she wasn't sitting, she'd have tripped over her own feet and fallen into a clumsy heap. Javier looked away and resumed the conversation with his buddies, so thankfully he didn't see Olivia's cheeks flush, her book tumble from her lap onto the ground and her awkward attempt to retrieve it. At least, she hoped he didn't see.

"Did you see that?" Mel jiggled with excitement and tugged at the loose sleeve of Olivia's summer uniform dress.

"Huh?" was all Olivia could manage as she tried to right herself and restore her composure. For how long had she forgotten to breathe?

"He looked right at me!"

"Huh?" Olivia was confused. "Who?"

"Javier." Mel gestured in Javier's direction as she turned her back on him to huddle in closer to Olivia. Her ponytail swished about her shoulders. "Javier Evans looked at me, Livvie. He looked at me and smiled!"

"Wow!" was all Olivia could manage. She could have sworn Javier had looked at her, but maybe she was wrong. After all, Mel was stunning with her long, black, shiny hair, nougat skin, deep brown eyes and tall, athletic build. She could easily have a career in modelling if she chose. The benefits of a biracial heritage. In comparison, Olivia was a mouse: mouse-brown hair, mouse-brown eyes, skinny and tanned like a Siamese cat—darker at the extremities and pale in the middle. Mel pulled straight A grades, when all Olivia could muster were (mostly) Bs. Mel was an athlete, a key member of the school swim team and she was musical too. She played the piano with great proficiency. Mel would be a far more worthy companion for Javier than Olivia. There was no contest.

Olivia resigned herself to being mistaken. It was surely Mel that Javier had smiled at and the thought dragged her into a well of disappointment. She fumbled through her book to find the bookmark and tried unsuccessfully to dispel the incident from her mind.

Olivia's eyes moved over the pages of her book, but she couldn't focus her attention on the words.

Mel's phone buzzed in her pocket and she checked the message. "My mum says your mum just delivered your bag to our place." She swivelled toward Olivia, beaming with excitement. "So great that you'll spend the first weekend of the summer holidays at our place, Livvie."

"Yeah." Olivia peered up from her book. "I'm really looking forward to it."

Olivia really was looking forward to it. Mel's family always spent the summer holidays with her mother's family in Singapore, so they would only have the weekend to hang out together before Mel flew out on Monday evening. Mel lived in a spacious modern home beside the beach and the shopping centre was only a fifteen-minute walk in the other direction. Pretty much a teenage girl's dream. They always had such fun together there too: swimming, surfing, lazing on the beach, shopping, shopping, more shopping and occasionally hosting parties for a small group of friends. Olivia would have to make an effort to drag herself out of her current mood if she was to be a tolerable companion for the next few days. She was relieved when the bell rang and everyone scurried off to class. In a matter of hours, they would be on holiday for the summer and Javier would be a pleasant memory.

The last two classes were outright dull. By the last day of school, all the curriculum was taught, the exams had been completed and most of the teachers had not bothered to devise any useful amusements for their charges. Students, particularly in senior high, were left to their own devices, literally. The rules regarding use of devices were tacitly relaxed in the final week. On a brief errand to the main office, Olivia glanced through classroom windows and spied rows of students quietly engaged with computers, tablets and phones. There was the occasional wave of stifled chuckles as students distributed amusing tidbits they had found online to their buddies. Olivia reckoned a particularly funny meme could work its way through the entire student body in about ten minutes.

In the final session of the day their homeroom teacher wished them all a safe and wonderful holiday. "Hats please!" She meticulously adhered to the uniform code to the very end.

The bell finally chimed—not one of those classic school bells, but an electronic chime impersonating the real thing. Olivia couldn't get out of there fast enough and she hastened to the pickup zone to find Mel.

* * *

A scattering of students were already assembled in the shade under the peaked walkway roof at the pickup zone. Olivia made her way to the metal pole that her friendship group used as a meeting point. She was the first of her group to arrive, so she gently—after all, it did contain her laptop computer—dropped her bag to the ground and looked around for any sign of her friends.

A shiny, pearl-white SUV was parked directly in front of her. A tall, loping figure with a loose tumble of curly blond hair approached the car and casually tossed his school bag into the rear compartment. He pressed the button to activate the automatic close without needing to stretch in the slightest, then made his way to the front passenger door. Olivia froze, for even from behind, everyone could recognise Javier Evans.

Javier perched on the front seat and closed the door, then fastened his seatbelt and lowered the window. He looked directly at Olivia and smiled. Olivia's knees went weak and she grabbed the pole for support. She looked around, sure Mel must be nearby and she was mistaken again. Mel was nowhere to be seen. She looked back at Javier and his expression transformed to an amused grin.

As the woman driver, in her thirties, glanced over her shoulder for an opportunity to pull out into the snaking school traffic, Olivia pointed to herself quizzically and mouthed, "Me?"

Javier laughed and mouthed back, "Yes, you!"

Olivia just stood in stunned silence as the car pulled away and Javier's still smiling face disappeared behind the rising tinted window. She hugged the metal post closer as insurance against falling and pressed her hot cheek against the cool metal. Her stomach churned and she wondered if she might vomit.

"Is that pole as cool as it looks?" Kate asked as she ambled toward Olivia.

Olivia wiped her sweaty palms on her dress. "Yep! Would you like a turn?"

"No thanks. But if the weather stays this sweltering all summer, I reckon I'm going to spend my days alternating between our pool and the beach."

"Excellent idea!" Olivia was happy to be distracted from the mush in her gut and grateful of the opportunity to regain some composure before Mel arrived.

Olivia tried to be friendly and pleasant as she wrestled with a dilemma. Should she tell Mel what just happened and deal with her disappointment and jealousy over the weekend? Or should she let it slide, at least for now?

Summer Holiday Starts at Home

Javier watched Olivia through the closing car window until the curve of the school driveway obscured her from sight. He was intrigued by her. Many of the girls in school fancied him, but they were careless. Olivia was different. She was clear and focussed, at least toward him. Much about her was yet unfathomable and he began to burn with curiosity. Was she aware of what she was doing, or was this just another case of carelessness that he wished otherwise?

"How was the last day of school?" Charlie scanned the intersection for oncoming traffic and pulled out onto the road homeward.

"Normal." Javier checked the side mirror in the hope of one more glimpse of Olivia.

"As talkative as ever I see." Charlie flashed him a smirk then returned her gaze to the traffic. "You're lucky I don't do this for the conversation."

Javier chuckled and turned toward the rear seat. "Hello, Henry. How was your day?"

The toddler, strapped securely in the safety seat, plied a colourful, fabric book in his fingers. He met Javier's glance with his brown eyes and grinned at him until a dribble trickled from the side of his mouth.

"Nor'l," Henry said, pushing a fabric page into his mouth.

"Excellent." Javier watched a band of wet saliva radiate through the fabric.

"See!" Charlie took her eyes off the traffic and cast a quick glare at Javier. "You're teaching him bad habits. Just because you teenage boys revert to a one-word vocabulary doesn't mean boys should be taught that from the beginning."

Javier grinned at Charlie and turned backward again. "Hey Henry, can you say the word 'bossy?'"

Charlie playfully punched Javier in the arm. "Very funny."

Javier liked Charlie. Her name was Charlotte, but she hated it and preferred to be called Charlie. Javier's father chose a young second wife so, at thirty-three Charlie was closer to Javier's age than her husband's. This also meant she was more technologically proficient than Javier's father and was more adept at the lingo of youth.

"Do you have training tonight?" Charlie's smile vanished.

"Yeah. On Monday they released the results of the November selection trials and Coach wants to see how the new team plays together before everyone scatters for the holidays."

"What time?" Charlie's frown lightened. "I mean congrats on making the team again." Her brows furrowed. "What time?"

For a moment Javier thought Charlie was interested in his sport, then he realised she had another agenda. "From five until seven. Why?"

"Your father is getting together with some mates at the pub after work..."

"So, you want me home before he gets back?"

"That would be great. If it doesn't interfere with your plans for the evening." Charlie glanced at him with pleading eyes.

"The team are going to hang out at the clubhouse for a couple of hours after training to see in the school holidays." Javier was looking forward to the camaraderie, burgers, chips and copious volumes of soft drinks. Besides, every time he excused himself early, his team members chanted, "Off home to Mummy."

Coach was more concerned. He regularly asked if everything was OK at home. Javier always gave the standard response: "Normal."

But things weren't normal. There was quiet desperation in Charlie's eyes. It would go better for her and Henry if Javier was there.

"Sorry Charlie." Javier pretended to focus on the car in front until the twinge of guilt passed.

Charlie's face went pale.

"You'll be right." Javier shifted in his seat and rubbed his hands on his knees. He couldn't bring himself to look Charlie in the eye.

Charlie was silent and focussed on driving.

"It's not my problem, Charlie. I have my own life and my own plans. It's not my job to look after everyone else."

Tears welled in Charlie's eyes. Javier slouched deep into the black leather seat, looked out the side window and pretended he didn't see. "Besides, it's not like I'm going to be living at Dad's house forever. What are you going to do when I finish school and move out?"

Javier planned to stay at the clubhouse with his mates till everything had settled down at home. Heck, he even wished he could head straight to his mother's house for the holidays—a thought he once considered impossible. His mother's house was isolated but would still be way less hassle. His mother said Charlie and Henry needed a hero right now. He didn't want to be a hero, it wasn't his job to look after anyone else. He was a teenager on holidays; he wanted to move out of his father's house for good and maybe find a way to get to know Olivia. Was that too much to ask?

* * *

The pedals yielded to Javier's legs, weary and sore from training and standing about for hours socialising with his teammates. Coach had pushed the players to their limit to measure the capability of his new team and he issued each player with a card listing activities for the holiday break to develop their skills and fitness. Coach was keen that the team be ready to spring into action at the start of next term.

The night air was warm on Javier's face and the sea breeze felt cool and pleasant as it evaporated the sweat from his shirt. Javier enjoyed the solitude of the bike ride home from training. The traffic of the workday was gone and the ten-minute ride from the soccer fields to his father's beachfront home was a weave through suburban back streets toward the steady roar of ocean waves.

Javier had his provisional driver's licence, so he could borrow Charlie's car if rain threatened on a training night. His father was against him getting his licence, so his mother had paid for lessons. Both she and Charlie put in the many hours of supervision required and his mother took him to the driving test in the week after his seventeenth birthday.

The serenity of the evening ride was shattered by the tacit tension Javier sensed as he walked through the front door of his house.

Charlie was wiping the kitchen benches and the dishwasher burbled. "Shh. Henry and your father are already in bed."

Charlie looked meek and shaken like she often did when Javier got home late. Her neck looked a bit red this time. Javier rationalised that it was from her activity in the kitchen.

She was fine, Henry was fine, and his late night spent with his mates wasn't a problem after all.

The TV was on at low volume. Charlie reckoned Henry slept better if there was some background noise in the house. The evening news was rarely of interest but one headline caught Javier's attention.

Two prisoners escaped while being returned from the courts to Goulburn gaol this afternoon after their parole applications were rejected. Blake Jonston was serving a twenty-year sentence for assault and armed robbery and Damien Jonston was serving ten years for armed robbery. The father-son duo carjacked a vehicle that was later found abandoned in a nearby state forest. Police are combing the area. The public are advised not to approach these men. Anyone with information as to their whereabouts is asked to contact Crime Stoppers.

The image flashed from the stoic newsreader to unflattering photos of the two men and a banner at the bottom of the screen displayed the Crime Stoppers phone number.

"They look like an unsavoury pair." Javier's eyes never left the TV. "Glad they're in New South Wales and nowhere near us."

"What?" Charlie rinsed a sponge under running water.

"Nothing important." Javier made for his room. With that level of TV coverage, the police should have them both promptly back in custody. Certainly nothing to bother Charlie with. Javier showered and put on underwear and shorts. He fired up his computer, caught up on some emails and videos, then went to bed.

Summer Starts at the Beach

Mel led the way through the gate in their back fence, along a shaded, inconspicuous path that wound its way through the bushes and undergrowth of the dunes. The area was strewn with old, dry logs from small trees felled by wild storms. The dark, brown bark of one log was decorated with the orange fans of fungi which slowly dismantled the wood. Where sunlight penetrated, the warm, moist air smelled of roasted leaves and wood. The vegetation eventually thinned to reveal a sapphire sky, with pale sand stretching into the distance in both directions.

The two girls spent Saturday morning, the first morning of the summer holidays, at the beach. They lounged on the warm, fine sand until uncomfortably hot, then pranced through the lacework of white foam to immerse and bob about in the teal-blue waves; a sequence they repeated until they were hungry. All the while, Mel spoke of nothing but Javier.

"I've checked the school's parent directory," Mel said, "and it only lists his father at a Warana address. I checked Maps and it's near the beach. I wonder if that means his parents are divorced? Or maybe it means his mum died? I'm going to walk the beach to Warana before we leave for the airport and walk by the house. But what if I do and he's outside? I'd positively die if he saw me! But what if I don't see him? Can I last the entire holidays without seeing him?"

"Mel!" Olivia interrupted. She heaved a sigh. "Enough already!" She toyed carelessly with a pumice stone pebble, a relic of a distant, Pacific volcano.

"What?" Mel seemed unaware there was a problem.

"You're obsessed, Mel," Olivia said. "Hunting down his address and loitering outside his house. That constitutes stalking!"

Mel's smile drained and her shoulders slumped. "I guess so."

"Besides, you can't be sure he really likes you yet."

"But he smiled at me."

"That may be so, but you can't be sure until he contacts you and says so. Until then, it's just speculation." Olivia's eyebrows twinged as she realised Javier hadn't called her either. But how could he? She hadn't given him her number.

"I suppose so." Mel slumped back on her towel.

"Now, can we talk about something other than Javier this weekend please? After all, we only have two days to hang out?"

Mel tried her best. She tried her best when they ordered lunch and Mel wondered out loud what foods Javier might like. She tried her best when they shopped for clothes and Mel asked Olivia which outfit Javier might like. She tried her best when they retreated to the cool, air-conditioned cinema, but couldn't help but speculate which movie Javier might like to see and repeatedly scanned the room in case he was at the cinema too. She was still trying her best on Sunday when they were back at the beach and she closely scrutinised every blond male in sight in case it was Javier.

* * *

By the time Mel and Mrs Lawrence delivered her to Nambour train station on Monday morning, Olivia was exhausted from Mel's preoccupation with Javier and she was keen to head to the family farm. Still, there was a twinge of melancholy on the separation.

"I'll miss you, Mel." Olivia hugged her best friend farewell. "I can't believe I won't see you again till February. Do keep in touch. I want to see photos, OK?" Tears welled in Mel's eyes as Olivia pulled away. "Don't worry, Mel. It's only a couple of months. How much could go wrong in a couple of months?"

Mel managed a weak smile and helped her mother unload Olivia's bags from the car boot to the footpath.

Olivia remembered to be polite. "Thank you so much for having me stay for the weekend Mrs Lawrence. I had a wonderful time and I hope I wasn't too much trouble."

"You welcome." Mel's mum gave Olivia a brief farewell hug. "Is always lovely for you to come visit."

Olivia gathered up her bags and made her way through the turnstile to the platform while Mel and her mum drove off to prepare for their flight. Mel waved vigorously from the passenger window until they were out of sight.

The deserted train platform was a quiet refuge for Olivia who was glad to be alone with her thoughts. She propped her bags on a shiny aluminium bench seat, checked the overhead screen to confirm her train would depart at 11:27 as scheduled, then plonked herself down beside her bags to mull over the events of recent days. Though she sat in the shade of the platform awning, the heat radiated from the bitumen and warmed her skin.

Olivia hadn't told Mel the truth about Javier and she was plagued with guilt. Still, he hadn't called or emailed her either, perhaps because she hadn't given him her contact details, or perhaps because he wasn't interested in her enough to seek them out. Sadness welled inside her at the thought. Why subject Mel to such disappointment if Javier wasn't interested in her? By the time the train arrived, Olivia was despondent and keen to escape to the simple peace and refuge of the farm.

The train tugged northward out of the station as Olivia typed 'Kilkivan' into the search engine on her phone. A listing came up for the Kilkivan Horse Ride. She had wanted to ride in the event for as long as she could remember, but each year her parents declared she was not old enough, or not experienced enough as a rider. She pondered a strategy to persuade them this time and tapped the screen to research information to support her case. The train beetled onward.

Summer Holiday at Home

It was nine o'clock on Saturday night when a key was fumbled in the front door lock. Someone bashed on the door when their attempt to use a key was unsuccessful. Javier emerged from his room as Charlie opened the door and an overweight, middle-aged man staggered in. His nose and cheeks were flushed red and his short, brown hair was awry.

"G'day wife." Andrew Evans pressed Charlie against the wall and forcibly kissed her on the mouth while wrestling to remove his jacket. Satisfied, he pulled away, tossed the jacket at her and made for the kitchen. "What's for dinner?"

Javier had seen this expression of resignation and revulsion on Charlie's face many times before.

As a boy, Javier blamed his mother for the breakdown in his parent's marriage. If she had been nicer, less argumentative, more compliant and hadn't left his dad, they would still be together as a family. As soon as he was old enough, he moved in with his father. He watched his father court Charlie. He took her out to fancy restaurants, bought her nice things and treated her like she was special. He proposed early and within a year they were married. The marriage appeared blissful and perfect and this confirmed Javier's theory that his mother had caused all the trouble. Then Henry was born.

Charlie tried to juggle it all. The birth had been difficult. Andrew often stormed from the bedroom and left the house. Little Henry cried a lot and Andrew yelled at Charlie to shut him up while he watched TV or spent time at his computer. When Henry slept, Charlie cooked and did housework and

Javier watched her become progressively more tired with each passing week. When Javier returned from time spent at his mother's house, Charlie looked particularly wretched.

Finally, Javier stepped up to help with some of the chores. Andrew would yell at him to go do something more productive than "women's work". Eventually Javier came to see his mother in a new light.

"What's this bloody stuff?" Andrew yelled from the kitchen, leaning over the stove.

Charlie hung the jacket in the hall closet and walked slowly to the kitchen. "Spaghetti bolognese."

"Hmpf. The pasta is overcooked and the sauce is freakin' cold."

"I didn't know when you would be home."

"What?" Andrew loomed over her, menacing.

"Sorry."

"So you bloody well should be."

Charlie set about reheating the sauce and tried to refresh the pasta as Andrew plonked himself down at the table, set for three with woven reed placemats, aqua tumblers and a neatly folded serviette under each mirror-clean silver fork. Andrew insisted that no-one ate dinner until he got home and that they all eat together. Javier was ravenous.

"You're lucky I bloody keep you, Charlie." Andrew turned toward his wife as she did her best in the kitchen. "You can barely cook a decent, hot meal and the house is always grotty." He turned back toward the table, expectant. "Yeah, no one else would want you."

Tears welled in Charlie's eyes. Javier smelled the alcohol on Andrew's breath from across the table. Andrew was worse when he was drunk, but drunk or sober, Javier had lost respect for him years ago. Now there was just a steadily growing resentment.

When the bowl was placed in front of him, Javier scoffed down the food. He winked and smiled at Charlie to signal that he, at least, thought it delicious.

Despite his vigorous complaints, Andrew ate his bowl clean and headed for the bedroom. Javier returned to his room and his computer.

If it wasn't for his curiosity about Olivia, he would stay with his mum for the holidays. Heck, if Wattlewood Grammar wasn't such a good school and if there was decent soccer competition in his mum's area, he would be living with his mum already. He had a life and career ahead of him and he wouldn't be held back looking out for people who should take responsibility for themselves.

Andrew slept through till morning and left Charlie and the household in peace.

Home on the Farm

Olivia lugged her bags off the train at Gympie North Station under the watchful eye of the stationmaster. His black trousers and crisp white shirt were not suited to the heat and humidity, so the stationmaster tried to stay inside his air-conditioned room and only ventured out when he needed to supervise a train. The slick, new, prefabricated station was built outside the north end of town to replace the ornate, old station in the heart of Gympie which was now only used for tourist trains, like the Mary Valley Rattler.

To save money, only a scant section of platform was shaded by awning. This was not the section where Olivia found herself. The hot breeze on the platform was a stark contrast to the cool comfort of the train carriage.

A woman in her late forties, with short, grey-flecked, brown hair, made a beeline for her. Sheree McKinnon had come straight from the farm. Her jeans were well-worn and a short-sleeved aqua blouse hung loosely from her muscular shoulders, the fit of the garments concealing her soft middle. Sheree's brown, elastic-sided boots still sported a layer of farm dust.

"Hello Livvie." She wrapped her arms around Olivia's shoulders and gave her a squeeze.

Olivia held her bags in each hand and waited patiently for the hug to stop. Parents could be so embarrassing. "Hi, Mum."

Sheree was wearing makeup for the trip to town. She was good with makeup, not too much and not too loud. Just enough to complement her chiselled features and lessen the laugh lines etched on her face by time.

"Here, give me one of those." Sheree took one of Olivia's bags and made for the exit. The quickest way out was a concrete walkway behind the station building. They walked by a tall, light-grey box humming with electric currents and a large water storage tank and passed through the rear verandah which was furnished with a few wood and wrought iron bench seats salvaged from the old Gympie Station and painted forest green.

Sheree led Olivia to the farm ute parked beside the woodland on the far side of the station carpark. The ute was parked near a grand old gum tree with clean, white branches and a tousled skirt of brown, fallen bark. Through the trees, Olivia made out a pink band of bulldozed earth that heralded a future housing or industrial development. The station was built to escape the town and the town was in pursuit.

"I've got a few errands to run before we head home." Sheree pressed the electronic key and the car responded with a flash of its lights.

Olivia sighed. Nothing she said or did would change her determined mother's plans. It wasn't so bad; the errands had their benefits. They drove into town and started with lunch at Sheree's favourite cafe, followed by shopping and the acquisition of some farm supplies. When they finally cleared the outskirts of Gympie at around four o'clock, the once-white, twin-cab farm ute was crammed full of groceries (the cold items in a portable camping fridge), bags of pelleted food for the chickens, an assortment of tools and wire and Olivia's bags. If her sister, Daphne, had come home at the same time, they would have needed two vehicles or a small truck to get them to the farm. Although Daphne's end of year exams had finished the week before, her part-time job in Brisbane would only see her home for the Christmas long weekend.

Once they were on the open road, with no distractions and no escape, Olivia didn't have to wait long for the interrogation to begin.

"So, how was the weekend?"

Olivia didn't like her parents knowing too much about her life. "I'm tired, Mum and I really don't want to talk about anything."

"I know, dear, but you know the routine. It's a safety thing." Sheree glanced at Olivia with a smug grin. "I need to stay alert for the trip home. We can have a conversation, or I can sing."

Olivia said nothing and gazed out the window.

Sheree pressed a button on the console and pumped a switch on the steering wheel. She began to bob her head and twist her shoulders to the music. "Well, she took her Daddy's car and she drove to the ice cream shop now!" Sheree sang with gusto and a flat pitch.

Olivia squirmed and rolled her eyes.

"Seems she forgot all about the study like she told her old Dad now!" Sheree happily bobbed her head to the beat. "Don't you just love surf music?"

Olivia heaved a sigh, reached forward to press a button on the console and abruptly extinguished the sound.

"Aww, I love that song," Sheree protested.

"OK, OK, conversation it is."

"Excellent." There was a familiar echo of victory in her mother's voice. "How is Mel doing?" Sheree began. "Is she excited about her trip?"

So, her mother wanted to talk about Mel? Olivia resolved not to mention Mel's infatuation with Javier. "She's fine. Not so excited these days. I mean, they go to Singapore every year, Mum and see the same family every year." There, that should be safe and keep her mum satisfied for now.

"Yes," her mother agreed. "I can see how the novelty would have worn off."

Olivia waited in silence. This wouldn't be the end of it. Her mother would insist on conversation all the way home, or it was surf music.

"Funny how that happens," Sheree slowed for the left turn onto the Wide Bay Highway toward Kilkivan. "When we get something regularly, especially with no effort on our part, we tend to take it for granted, no matter how amazing it is."

Sheree's conversations were often laced with implied meanings and life lessons. Olivia wondered whether all mothers were like that, resolved not to take the bait and remained silent.

"I reckon Mel will appreciate it a whole lot more when she has to earn the money herself to go and visit her family in Singapore for Christmas."

Olivia could have responded with a simple 'yes, Mum' and let the issue and the conversation thread die there, but her mother would simply move to another, probably more uncomfortable, topic.

"Mum, that's never going to happen. Mel's family are totally rich and they all work for one big family company. The company pays for everyone to come to the Singapore base every year for a big family board meeting. Mel's greatest challenge is to have a life outside the company and independent of her family's control." Olivia stopped there. That was already more than her mum needed to know.

Sheree gazed at the road ahead for a few moments. "I had no idea it was that ... intense."

"Well, it is." Olivia looked away and watched the landscape as it whizzed by the window.

Sheree's brow furrowed. "She's not going to be forced into an arranged marriage, is she?"

Mel had discussed this, so Olivia had some idea of what her friend's life had in store. "I don't think so." She watched an oncoming truck until it whooshed past. "But I think the family intends to have a say in who she dates and whether or not they are suitable."

Sheree's frown melted. "Poor Mel."

Mel had stunning looks, athletic ability, academic prowess and family wealth. Mel may be many things, but poor wasn't one of them. Olivia hoped her mother would drop the subject and said nothing.

"I guess you and Daphne have it pretty good?" Her mother headed off on a tangent. "I mean, the family farm is there if either of you want to take it on, but there's no obligation."

"You know I want to take it over, Mum." This was a replay of previous conversations. Sheree regularly fished for reassurance that Olivia had not changed her mind. "After all, that's why I'm doing Ag at school and plan to study it at uni when I graduate. I'm just ticked off that the school doesn't offer agriculture as a subject beyond Year Ten."

"I know, dear, but it really is the best school in the region, so it will give you your best chance of getting into the course. That's why we go to all the trouble of owning a townhouse near the school and only come home on weekends."

"I know, I know," Olivia said. She'd heard that lecture before. "That's why I chose the subjects that I did for the next two years. It's part of a plan."

"Excellent!" Sheree sounded enthused. "Let's hear it."

"Well ... I chose to study biology instead as it should give me the basics. I'm doing business studies and economics because they are relevant and my grades are good. I get good grades in English and maths too, especially English, so I'm doing an extension level in English. Apparently, my teachers think I'm an effective communicator." She glanced at Sheree to see if that comment hit home. No reaction. "I've also tracked down the textbook that the other schools use to teach Ag in Years Eleven and Twelve and I'm going to use it for holiday reading over the next two years so I'll be well equipped for uni."

"That sounds like a great plan." Sheree beamed with the satisfied smile of a mother who had suggested something similar many months before only to have Olivia adamantly argue that it wouldn't work, that she was doomed to miss out on a place in the Ag course at uni and that her mother didn't know what she was talking about as it had been decades since she faced such choices and the world had changed since then. "But what if you meet a boy?" Sheree's expression hinted that the issue had niggled at the back of her mind for some weeks now.

Olivia's eyes widened and she turned to her mother with an expression of both incredulity and disdain that only a teenager can really master. "Well, he'd better like living on a farm if he's truly serious," she said with the matter-of-fact tone of someone still oblivious to the vagaries of life and the heart.

Sheree responded with a knowing smile and seemed reassured that that Olivia at least intended to further their rural legacy. To keep the conversation on safer territory, Olivia opened a discussion on the latest movies in the cinema and pleaded her case for a day trip to Gympie in early January when a movie she was looking forward to would open in Australian cinemas.

When that topic was exhausted, Sheree brought Olivia up to speed with recent goings-on in the local area. After all, not much happened in a farming community that wasn't widely known within a day of the event. Daphne found such a society probing, intrusive and stifling, and preferred to be in cities. Olivia understood that this type of society could also provide considerable amusement, especially when they got the story wrong. It also ensured that someone in difficulty was soon noticed and the community would come to their aid. It was a double-edged sword that she was learning to work with. In rural communities, news was currency ,and in the absence of news, gossip would suffice.

Olivia was reassured by how green the countryside was. The first of the summer storms had come and the dry earth had sprung to life. Bushfire season was now well and truly past and the grass in the fields was already knee-high and taller still by the roadsides.

"You remember the property across the creek from us that was sold a couple of years ago?" Sheree started a new thread of conversation in the local news update.

Olivia nodded, then remembered to mutter "yeah" so that her mother would know she was following the conversation without the need to look away from the road. When you're a passenger in a car travelling at one hundred kilometres per hour in the country, you want the driver to pay attention to the road.

Olivia recalled the events. First the news of a one-thousand-acre property that had been in the same family for four generations coming on the market. Her father spent some days and nights shuffling papers, tapping away on his calculator and making phone calls before he ceded that he would not be able to afford it. At six hundred acres, the McKinnon property was substantial, had a secure water supply and was very productive, but the banks did not see it as sufficient equity to support the massive debt that would be needed to secure such a purchase. Olivia attended the auction with her parents. They stood helplessly silent as the property was sold at well above the reserve price to an anonymous buyer represented by a bidding agent. The small gathering of townsfolk at the auction were curious to discover who the new, wealthy addition to their community would be, but had no satisfaction at all beyond the bidding agent's comment that that the buyer at the other end of the phone was thrilled to have acquired the property.

The property in question was what Olivia's father called a "nice patch of dirt". It was visible from the north end of their verandah. Set back from the creek flats used for cropping and growing lucerne for hay was a gentle rise on which stood the original Queenslander-style homestead and outbuildings. Beyond this, the land sloped steadily upward culminating in hills wooded with grey-green eucalypts. Just north of the track from the property's east gate to the homestead was a modest, modern, low-set timber home that served as a caretaker's residence.

Sheree continued. "You remember that the new owners moved the caretaker's residence off the property and sold it?"

"Yes." Tales of the mysterious new neighbours were always interesting.

"Then they brought in a big truck and a work team and moved the old homestead to where the caretaker's cottage was."

"I remember," Olivia said. "I've watched them build a new house on the old homestead site. Is it finally finished?"

"Yes and it's really weird. Your dad got the binoculars out and the part that faces our place is a two-storey wall of windows. I've never seen anything like it!"

"Has anyone found out more about them?"

Much to the frustration of everyone in the district, details about the new owners were scant. The real estate agent was no help. He said the buyer of the property was a family trust. They employed a new farm manager who was reticent to reveal any details about his new boss. The locals waited to see if they could prise some information from the farm manager's wife, but it turned out the new farm manager was gay—something the community was still adjusting to—so he was not often engaged in conversation.

"Only a snippet. The builders say the new owner's wife seems to be overseeing the whole project. Apparently, her name is Lauren. They said she was fairly young and she has blonde hair. No sign of the owner yet."

"Well, at least that's some progress." Olivia glanced at her mother. "More than we knew last term."

"Yes, but it's taken us over two years to find out that much."

A familiar sixty-kilometre-per-hour speed sign marked their arrival at Kilkivan and Sheree slowed the car on the downhill approach. The first houses came into view, followed soon after by the football oval on the right and the town sign on the left. It read:

KILKIVAN
Pop 800
HOME OF THE GREAT HORSE RIDE

They drove past the Bowls Club. Just before the local school, the highway turned abruptly right and revealed the wide main street lined with old shop buildings, each sporting a verandah over the concrete footpath. The parking areas were broken up by discrete garden beds planted with mauve flowers. It was a well-tended town.

"Ice-cream?" Sheree asked as she parked the car near the general store.

"Yes please, Mum!" Olivia sat upright and beamed. It was a family tradition; they would stop in for an ice cream on the way through town on the return from school. Despite being sixteen, it was a tradition she was in no hurry to grow out of.

They enjoyed their confection seated at a table on the store verandah. Olivia used a serviette to wipe drips of ice cream off the bright tiles laid out in a mosaic on the table top.

"Oh and Mike, in the shop, reckons they are putting up exclusion fencing around a large chunk of the property," Sheree said in between mouthfuls.

"Who?"

"The new neighbours of course!"

"So, we're back to talking about them?"

Sheree grinned, ice cream at the corners of her mouth. "Did we ever stop?"

"Not for at least the last two years!"

"Very funny!" Sheree faked a smile. "Hurry up and finish your ice cream." She tried too hard to sound serious and they both giggled.

Olivia mulled over the new information. Perhaps she could investigate further during the holidays? After all, the mysterious neighbours lived just across the creek. It was almost walking distance.

The last leg of the journey passed quickly and every kilometre felt more like home for Olivia. They headed out of town on the Wide Bay Highway and eventually turned off onto a bitumen road. The road became narrower with each successive turn off until the bitumen gave way to a graded dirt road. At the final crest, Olivia's home appeared; a neat white Queenslander nestled among outbuildings and a skirt of trees. The cluster was edged along one side with a row of mint-green silage round bales stacked two bales high. As the ute shuddered over the last cattle grid into the house yard, Olivia's father emerged down the verandah steps.

Arthur McKinnon was a tall sinewy, muscular man. He was clean-shaven with short, red hair, ruffled and sweaty from the moth-eaten Akubra hat he wore for most of the day. His green, cotton drill shirt and worn, loose, khaki work shorts were coated in a fine layer of red dust. His face still bore the dried sweat and dirt of a solid day's work in the fields. He smelled like diesel, aftershave and dad. He gave Olivia a warm, welcoming hug and insisted on carrying her bags inside. She was finally home.

Arthur hauled her luggage up the steps and paused at the top. "Have you heard about the neighbours, Possum?"

"I think so." Only her dad got away with calling her Possum these days.

"It's OK, dear." Sheree carried a bag of groceries and followed behind. "I brought her up to date on the way home."

Arthur's expression sank, then brightened again. "I reckon Mum didn't tell you about the new bull."

Olivia shook her head and Arthur came to life as he described the benefits and features of his new acquisition. She tried to pay attention but her mind drifted to how she might win more freedom to ride and investigate.

Riding Alone

Olivia devoured her breakfast of eggs and toast. She had timed it perfectly. Her dad usually left for the fields at sunrise and her mother would be busily tending the veggie garden before the heat of the day. It was her best opportunity to sneak away - or so she thought until the screen door clanged shut. Olivia started and the jolt pushed the egg, skewered on her fork, almost off her plate. She juggled to rescue her breakfast.

Sheree appeared in the kitchen with tousled hair, sporting a blue polo shirt and loose jeans; both were stained and dusty. The family were trained to leave their boots at the door, so Sheree moved almost silently across the room in her thick cotton socks.

"Just came in to put the air-conditioner on," she said as she marched through the dining room. "Can you check your bedroom window is closed please, Livvie?"

"OK." Olivia hastily put a forkful of egg and bread into her mouth and got up to check the window in the room she shared with her sister. It was much quieter now that Daphne was away at uni. She also closed the door to the ensuite bathroom, to save a second trip to the room when her mother thought of it. When Olivia emerged, Sheree stood in the kitchen, eyeing her clothes with consternation.

"What?" Olivia gathered the last morsels of her breakfast into her mouth and made for the kitchen with the plate.

"So, you're planning on riding?"

Olivia looked down at the pink polo shirt and jodhpurs that gave away her intentions. "Yeah, is there a problem?"

"You know I don't like you riding alone. Anything could happen and it could take hours before you were found."

"I'm careful, Mum. I take my phone. I stick to the tracks and Vanilla is a reliable horse."

Sheree sighed in dismay, her frown unmoved.

"Mum, I've been fine riding alone most weekends for the entire year. I'll be fine riding alone today." The persistent frown meant her mother was not convinced. "I'll take my phone and I'll keep clear of the creek."

"Just be careful." Sheree's frown softened, defeated. She gathered up the egg basket from the kitchen and made for the door.

"I always am, Mum. Don't worry. I'll be fine."

"Oh, and shut the door to your bathroom to keep the cool air in."

"Yes, Mum," Olivia called behind her as Sheree disappeared onto the verandah.

* * *

Vanilla had been Olivia's trusted buddy since Olivia was twelve. Technically Vanilla was a grey mare, but to the casual observer she was creamy white with dappled grey legs, tail and muzzle. When Arthur first unloaded Olivia's birthday gift from the horse float, Olivia declared the pony was the colour of vanilla ice cream and the name had stuck. At fourteen hands Vanilla was the ideal size for an ambitious twelve-year-old and was still adequate and comfortable for a sixteen-year-old.

With the pony securely hitched to the yard railing, Olivia pushed a brush along Vanilla's back. The short, glistening summer coat still reminded her of ice cream, though the pungent smell of 'horse' did not.

"Stand still!" Olivia tried to be stern as Vanilla danced about on the spot. "I know you're keen to get out. Me too. But try to be still so we can be out faster."

Vanilla's ears flicked toward Olivia as if she was listening, but with each stroke of the brush, the excited mare danced a little more.

The dancing intensified as Olivia approached with the saddle blanket.

"That's it." Olivia hung the blanket over the fence, stepped away and leaned against the fence. "I'm not doing anything more until you stand still."

Vanilla tried to toss her head up but was constrained by the tie to the rail, so she danced about some more and pranced on the spot. Olivia just stood quietly and waited. Vanilla paused to glance at Olivia, then kicked out a few times with her hind legs. Finally, she exhaled in a huff and stood still.

"Are you done?" Olivia asked. She dared not move lest the stillness was a ruse.

Vanilla stood motionless. Olivia took up the saddle blanket and stepped toward Vanilla. The excited horse danced about and Olivia stepped back.

"If you're not done yet, I can wait." She moved to hang the blanket back on the rail. Vanilla instantly stood still. "Are you sure?"

Vanilla lowered her head in quiet defeat.

"Good." Olivia stroked Vanilla's warm, soft neck, then gently tossed the blanket onto the horse's back. Vanilla didn't flinch.

"Good girl," Olivia said as she gently placed the saddle on Vanilla's back. She reached underneath Vanilla's belly to retrieve the dangling girth strap. "I know you're excited, but do we really have to play this game every time?" Olivia pulled the girth strap tight and secured it.

Vanilla offered no resistance to the bridle, but once it was securely in place, she nudged Olivia in the chest, forcing her to take a step backward. Olivia wrapped the reins around the rail and stepped away.

"I can wait," she said, resuming her position leaning on the fence.

Vanilla pawed the ground with a front hoof.

"Well?" Olivia breathed deeply. There was no point getting frustrated. Both of them behaving badly would not improve the situation; it was bad enough that one was. Besides, it was school holidays; no one was waiting for them, so Olivia had plenty of time to outlast Vanilla's impatience.

Finally, Vanilla stood quietly again, with her ears pointed forward and her head lowered a little. Olivia transferred her phone from her back jodhpur pocket to her breast pocket, donned her riding helmet and checked one more time that the girth was tight. Olivia walked Vanilla to the mounting block. "Are we good now?" Vanilla walked placidly beside her, so she took that as a yes. When she was comfortable in the saddle, Olivia walked Vanilla once around the yard to ensure that all was secure and functional before she turned out through the open yard gate. She manoeuvred Vanilla through the horse gate in the house area fence and headed along the track toward the creek.

Vanilla felt strong, excited and confident beneath Olivia, and she pulled against the reins, keen to canter. Olivia was happy to walk and take in the splendid summer morning. On the other hand, perhaps a little exercise would get the energy out of Vanilla's system? She nudged with her heels. Vanilla's response was brisk and they trotted along the track toward the creek.

Vanilla knew the route well. Olivia relaxed into the steady pace and the secure grip of the stock saddle. She gazed out into the distance and surveyed the green fields of pasture and lucerne along the length of the valley, the grey green of the eucalypts on the nearby hills and the contrasting smoky blue of the distant hills. The sun lightly stung her arms and Olivia was glad her morning routine had included sunscreen. Big puffy clouds wafted through the blue sky overhead and a cool breeze made the ride more pleasant for both horse and rider.

Olivia's thoughts drifted to Javier. She wondered where he might be and imagined him off skiing in Canada or the Swiss Alps like many of her school friends. She replayed the strange but precious moments of the last day of school over in her mind and it stirred a yearning deep inside her. This was drowned by a wave of despondent sadness that he hadn't contacted her. Maybe he toyed with girls that way, raising their hopes with a smile then rendering all hope futile by neglect. Her sadness was thus quashed by anger and Olivia resolved not to waste any more thoughts or feelings on Javier, unless he contacted her. She wondered if Mel was doing the same.

Olivia closed the gate to the creek run behind her and ambled her horse down the trail that crossed the creek bed. Recent rain filled the low pools, but there was not enough water to get the creek running. It had been a very dry winter and spring.

On either side of the crossing, the creek bed was obscured by a forest of bottlebrush bushes. Their writhing, tangled trunks and branches formed mysterious woody grottos in both directions. Entwined between their exposed roots were driftwood branches of diverse size that had been washed down by previous torrents.

Olivia guided Vanilla across the graded crossing and up the trail on the far bank. From the top, Olivia could see the neighbour's fields to her right; their boundary fence came in from the west to meet the fence at the creek run. Before the property was sold, the neighbour had installed a gate in this fence just near where it intersected the creek run fence, ostensibly so that stray cattle could be more easily returned to their rightful owner. To her left, the Kinbombi Creek sliced through the western third of the McKinnon farm, flanked by large, flat fields suitable for irrigated cropping. The field ahead of her contained stubble from a recent lucerne harvest and the ones further left and behind were expanses of green lucerne with white veils of irrigator spray wafting over them. Along the creek bank to her left was a disused windmill. It stood forlorn, its blades broken, but Olivia could just make out the gentle whoosh of water in the new plastic pipes, pumped using solar power from deep underground to a distant storage dam.

Olivia inhaled the serenity of the idyllic landscape. Without warning, Vanilla suddenly tensed beneath her. The horse let out a screeching neigh and reared. Caught off guard and before she could even scream, Olivia slid backward out of the saddle and hit the unforgiving ground, hard. To Olivia, the fall played out in slow motion, yet she was powerless to react. Her head flew back and hit the ground with a sharp ping as her helmet connected with the rocky dirt. Her right ankle connected with a rock, with a snap and immediate stabbing pain. Olivia was dazed, kept conscious by the acute pain in her ankle.

"Bugger!" She winced as she tried to move and triggered a fresh burst of agony. "Mum is going to be so pissed off."

Helpless

A warm muzzle nudged Olivia's neck. At least Vanilla hadn't run off. Olivia moved to grab a rein, but stabbing pain in her ankle deterred her and she lay back down. She was able to retrieve the phone from her breast pocket and turn it on … no signal.

"Damn!" Olivia cursed. "This had to happen in a signal black spot!"

Vanilla responded with another nuzzle. It was comforting but not otherwise helpful.

A tear rolled down Olivia's cheek, partly from the pain in her ankle but mostly from the sunken feeling in her gut as the opportunity to participate in the horse ride this year frittered away. The baking sun reminded her that more than a missed opportunity was at stake and Olivia began to work through her options. She called out for help for a while to no avail. She was well out of range of the farm and her father was working a distant field that day. She tried to instruct Vanilla to go home and get help, but no matter how stern or imploring her instructions were, the horse wouldn't leave her side.

Olivia looked around for something to splint her leg, but any useful sticks were down in the creek bed and well out of reach. She didn't like the idea of army-crawling down to reach them; it hurt too much to move. Olivia decided her best option was to simply lie there and wait. She would eventually be missed and her father would come searching. She only hoped that he would find her before the meat ants did. So, she lay there, defeated and wretched. To pass the time, she imagined she could somehow send out a signal to someone, anyone, to come to her rescue.

* * *

It seemed like an hour had eked by but, depressingly, when Olivia checked the time on her phone only fifteen minutes had elapsed. The sun blazed down on her; she was thirsty and her right foot swelled inside her boot. She moved to remove the boot, but it hurt too much. She considered dragging herself to some shade closer to the creek bed, but it was at least twenty metres away and her leg hurt when she moved it even an inch. She brushed a few meat ants off her arms as they arrived and hoped they didn't go back to the nest to tell their friends about the large carcass of fresh flesh they had found. Vanilla, still by her side, suddenly raised her head in surprise, rotated her ears about and listened for a faint sound.

Soon Olivia heard it too; the sound of hoof beats. She raised herself onto her elbows and craned to see a rider approach across the neighbour's fields toward the gate. Should she be relieved or scared? This was a chance at rescue, but the neighbours were a mysterious lot. What if they weren't nice people? What if they were hiding dark secrets? An organised crime gang? Serial killers? Olivia was in no position to defend herself. Maybe she should just lay low and wait until her father found her. She lowered herself back to the ground while Vanilla stood as a riderless sentinel over her, revealing her plight.

The boundary gate clicked twice as it unlatched and soon relatched. Steady hoof beats approached, followed by the thud of boots hitting hard earth when the rider dismounted. Vanilla relaxed as if relieved and took a few steps back as the rider approached. The mint green blouse and cream jodhpurs revealed the rider to be a woman. Olivia relaxed a little. After all, most serial killers weren't women. Her muscular, dun quarter horse was a gelding whose brushed coat almost glowed in the sunlight.

"You're hurt," the woman observed as she removed her wide-brimmed hat to reveal platinum blonde hair tied back in a short, loose ponytail. "I'm Lauren by the way."

"Olivia," was all she could reply.

"Pleased to meet you, although it would have been more pleasant in different circumstances no doubt. What happened?"

"Not sure." Olivia started to feel more relaxed. "One minute I'm having a quiet ride and next minute my horse rears and I hit the ground. I think I've broken my ankle."

Lauren gazed toward the pony for a few moments. Vanilla lowered her head as if in shame.

"She was probably spooked by something." Lauren looked around her. "A snake maybe? She looks very sorry to have thrown you."

Olivia cast a sideways glance. Vanilla still stood with her head lowered. Lauren's horse walked over to her and nuzzled her neck as if in reassurance.

"May I have your permission to check your injuries?"

"Sure."

"The ankle injury is obvious, but I'd like to check for head or neck injuries before we try and move you."

Lauren asked Olivia to wiggle her fingers and the toes on her good foot. They both saw some evidence of toe movement even through the boot. Lauren reached out and touched Olivia on the forehead. It was a weird sensation, like watching a movie skip a few frames, then continued as if nothing had happened. Olivia thought the horses had moved a little and Lauren's head had suddenly moved to a slightly different position, but it was nothing she could really be certain of. Her right boot wasn't quite as tight now and the throbbing had subsided.

"Is there any pain in your back, neck, or head?"

Olivia shook her head. They all felt fine.

"Can you bend your good leg at the knee and raise it up?"

Olivia dutifully bent her left leg up with no discomfort.

"That's great, Olivia." Lauren's expression softened, satisfied. "Your lower half seems fine—except for the bung ankle. How many fingers do you see?"

Lauren held up her fingers with her palm facing away from Olivia.

"Four."

"Excellent! And now?" Lauren lowered the fourth finger.

"Three."

"Very good. And now?" Lauren lowered her third finger.

"Two."

One side of Lauren's mouth drew into a half smile. "And now?" Lauren lowered her first finger.

Olivia giggled and blushed. "One!"

"Wonderful! Sense of humour is intact and that helmet may have saved you from a nasty concussion or worse. We'll be more certain once we get you vertical."

Lauren now turned her attention to the ankle. It was still sore when Lauren touched it and more so when Lauren gently moved it about, but somehow not as sore as before. Lauren placed her fingers over the tip of the boot.

"Try moving your toes now."

Olivia tried to wiggle her toes. They both felt the movement and smiled at each other.

"Looks like it's sprained rather than broken. We'll leave the boot on as a splint and get you home. I reckon a doctor will probably want to x-ray to be sure there are no breaks."

Olivia was in no position to argue. "OK."

"Now let's get you up." Lauren moved into position near Olivia's feet. "Bend your good leg again and give me your hands. I'm going to step on your boot and pull you up without touching the sore one, OK?"

Olivia obeyed. She soon stood on one foot with tolerable discomfort in the sore ankle, while Lauren moved to her side to support her in the upright position. As if knowing what was required, Vanilla moved into position in front of them, the reins dangling under her head.

"Put your arms over the saddle. I'll hoick you up and we'll swing your good leg over her back."

Vanilla stood stock still as the manoeuvre was completed. Olivia let her legs hang loose beside the stirrups while Lauren handed her the reins.

"Good to go?"

"Surprisingly, yes." Olivia took up the slack in the reins.

"Good." Lauren launched herself up into the saddle of her own mount, a feat that appeared effortless, even without a mounting block. "Let's go."

Lauren took the lead as they plied their horses back down across the creek. Olivia did nothing but let Vanilla follow behind Lauren's horse and cringe with pain at every jolt and bump. It was a long ride home.

* * *

Sheree came into view first, her back toward them as she tied tomato plants to a frame in the veggie garden. Her head popped up and her expression transitioned rapidly from confusion at the sight of two riders to anguish at Olivia's wincing face and her legs dangling outside the stirrups.

"Art!" she cried out and Olivia's father promptly emerged from the hay shed. They ran toward the horses.

"Livvie! Are you OK, Livvie?"

"I'm fine, Mum." Olivia tried to look calm and controlled to avoid agitating her mother further. "It's just a sprained ankle. I'll be fine."

Lauren pulled up her horse and slid gracefully to the ground. She strode up to Sheree, removed her hat and held out her hand. "Hello. I'm Lauren, your neighbour from across the creek." She tilted her head in the direction of the strange house with the glass wall.

Sheree shook her hand awkwardly. "Sheree McKinnon and this is my husband." She glanced in Arthur's direction.

"Art," Arthur said and eagerly held out his hand. "Good to meet you."

Her father looked most distracted and her mother suddenly frowned at Lauren.

"Ahem!" Olivia interrupted, worried that her father might shake Lauren's hand clean off.

"Sorry, Possum." Art darted to her side. He held Olivia's waist to provide support as she threw her good leg over Vanilla's neck and slid to the ground, her sore leg protectively bent.

"What happened, Livvie?" Sheree wrapped Olivia's arm around her shoulders and relieved Art of support duty.

"I came up the far creek bank," Olivia said. "Then Vanilla suddenly reared up and I hit the ground. I must have landed on my ankle and it was too sore to walk. I couldn't get a phone signal to call you and next thing I knew Lauren arrived and helped me home."

"Bloody dangerous pony!" Art blurted out. "I never trusted it around kids. Too dangerous for you to ride again, Possum. I wouldn't want to sell her either, in case some other kid gets hurt. I'll dig a hole and shoot the bloody nag by morning!" He moved to grab the horse's reins.

"No!" Olivia lunged toward them but was restrained by her mother's grip and the pain in her ankle.

Lauren turned to Olivia and gave her a reassuring half smile before she turned her attention back to Art, who was roughly leading Vanilla away.

"Snake!" Lauren shouted, pointing to the ground near Art's feet.

Barely glancing down, Art leapt high into the air and off to one side, tugging the startled horse with him. His gaze darted about the dusty driveway, looking for the offending reptile. There was no trace of it. Olivia, then Sheree, began to giggle. Art blushed and looked sheepish.

Lauren looked smug. "Reckon that's what Vanilla did when she unexpectedly saw a snake too." Lauren walked over and patted Vanilla on the neck. "And to her credit, she refused to leave Olivia's side until help arrived. Sounds like a pretty reliable kids' pony to me." There was a moment's silence. "If you're still determined to get rid of her in the morning, give me a call and I'd be happy to take her off your hands."

"And that's the end of riding alone," Sheree said with authority. "You'll just have to wait until your sister comes home."

"But Mum!" Olivia slumped onto Sheree's shoulder, crushed. "She's hardly ever home. I'll never get to ride. How will I get to join in the Kilkivan Horse Ride in April if Vanilla and I never get to practise?"

"You'll just have to wait until your father can ride with you."

"Dad never has any spare time. He's always working. I'll never get to ride." Olivia was both despondent and helplessly wounded.

"Actually," Lauren piped in. "I like to ride parts of my boundary fence a few times a week and I wouldn't mind some company."

Olivia's face lit up, but her parents looked wary.

"If it's OK with your parents," Lauren added.

"Mum? Dad? Pleeaase!" Olivia employed her most sincere 'puppy dog eyes' in her dad's direction.

"If it's alright with your mum, it's alright by me," Art conceded.

All eyes turned to Sheree, who now looked uncomfortable. "Well, alright then. But don't go making a nuisance of yourself."

"I won't!" Olivia said, triumphant.

"Pass me your phone and I'll add my number." Lauren walked toward Olivia.

Olivia pulled her phone from her breast pocket, brought up her contact list and passed it to Lauren, who tapped in her details and passed it back. Olivia looked at the screen. Only two fields were entered; the name 'Lauren' and the mobile number.

"If you send me a text, then I'll have your number too." Lauren settled her hat back on her head, a sign she was preparing to leave.

Olivia obediently tapped away at the screen and within moments a reassuring beep emanated from the breast pocket of Lauren's shirt. She walked back toward her horse, gathered up the reins, placed a foot in the stirrup and launched herself into the saddle.

"I'm pretty sure it's just a sprain," Lauren said as she took up the slack in the reins. "But you may want to take Olivia to Gympie Hospital and have it x-rayed, just to be sure."

They all stood in silence and watched Lauren ride off.

Sheree cast disapproving glances at Art. "Stop staring, dear."

"Did ya see her?" Art's eyes were still transfixed on the figure as she disappeared into the distance. "She's a looker, that one!"

"That she is," Sheree said. "Definitely a trophy wife if ever I saw one!"

"Y'know," Art finally turned to his wife, "for a minute there, I really thought I saw a snake, but when I looked again it was gone."

Later that evening, Olivia lay on her bed with her strapped ankle propped up on a pillow, watching the trees outside thrash about in the howling summer wind. She recalled the cry of despair from her mother when the nurse cut the boot from her injured foot.

"But they're R.M. Williams! Do you have any idea how expensive R.M. Williams boots are?"

"I'll just cut the elastic bit," the nurse replied in a matter-of-fact tone as she cut away at the boot with large, sharp scissors.

Olivia also recalled the doctor explaining the x-ray findings.

"She was lucky it was just a sprain this time," the unshaven young doctor in scrubs had said.

"What do you mean 'this time'?" Sheree asked.

"Well, it looks like she had a bad fracture of the ankle about a year ago." The doctor pointed at one of the bones on the x-ray. "But it has healed really well. You can barely tell it happened at all."

"I don't remember Olivia breaking her ankle a year ago." Sheree frowned and looked confused. "Are you sure this is the right x-ray?"

"Definitely the right x-ray, Mrs McKinnon." The doctor was indignant. He pointed at the name on the image with his pen. "It was the sort of injury you wouldn't forget either. She would've barely been able to move for pain."

Olivia worked to make the pieces of the puzzle fit. She fell asleep trying.

Research and Other Bruises

On the first Monday of the school holidays, Javier had time on his hands. Unlike most of his school friends, he wasn't holidaying with his family at some exotic location. He was thankful none of his friends were the type to continually bombard him with images of their wonderful holiday adventures, except maybe the occasional gory bit where someone was injured and there was visible blood.

Most of Javier's soccer buddies also stayed local for the summer holidays and they were keen to get together a few times a week to see a movie, hang out at the mall or go to the beach. The beach was the most popular because they could do most of coach's fitness exercises together on the sand. Though it was never discussed, Javier wondered if he wasn't the only one keen to spend time away from a troubled home.

Javier was at his computer, ignoring the warm sunshine as it tried to lure him outdoors. He wasn't gaming, as he and his friends often did, but researching. He worked his way through the social sites and typed "Olivia McKinnon" at each one. Although there were some name matches, like a woman in Oregon USA who kept goats, it was never the Olivia he was looking for.

He tried again with "Livvy McKinnon" as the search term, but still no luck. "She sure keeps a low profile," Javier muttered.

It was time to get more creative. He didn't know her parents' names, so a search of the phone directory proved fruitless. A thought occurred to him. "Maybe." He picked up his phone and dialled a soccer buddy. "Elton, mate. Is this a good time?"

"Sure, Javier, what's up?"

"I've got a bit of a problem and seeing as your computer skills are legend..."

"I see. Tell you what, how about you come over? We can work on your problem and then maybe go grab some pizza or something?"

"Sure. What's your address?" Javier's phone pinged as the details promptly arrived by text. "See you in about an hour then?"

"Works for me."

* * *

Javier had not been to Elton's house before. It was a bit of a ride northward, at Point Cartwright. Javier rode through the dappled shade of she-oak trees along a section of the street, then a section where there were no trees and the sun scalded the short-mown lawns dotted with ant mounds of fine beach sand. He passed a basketball hoop and stand set up on the kerb, complete with ball. It gave the street a neighbourly trusting atmosphere. He rode past houses with boats parked on trailers at the kerb or in carports and along a section with draping, old paperbark trees shading the footpaths. Elton's house was a modest three-bedroom, brick-veneer dwelling one street inland from the beach. The house was on the low side of the street. The houses on the high side of the street were overlooked by the grand mansions along Pacific Boulevard and were more modest than those on the low side.

Javier leaned his bike against the porch and knocked on the door. Locks were fumbled and the door was opened by a tall, gangly teen with pasty skin and greasy tousled brown hair. His loose grey t-shirt and baggy shorts looked crumpled, as if slept in.

"Elton. Good to see you mate." Javier tried to conceal his shock at his friend's dishevelled appearance. Clearly, Elton was having even more isolation issues this holiday than he was.

"Yeah, Javier. Come on in." Elton stood to one side and gestured for Javier to pass.

"Is there somewhere I can put my bike?"

"Absolutely. I'll meet you at the side gate and we'll put it in the backyard." Elton pointed toward a wooden gate at the side of the house.

Javier moved to take up his bike. Out of the corner of his eye, he glimpsed Elton pinch and sniff the shoulder of his t-shirt before he closed the door. He wondered how long it was since that shirt had seen a washing machine.

Inside, the house was clean and quiet. A lazy, ginger cat lounged on the sofa, not bothering to move as they passed through.

"My parents are both at work and my sister is at the shopping centre with some friends." Elton led Javier down a short corridor that exited off the kitchen. "So, we've got the place to ourselves for a couple of hours."

If Javier hadn't known Elton from the soccer team, he may have thought it all a bit sinister. As it was, nothing was unusual until he entered Elton's room.

The room was tidy enough, but Javier spied the edge of some underpants protruding from under the wardrobe door. He wondered if opening the door would start an avalanche of dirty clothes. The room smelled of musty socks and teenage boy. But what really caught Javier's eye was the tech. A large,

L-shaped desk in one corner housed three video screens, the central one curved around the desk corner. Between and behind the screens were black boxes with flashing lights and a maze of black cables. In front of them were keyboards, game controllers, a couple of mouse pads and an empty plate dusted with crumbs.

"Wow, Elton." Javier tried to take it all in. "This quite a setup. It must have cost a bit."

"Yeah." Elton pushed some clothes off a small chair next to his bed and dragged the chair toward the desk. "I've had a job at the local fast-food place for a couple of years now. It pays for some really good gear." He positioned the small chair beside one that resembled the love child of a racing car seat and an armchair. Elton settled into the fancy chair and gestured for Javier to sit on the small one.

"So, what can I do for you?" Elton swivelled his chair to face Javier.

"I want to get into my school's computer system."

Elton frowned and looked disappointed, as if this was something he had been asked to do before and loathed. "Problem grades last semester?"

"No." Javier blushed. "It's a girl."

"Ooh!" Elton's face lit up. "Much more fun." He swivelled to face the central screen and started typing. Soon, the home page for Javier's school appeared on the screen.

"You know which school I go too?"

"We're on the same soccer team; I pay attention."

Javier raised his eyebrows and tightened his lips. He began to see why the team whispered about Elton's computer prowess.

"Is this the student login page link?"

"Yeah."

"ID and password." Elton pushed his chair back and allowed Javier to lean forward and type in his details. As soon as Javier hit the return button, Elton swooped back in. Pages flashed on the screen in rapid succession and soon they were pages Javier had not seen before. "Not so difficult to get behind the system. All the government schools use the same template and looks like the private schools do too. I guess it's so they can interface with the government system."

Javier leaned forward and tried to take in each page before it was promptly replaced by another. Finally, a relatively blank screen with a small box appeared.

"Her name?"

Javier took a deep breath. This was the point of no return. "Olivia … Olivia McKinnon."

"Nice name." Elton keyed in the letters at lightning speed. Pages promptly appeared and Elton scrolled through them. "Good grades. She's bright. Sure you want a bright one? They can be difficult to handle." Elton scrolled further through the pages. "Not bad looking though." Olivia's most recent ID photo appeared. "Probably even better looking in real life. ID photos never do anyone justice."

Javier winced. Someone he hardly knew was trawling through Olivia's private information and passing judgement. It felt as if his own personal details were being exposed to the world. "Look mate, this is kinda private stuff."

Elton glanced sideways. "Sorry mate. Didn't mean to intrude." He turned back to the screen. "What was it you were after?"

"Her address and contact details." Javier pulled out his phone ready to take down the information or photograph the screen.

"Easy," Elton announced. "No need to type it. I'll screenshot it and message it through."

Within seconds, Javier's phone pinged receipt.

"Anything else? Her photo maybe?"

"Yeah, that would be great." Seconds later a ping announced arrival of the item on his phone. Javier would wait till later that evening to gaze at it.

"So," Elton said, exiting the school's system. "Fancy some pizza?"

"Yeah, mate, my shout. I owe you."

Elton face lit with enthusiasm. "Maybe we could come back later and play a game? I have a second controller."

"Sounds great." It did sound great. After all, it wasn't as though Javier had anything else planned and he was in no hurry to get back to the tension at home. There would be plenty of time to check out Olivia's house tomorrow.

* * *

When Javier finally did get home, the house was dark and quiet. The living room still reeked of alcohol. Javier felt suddenly guilty about having stayed away. He hoped that Charlie was OK. Oscillating between weariness, unease and hopeful anticipation, Javier went to bed.

Javier was woken by the routine morning sounds of the household and the aroma of a cooked breakfast wafting under the door. He didn't need to be at school and he didn't have a holiday job, so he lay there and gazed at the photo of Olivia on his phone until after his father's loud car pulled away from the driveway. He emerged to find Henry gleefully eating half of his breakfast while spreading the other half on his face, his clothes and the table. Rather than a separate highchair with its own tray, Charlie preferred the type that attached to the edge of a normal table and insisted it was more efficient to wipe down one surface instead of two.

"Morning Charlie." Javier opened the fridge to get the milk for his breakfast cereal, without actually looking at Charlie.

When his gaze finally moved across to her, he was gutted. She sported a large bruise on her upper left arm in the shape of the powerful fingers that had clearly grabbed her too tightly and muscled her about. The shock continued as his gaze moved up to her face, where a similar bruise and swelling on her left cheekbone pushed her eyelids shut.

"Charlie!" Javier put down the milk and walked tentatively toward her. "What happened?"

"It's OK, Javier. He apologised. He said it won't happen again."

Javier stopped right in front of her. "Just because he apologised doesn't make it OK."

Charlie's expression of firm resolve melted and tears began to well in her eyes.

"Oh, Charlie," Javier said as she launched forward to hug him. He awkwardly placed his arms around her and patted rhythmically on her back. She began to sob. "I think you need to leave him, Charlie. I'm worried it's not safe for you and Henry here."

"No, Javier," Charlie left a patch of salty tears on his shirt. "He apologised. Besides, marriage is for life."

"That doesn't mean it should cost you your life."

Charlie pulled away, sniffling and found a tissue in her pocket to stem the flow. "Don't worry Javier. It'll be OK. You'll see." She resumed tending to Henry's breakfast.

Javier moved back into the kitchen. He was out of his depth and he knew it. Charlie was a good friend and he couldn't bear to see her harmed, or little Henry either. Whether it was his problem or not, he was in no position to help resolve this. Maybe his mother would know what to do.

* * *

Fed, showered and dressed, and with the mid-morning sun streaming onto the pool, Javier took his phone outdoors. The entire backyard was taken up by the pool, so Javier went through the gate in the back fence onto a lawn area that was "stolen" by the residents from the council-owned dune bushland. On his left the neighbours had constructed a cubby house; on his right stood some citrus trees, behind which a hammock was strung between two paperbarks. It was more private there. He checked that his mother was available to talk. She was and he pressed her number.

"Mum."

"Hi Javier. Tell me what happened."

Javier recounted how he had stayed out late and what he had woken to in the morning. "I'm really worried about Charlie and Henry. I think she should leave him."

"I think you're right. But she won't."

"Why the hell not?"

"First, he'll give her false hope. He'll apologise profusely and swear that it will never happen again."

"Yeah, he's done that already. But it will happen again, won't it?"

"Yes, it will, repeatedly, and it will get worse each time."

"Oh crap!"

"Exactly. If he's still playing the same games, he's probably disconnected her from her family and friends, so that she feels like she has nowhere to go."

"Now that you mention it ... Look, this shouldn't be my problem, Mum. Can I just report it to someone and get on with my holiday?"

"You could contact the police. If they arrive during an incident, they may arrest your father, remove him from the house, charge him with assault and arrange a DVO. If you call them after an event, especially while she still has the bruises, they can organise an immediate DVO. A DVO would require him to stay at least 100 metres away from her, Henry and the house. Both of these options are possible without Charlie having to press charges herself."

"I've watched the news, Mum. A DVO is just a piece of paper. If he was determined, he could still take revenge on them. Besides, he owns the house. At the very least he'd want to get me out for dobbing him in and then..."

"I know, she would probably take him back despite the DVO."

"Then, she'd be here alone. With him."

"Yes, Javier. I'd have the surety of knowing you were safe, but..."

"But Charlie and Henry could be lost?"

"Yes."

The conversation lapsed into brutal silence as Javier came to terms with the situation. Every scenario he pondered ended with him leaving the Sunshine Coast and having to quit the soccer team and his school. "Not acceptable. So, what else can you do?"

"You mean, what can we do? This is going to take teamwork and close communication. Are you up for it?"

Looking out for Charlie and Henry was not what Javier had planned for this holiday. This was all so inconvenient, but it wasn't like there was anyone else in a position to help them. "Yes, Mum." Javier released an exasperated sigh. "I don't see any other good options."

"You're smart and capable; you've got this. I'm going to organise a safe place for her to go to. Meanwhile, keep a close eye out. After each incident, and there will be more incidents, remind her that it's getting worse, not better, and start to suggest that she will need to leave with Henry at some point. Emphasise keeping Henry safe. I'll keep you posted on what to look for. When it all comes to a head, you must get them out. I'll tell you what to do. Once she and Henry are safe, we call in the police. OK?"

"OK." Javier fidgeted, peeled some bark off a paperback tree and pressed the crispy flakes between his fingers. Why couldn't he have a normal holiday, like Elton?

"We must find a time for you to come and visit. You'll need some time away from that pressure cooker to take care of yourself. More than just the time while your father is at work."

"That would be great, but I don't see how." Javier flicked the bark into the bushes.

"Isn't there a real estate agent conference around the middle of January each year?"

"Yeah." Javier saw a glimmer of hope. "I think you're right."

"Glad you're feeling better."

"I've got to go Mum. Charlie's coming outside."

"Love you."

"Love you, too." Javier put the phone into his pocket as Charlie approached.

"Chatting to a secret girlfriend?" Charlie tried to wink her good eye. It came over as more of a blink.

"I wish." Javier sighed and moved to walk past her. "That reminds me though, I need to go for a drive. Can I borrow your car?"

"Sure. Just don't tell Andrew."

Her words tapered away as he went inside to collect the car keys from a sideboard drawer. He had an address to check out.

Expedition

Javier pulled the vehicle up to the kerb opposite the address Elton had given him. It was a white, rendered townhouse, one of five in a neat row in Buderim. Developers had built a multitude of such dwellings to accommodate students and staff from the university in the adjacent suburb. Families who lived in these townhouses usually couldn't afford to attend Javier's school. He began to speculate. Maybe her parents were divorced and her dad was paying the school fees while her mother provided basic accommodation?

In any case, the curtains were drawn even though it was the middle of the day. There was no car in the driveway. A few store catalogues poked through the letterbox slot. It was a house deserted. Or maybe they had moved to another house at the end of the school year?

The school had listed a post office box number as part of Olivia's contact details. Javier drove to the Buderim shops and parked the car in a shady spot under a tree where he could sit and observe the door to the PO boxes. Perhaps if he sat there for few hours each day, he would catch a member of her family checking the box and be able to follow them to the new address? He resolved to start tomorrow. First, he had a gaming appointment at Elton's to keep.

* * *

"Any luck tracking down Olivia?" Elton asked, as they completed their first game of the afternoon.

Javier wasn't convinced it was such a good idea to involve Elton, but it was nice to have a buddy to share the secret with. He was going nuts thinking about it alone.

"Not yet," Javier replied, setting the console down on the desk and leaning back in his chair. "The house looks deserted."

"Maybe they've gone out of town for the holidays?" Elton set his console down and swivelled toward Javier. "Most of the kids from your school do."

"That could be it." Javier folded his hands on his lap. "I'm planning to stake out the PO box for a few days in case one of the family goes to collect the mail."

"What then? Follow them home?"

"That's the plan."

"That's stalking, mate." Elton took a sip from a can of soft drink on the desk. "Careful you don't get yourself arrested. I'm not sure, but I think most girls prefer their boyfriends not to have a criminal record."

"Yeah, mate, I guess so." Javier's shoulders slumped.

"Has she actually shown any sign that she likes you? I mean, has she said anything?"

"She smiled at me." That was all Javier was prepared to share.

"Strewth, mate!" Elton raised his eyebrows. "Pretty much threw herself at your feet?"

"Very funny." Javier turned back toward the screen.

"You're used to getting what you want, aren't you?'

Javier sat upright in the chair, then frowned. "No. I don't always get what I want."

Elton stared him down. "Do you get an allowance so you don't need to get a job?"

"Well ... yes."

"Did your parents buy you a car?"

"My mum bought a..." Javier could see where this was going. "But it stays at her place for now."

"When you wanted to join the soccer team, who paid for the gear and paid the fees?"

Javier's shoulders slumped. "Mum."

"Look, mate." Elton took another swill of his drink. "I like you, but you're at risk of turning into just another selfish, overentitled, rich, private school kid. Instead of thinking about what you want from your family and this Olivia girl, maybe you could think about what you could do for them?"

Javier sat silent, stunned.

Elton set the can on the desk. "Just be careful. A broken heart is one thing but getting arrested is another, even if you reckon you can count on your mum to bail you out."

"Words of wisdom coming from the guy who illegally hacked into the school computer system to get her details."

"Touché." Elton mock-saluted and swivelled his chair back to face the desk. "Ready for one more game before we go hunting food?"

"Sure." Javier moved into position and took up the controller. "Reckon it's my turn to win one."

"Good luck with that." Elton worked the keyboard to set up the next game.

Back in the Saddle

Olivia went out to the horse yard nearly every day, leaning heavily on her crutches. She would pat Vanilla and offer her a carrot or an apple. As soon as Olivia could put her bulky, strapped foot to the ground, she began to give Vanilla a thorough brush down every morning. Vanilla thrived on the attention. On a warm, windy morning three weeks after her fall, Olivia gazed wistfully at the house yard gate and beyond. She wanted to be out there, riding and roaming the fields. Instead, she was cooped up with a strapped ankle.

Vanilla also gazed toward the fields.

"I know, girl," Olivia said and resumed long, even brush strokes along Vanilla's back. "You'd rather be out there too."

The phone in Olivia's back pocket chimed. Olivia placed the brush on Vanilla's back and fumbled to check the message.

Riding the boundary fence down your way tomorrow morning. Are you up to joining me? 🐎
Lauren

Olivia didn't hesitate:

Yes! 😃 🤚
Great! 👍 Meet you at the creek boundary gate 8:30 a.m.?

"Our ticket to freedom just arrived." Olivia slid the phone back into her pocket and wrapped her arms around Vanilla in a mighty hug. The horse softly snuffled. Olivia retrieved the brush and stepped back to admire her handiwork. "At least you'll look the part."

Vanilla's ears flicked about and she turned her head to face Olivia.

"Come on then, let's get you fed."

Vanilla's head popped up. Olivia unclipped the halter and Vanilla cheerfully followed Olivia toward the hay shed.

* * *

Olivia rose early and made breakfast for Art.

"You're chirpy today, Possum," Art said, munching happily on a sausage. "You've been pretty quiet lately."

"I'd rather be out riding than cooped up in the house." Olivia bit off a piece of toast.

"You're riding today then?"

Olivia nodded as she chewed.

"Are you sure you're ready?"

"Yes, Dad." Olivia waved the toast toward her leg. "The ankle is pretty much healed. I've been walking on it for a few days now."

Art shook his head. "I dunno, Possum. I'm still worried about that horse."

Olivia rolled her eyes. "Dad..."

"I'd ride with you, but I have to go into town to get a pump fixed." He finished off the sausage.

"Don't worry, Dad. I'm riding with Lauren. I'll be fine."

Art picked up his empty plate and took it to the sink. "I'd rather be riding with you." He winked in Olivia's direction as he made for the door. "Be careful, Possum," Art called out as the screen door clanged closed behind him.

"I will." Olivia popped the last of the toast into her mouth.

Already dressed in her riding clothes, Olivia set about replacing the thick bandage on her ankle with a much lighter version that would fit inside a riding boot. Sheree entered the kitchen as Olivia pressed down the cut edge of the self-adhesive strapping to secure it.

"You're not healed enough to go riding yet," Sheree said on her way to the kettle.

Olivia gently unrolled a sock over the strapping. "I'm fine, Mum."

"But you can barely walk."

"I've been walking on it for a few days, Mum. I'll be fine."

"What if you fall again and worsen the injury? You could be laid up for the rest of the holidays." Sheree pulled a cup from the cupboard and flipped in a teabag.

"I'm riding with Lauren." Olivia pulled her repaired boot gently into place. She tentatively put her foot to the ground and the boot provided sufficient support to replace the thick bandage. "If I fall, she'll make sure I get home safe."

The kettle bubbled, then clicked off. Sheree poured the steaming water into her cup. "There's something strange about that woman. I don't trust her."

"Don't trust her, or don't trust Dad around her?" Olivia raised an eyebrow and walked gingerly toward the door.

"Hmmfph." Sheree dangled the teabag over the cup, then dropped it into the bin. "Just be careful."

"I will," Olivia called back, as the screen door latched behind her.

* * *

It was good to be back in the open. Olivia was sick of being cooped up, checking her emails and texts at least four times a day for any messages from Javier. The pang of disappointment she felt each time was already too familiar, like a persistent, uninvited visitor. The still air was warm, but in the shade there were still dew droplets on the grass, glinting like diamonds when the morning sunlight caught them. Her ankle felt remarkably good and Vanilla was secure and confident under her. Olivia's spirits were as high as the eagle that drifted over the nearby fields. Her curiosity had festered during her convalescence and she was excited at the opportunity to discover more about their mysterious neighbour.

Lauren sat sentinel on her horse on the far creek bank and remained motionless as Olivia plied her way through the dry creek crossing and up the far side. Olivia spied two plump saddlebags behind Lauren's saddle.

"Good morning," Lauren called out at Olivia's approach. "How's the ankle?"

"Much better, thanks. I'm noticing it even less now that I'm back on horseback." She pulled Vanilla up beside Lauren's horse. "Thanks again for the rescue … and for saving Vanilla's life."

"No worries." Lauren smiled and patted Vanilla's neck.

"Your horse is beautiful by the way. What's his name?"

"Aztec."

"That's such a cool name."

"I thought so too." Lauren turned Aztec and began to walk off. "Ready to go?"

"Yep." Olivia turned Vanilla to follow them to the boundary gate.

"I hope your dad won't mind, but I asked my farm manager, Wayne, to install a gate that can be opened and closed without dismounting. I figured it would be a good investment if we're going to do this regularly." Lauren opened the new metal gate using a vertical attachment at the latch end.

"I'm sure that'll be fine." Olivia walked Vanilla through the gate that Lauren held open for them.

"Self-closing too!" Lauren released the gate and it swung slowly shut with a loud click.

"Cool!"

Lauren turned Aztec to the left and they rode two abreast along the fence line for a while until Lauren pulled Aztec up beside an old fence post that stood at a dubious angle. She took her foot from the stirrup and gave the post a kick. It dangled about, suspended from the wire it was supposed to be holding stable and a few splinters of old, rotten wood fell away.

"Well, that's not doing much is it?" Olivia said.

"Not much at all." Lauren took a bright yellow clip from her breast pocket and attached it to the fence. She took out her phone and tapped the screen. "Just logging the GPS coordinates of the post and dispatching it to Wayne so he can attend to it."

"Do you do this often?"

"I try to get out for a fence check a few times a week," Lauren replied. "I get to go riding—which I love—and Wayne doesn't have to waste time checking fences. He can just focus on fixing the broken bits. With a thousand acres here, there's a lot of fence line to check." Lauren changed the subject. "What year are you in at school?"

"I've just finished Year Ten and I go into Year Eleven after the holidays."

"What's your school like?"

"I go to Wattlewood Grammar on the Sunshine Coast."

Lauren raised an eyebrow and listened with interest as Olivia discussed the pros and cons of school, the teachers and the range of subject choices. Lauren paused when necessary to mark fence defects and the discussion resumed. Eventually Lauren pulled Aztec up in the shade of a tree.

"Fancy a snack?" Lauren gestured toward her saddlebag.

"Sure." The conversation was free and easy and Olivia found her neighbour to be less mysterious and suspicious and more amicable than she initially expected. "So how long have you had this place?"

"Who wants to know?" Lauren slid smoothly from the saddle. "You, or the entire town?"

Perhaps not so amicable after all.

"I do," was Olivia's cautious response.

Lauren considered her with suspicion for a few moments before her expression lightened. She began to remove items from the saddlebags. "I prefer the people I spend time with to practise discretion. Do you think you could manage that?"

"I think so." Olivia alighted from Vanilla, careful to land on her good leg.

"I grew up in a country town and I know how people talk." Lauren spread a rug on the ground. "If they don't get information, they tend to make up a story instead. Very amusing most of the time. So, what are they saying about me in town?"

"I don't know exactly what they're saying about you in town. I only know what my parents are saying about you."

Lauren glanced at Olivia expectantly and laid out a rectangular plastic container filled with pieces of cake, a bottle of cool water wrapped in a tea towel and two enamelled tin cups.

"Well, my dad thinks you're very attractive. My mum thinks you're a trophy wife. The whole town is waiting to meet your husband." Not seeing any reaction at all from Lauren, Olivia pressed on. "And everyone is frustrated because they usually try to get information from the farm manager, but they're all uncomfortable about talking to an openly gay man."

Lauren looked thoughtful for a moment, smirked a little and broke into a melodic laugh. "The whole town is stymied because Wayne is gay?" She offered Olivia some cake and a cup of water.

Olivia accepted as politely as she could manage. She got the impression that Lauren wasn't someone to be taken lightly. She nibbled on the cake.

"And what do you think, Olivia?"

Cornered, Olivia resolved to choose her words carefully. "Well, I think everyone is making a lot of assumptions based on very little information."

"Interesting," Lauren said between a mouthful of cake and a sip of water. "Do go on."

"Well, they're assuming you're married when you could be single or even divorced. Though you look too young to be divorced. And just because there are no other female owners of significant property holdings in the district, doesn't mean that you aren't the first." Olivia paused to take a breath. "Homophobia is so twentieth century. I mean you probably employed Wayne because he's a really capable farm manager and just because he's gay doesn't mean he's going to make a pass at every man in town! I mean he's probably a really nice bloke and he makes a good horse-riding gate too!"

Lauren swallowed a large bite of cake. "Wow! You know James would be totally pissed off if Wayne made a pass at any of the blokes in town?"

"Who's James?"

"Wayne's partner. He manages the household."

Olivia's eyes widened and they both chuckled.

"I like you," Lauren said. "You're honest."

Olivia fell silent.

"No need to worry girl. I'm not a lesbian."

"Excellent!" Olivia gave a sigh of relief. "Neither am I!"

"And you know it's the twenty-first century when it becomes necessary to clarify that!" Lauren raised her cup toward Lauren and resumed eating cake.

* * *

After their little picnic, they conspired to trot and canter the horses back to the boundary gate. Lauren trotted slightly ahead and Olivia saw there were no flies on the back of Lauren's shirt or buzzing around her face. Despite applying insect repellent, Olivia spent a good part of the morning brushing away flies. She twanged her shirt and a black flurry of flies briefly tumbled in the air behind her before they disappeared from view, back onto her shirt. That's how it usually was in these parts in summer; anyone outdoors was soon clad in flies. Insect repellent usually deterred them from faces, but the back of a shirt was a prime target. Olivia concluded Lauren must be using a really effective brand of insect repellent and had sprayed it from top to toe.

They pulled up at the edge of the paddock and Lauren held the gate open for Olivia and Vanilla to pass through.

"Thank you for the ride," Olivia said as the gate clicked shut. "I really enjoyed it. The cake was yummy too."

"You're welcome. I'll be in touch about the next one soon."

"Looking forward to it already." Olivia turned Vanilla toward the creek crossing.

"Before you go. I was considering inviting your family over for a barbeque. Sort of a housewarming. Do you think they'd like that?"

Olivia grinned as she considered her parents' likely reaction. "They are way too curious to decline an invitation like that!"

"Excellent! Text me your mum's email address and I'll send the invitation.

Olivia pulled her phone from her breast pocket and tapped away. "Done."

She returned the phone to her pocket, took up the reins and urged Vanilla on toward home. It wasn't until she was in sight of the house that she realised Lauren had learned a great deal about her that day, while she had learned little except that Lauren had a farmhand called Wayne whose partner's name was James. Obviously, Lauren was very good at protecting her privacy. Perhaps more would be revealed at the barbeque?

Under Control

For the next few weeks, Javier had everything under control. He spent mornings on the beach where he trained with his soccer mates. In the afternoons he hung out with Elton and gamed on Elton's computers. He was careful to be home in time for dinner.

When not distracted by his mates, Javier's thoughts drifted to Olivia. In quiet moments he gazed at her photo on his phone. He entered the details Elton retrieved from the school records into his phone contacts. He wanted to call her, but the mobile number in the school records probably belonged to one of her parents and he couldn't be sure they weren't overprotective. He knew from the format which email address on the school's record was hers and, every few days, yearning left him poised to email her. Then Elton's voice would echo in his head. What did he have to offer her? A boyfriend with a screwed-up family, no job and an uncertain future was probably the last thing she needed.

"So, how come we never go to your place?" Elton asked one day over a burger at the shopping centre.

Javier winced at the thought.

"Something you don't want me to see?" Elton took another bite of his burger and waited for a response.

"It's my dad and my stepmum." Javier glanced around to check no-one else he knew was within earshot. "They're not getting along so well."

"That's nothing new. A few of the guys we train with on the beach have similar problems."

"Well, it can get a bit tense." Javier picked up a potato chip and dipped it in sauce. "I didn't think you'd enjoy being subjected to that." He popped the chip in his mouth.

"I'm game." Elton grinned as sauce dripped from the side of his lip. "My curiosity about where you live is overriding my survival instincts."

Javier never brought friends home. It felt dangerous when his mum and dad didn't get along, it felt awkward when his dad was single, it was embarrassing and cringeworthy when Charlie and his dad had been unable to keep their hands off each other and now it felt dangerous again. He guessed what would happen if Elton encountered Andrew on a bad day and he was worried he would lose another good friend. He really liked Elton.

Javier swallowed and cleared his mouth. "Well, if you're game, how about next week then?" Maybe that would be enough time for Elton to forget about the idea?

"Deal." Elton took another bite of his burger.

Barbeque

Olivia enjoyed one more boundary fence ride with Lauren before the day of the barbeque. She came away with new information about the property and the drawn-out process of building a new house, but nothing of Lauren and her family. Sheree bombarded Olivia with probing questions but she revealed nothing.

The McKinnon family drove to Lauren's house all curiosity and excitement. Art drove Sheree's SUV over the first cattle grid. There was no property identification, no name and no number. Just white, freshly painted fencing and side guards. The road from the gate to the house was sealed for the full two-kilometre length — a contrast to the dirt track that led to their own house.

The relocated homestead stood proudly refurbished off to their right side. It sported a white post and rail fence lined with wire mesh to keep out livestock, which enclosed a veggie garden and a manicured lawn with some strategically placed shrubs and trees. The carport was carefully placed so cars could drive straight in, without the need to open any doors or gates, and a side door gave access to the house yard and the path to the back door of the house.

The burring sound of the wheels on another cattle grid marked the boundary between two paddocks and a third grid marked the entrance to the main house yard. The road opened out into a sealed circular driveway enclosing a patch of lawn with a bottle tree sapling, solid and rotund, at its centre. The garden layout was professionally designed, but most of the plants were only young.

"This bloke's not short of quid," Art said, pulling up the car near the entrance.

Olivia smiled; her father's stereotyping was off the mark and because she already suspected that someone who could afford a farm manager and a household manager was probably well-to-do.

Daphne, finally home for Christmas, looked up from her phone and flicked her bright purple hair to one side. "Yep, reckon he's loaded." She finally turned off the device and stowed it in a large pocket of her loose, green dress as the car pulled to a stop.

The verandah along the north face of the house was at the base of a massive, sloping roof, nearly completely covered in a shiny matrix of solar panels. Art pulled up close to the house. As Olivia and her family alighted, a small group appeared from under the verandah. Olivia recognised Lauren, who walked toward them with a welcoming smile. She wore a white linen shirt dress, cinched by a belt at her waist, and her hair swished loose and straight about her shoulders. An angelic vision in white and a dramatic contrast to her riding attire.

"Welcome." Lauren looked at them in turn. "So glad you could come."

"Thank you for inviting us." Sheree gushed forward and presented Lauren with a bowl of the McKinnon's favourite pasta salad. She glanced around the scene and the members of Lauren's household.

"Thank you, Sheree. This is my daughter Elise." Lauren gestured to an elegant young woman wearing a loose-fitting, striped, boat-neck top and tight white jeans.

Olivia blinked in surprise at the word "daughter"; Elise looked no more than a decade younger than Lauren, if that.

"And this is our farm manager, Wayne, and his partner, James." Both were suitably showered, combed and dressed for the occasion.

Sheree introduced Art, Daphne and Olivia in turn. Daphne flicked her gaze to each in turn and rolled her eyes.

Lauren led them past the barbeque, all set up and ready on the verandah, into the house.

Art piped up. "Is your husband about?"

Lauren and her household glanced at each other and smirked as if sharing a secret joke. Lauren winked at Olivia. "There is no husband. I'm happily divorced."

Art blushed and looked decidedly sheepish. Sheree glared at Lauren as if monitoring a predator. It took all Olivia's effort not to giggle at their awkwardness as they passed through the large doors into the house. This promised to be more entertaining than even Olivia expected.

Lauren turned. "I have a son too, but he is spending the Christmas break with his father in town."

Beyond the entrance, the room opened up into a grand space with a cathedral ceiling and a suspended mezzanine level. Before them a long dining table was immaculately set for eight. Lauren moved toward the large kitchen island on the right, adorned with covered platters and bowls and carefully placed Sheree's salad among them. Not that anyone noticed; the McKinnons were mesmerised by the wall of windows and the spectacle of landscape beyond.

Outside the windows was a paved area with a rectangular central swimming pool, beyond which the paving, gardens and lawn dropped out of sight to reveal the wide landscape.

"This is freaking awesome!" Daphne blurted out.

Sheree elbowed her in the ribs and whispered, "Mind your language!"

Art moved to Daphne's other side and leaned in. "Yeah, mind your bloody language." He grinned and winked at her.

Daphne glared at her mother and elbowed her father in the ribs. Olivia and the others stifled giggles.

"I just love the view too," Lauren said, breaking the awkwardness with a smile.

"That's our place." Olivia pointed off into the distance. From here their home was a small cluster of trees and a few outbuildings, the edge of their verandah just visible, poking out from behind the greenery.

"Yep!" Elise said. "Mum thought you might like to see for yourself that despite all the windows, we're not spying on you from here." Elise was tall, with long, wavy, strawberry-blonde hair tied back in a loose ponytail to reveal her pale and lightly freckled complexion. Seeing the two of them together, Olivia decided that Lauren definitely looked too young to be Elise's mother. There was some resemblance in their faces; same nose and chin maybe. They looked more like sisters.

Wayne was muscular, his skin dark-tanned from working outdoors. He was tense, as if unaccustomed to indoor events, so Olivia assumed he had shaved, showered and gelled his dark wavy hair especially for the occasion. He stood awkwardly for a while. Clearly mixed company and conversation were not a strong point. Eventually Wayne made his way to the refrigerator and retrieved a tray of meat and a couple of beers. "Time to fire up the barbeque." He looked Art in the eye and held out a beer. "Would you like to help?"

Art paused, awkward; torn between the tradition of doing the "bloke" thing of congregating around the cooking of meat and trying to avoid the company of a gay man.

"What varieties of lucerne have you got in, mate?" Wayne asked in another attempt to break the tension. "I've got two in and I'm trialling them under irrigation and dry land."

Art finally relaxed; lucerne and farming were his passions. He stepped forward and took the offered can. It dripped with condensation. "I've had the same varieties in for a few years now and I'm getting good yields..." Art's voice trailed off as the two men and the meat tray disappeared to the verandah.

The immaculately groomed and dressed James served drinks and a platter of canapés. With tidy, brown hair, smart casual clothing and concise diction he was blatantly out of place in a rural backwater like this.

Elise and Daphne discovered they were attending the same university in Brisbane and promptly made for a nook in the living room where they could compare observations while they availed themselves of James's food and drink service.

Lauren passed by Olivia enroute to engage Sheree in conversation and whispered, "No one in town seems to know that James exists yet. I'm impressed!"

"They will tomorrow," Olivia whispered back. She had passed the first discretion test. Olivia took her sparkling apple juice drink and perched on a stool at the kitchen island, happy to watch the interactions in the room while James fussed nearby and periodically tried to engage her in conversation about the food, the décor and her school.

* * *

By the time they were all seated at the table, everyone was relaxed in each other's company.

"Would you mind passing the green salad?" Olivia asked.

James promptly passed it to Olivia. He picked up the pasta salad and passed it to Lauren.

"Wouldn't mind some of those potato thingies," Art said, passing the platter of meat on to Sheree. "They look pretty good."

"The potato wedges?" James verified, retrieving the green salad from Olivia and passing it to Lauren.

"That's them." Art received the platter from Wayne.

Elise took the platter of meat from Sheree, put a couple of sausages onto her plate, then passed it to her mother. Wayne sent a bottle of sparkling apple juice down to Lauren. It looked appealing, and before Olivia could ask for it, Lauren placed it on the table in front of her.

Olivia paused to take it all in. A blue-sky day, spectacular views, sumptuous food and convivial conversation. So far, her family had managed to avoid saying anything overly embarrassing and she felt happier and more content than she could remember. She wondered if this was how Mel felt at her large family gatherings.

James beamed with satisfaction as the food was repeatedly declared delicious.

Olivia ate and drank and observed the "dance" of food, fine wine and soft drinks passed among friends and family. As she watched, she sensed that something wasn't quite right. Something about the dynamic irked her, something unusual but subtle. She couldn't quite put her finger on it.

After the meal, Wayne took Art on a quick tour of the outbuildings and house paddocks while Lauren and James treated Sheree and the girls to a tour of the house and garden.

After the tours, Sheree suggested it was time to leave.

"No, you must stay for afternoon tea." Elise was adamant. "James has baked." Her tone had the authority of someone stating a self-evident fact.

"Very well," Sheree quietly acquiesced.

James was delighted to present a pavlova adorned with mango, kiwi fruit and finger lime balls, and a black sapote chocolate cake glazed with a chocolate ganache.

"I'm in!" Art took up a plate and started the queue for slices of the confections.

"All the fruit's from the garden." Wayne grabbed a plate and lined up behind Art.

"Impressive!" Sheree nudged in front of Art. who made space for his wife to go first.

Lauren gestured for Olivia to take a plate and join the queue.

Olivia complied and observed the ritual. Art asked for and received a generous slice of each confection. Wayne said nothing. He just presented his plate and received the same. Sheree and Daphne asked for pavlova. Lauren and Elise said nothing and received a thin sliver of chocolate cake and pavlova respectively. It all seemed ordinary, yet somehow not. Olivia still couldn't pin down what irked her about it all.

* * *

Taste buds, bellies and curiosities sated, Sheree finally placed her napkin on her empty plate and stood up. "We should be going now. There are chores that need doing."

From a pose of slouched contentment, Art forced himself to his feet. "Yep. Must be going." He glanced at his daughters; it was a signal for them to follow suit.

By the time they reached the car, they were gushing out their thanks. Sheree vowed she would organise a reciprocal gathering at the McKinnon's farm soon. James looked smug and satisfied with how the event had played out and Lauren's household seemed politely pleased at their departure. Olivia thought she heard a sigh of relief as they bundled into their car for the trip home.

"What an amazing home!" Sheree started the debrief, still waving as the car burred over the first cattle grid.

"Yeah, you don't see many houses like that around here," Art chimed in.

"You don't see any houses like that around here … period." Daphne retrieved her phone from her pocket and flicked on the screen.

"Agreed," Sheree said and no one argued the point.

"The food was bloody good, wasn't it?" Art said.

"City restaurant quality, I'd say," Daphne replied, while her eyes remained on the screen.

"That Wayne's not a bad bloke after all," Art added. "I mean Lauren has some crazy ideas about what to grow on the place, but Wayne reckons he can make it work. If they can turn a profit on some of these new ventures, it might be worth us giving them a go too—after they've ironed all the bugs out."

"Apparently, Lauren bought the place using a family trust and visited regularly during the set-up phase, but only moved in after the new house was ready." Sheree looked smugly satisfied to have gleaned information that no one else in town knew … yet. "She seems nice enough, but she doesn't look a day over thirty. Way too young to be Elise's mother."

"Absolutely!" Daphne glanced in her mother's direction. "I reckon she's had some work done. With all that money, why wouldn't you?"

"I wouldn't!" Art said. They all laughed.

"What do you think, Livvie?" Sheree turned toward the rear seats. "You've been rather quiet there in the back."

Olivia was indeed quiet. She gazed out the window, listened to the conversation and smiled at how her family's opinions about their neighbours had transformed in a single visit. "I like them. I think they're going to be excellent neighbours." But there was something about them that still needled away in the back of her mind.

"Did anyone catch their last name?" Art glanced at the girls via the rear-view mirror.

"Never thought to ask," Sheree replied.

Daphne, thoroughly engaged with her mobile phone, shrugged. Olivia looked out the window, trying to hide her amusement.

Detective Olivia

Olivia lay restless in bed that night in the room she shared with Daphne. She listened to the quiet whirr of the ceiling fan and replayed the barbeque over and over in her mind. She tried to pinpoint what it was that seemed odd, but eventually fell asleep without any success. She woke with a start before dawn and recalled fragments of a dream about bees. As echoes of the quiet buzzing faded, she remembered how the queen bee moved around the comb, attended by a team of worker bees that moved with her and tended her without any discernible means of communication. Olivia sat bolt upright.

Once again, she replayed the barbeque in her mind, but this time it was clear: the entire process from greeting to departure had occurred without Lauren uttering a single word to Elise, Wayne, or James. Wayne and James had spoken to Lauren, but Elise hadn't uttered a word to her mother either. The whole operation had run with clockwork precision, with barely any discernible communication! She considered the possibility that they may have arrived during a family dispute, but their body language wasn't hostile. Lauren had placed a reassuring arm around Elise's waist during the introductions and Elise had reciprocated during the farewells, both without a hint of antipathy. The entire group was friendly and relaxed for the whole event.

At the table, condiments and bowls were passed to Lauren and between Lauren and Elise without Lauren uttering a single word. When Olivia or Sheree offered to pass items to Lauren that she had not yet received, she had politely declined; presumably, she was not fond of those.

Olivia couldn't get back to sleep. She pondered her discovery and its implications over and over. It haunted her all day too, but she said nothing to her family. Over the next couple of days, Sheree noticed and repeatedly asked, "Are you OK?" To which Olivia consistently replied, "I'm fine." The following day a text arrived:

Boundary riding tomorrow.
Would you like to join me?
Same meeting place. Same time.
🐴 ☺
Lauren

Olivia replied:

Thanks. I'll be there 😃 👍 🐴

* * *

Olivia saddled up Vanilla and made her way toward the boundary fence in the same way she had done on every other ride with Lauren, but this time was different. This time she had butterflies in her stomach. This time she rehearsed what she might say over and over in her mind. This time she questioned whether or not she would have the courage to ask.

As Olivia walked Vanilla up the creek embankment, she saw Lauren on Aztec as she waited patiently by the open boundary gate with a welcoming smile.

"Good morning!" Lauren called out when Olivia was within earshot.

"Hi!" Olivia replied as she made her way through the open gate. This time she felt more nervous around Lauren than ever before.

Lauren released the gate and the pair set off toward a distant hill. "Wayne reckons I should check the fences of the west hill paddock today. I hope you won't mind riding some bush country."

"Sounds like fun." Olivia tried to sound enthused.

Lauren glanced at Olivia with a wry, knowing smile. "We'd better get a shuffle on, or we'll spend most of our time just getting there."

Lauren urged Aztec to a trot, then to a gentle canter. Olivia did the same with Vanilla and followed a short distance behind.

The firebreak cut on either side heralded the fence line as it sliced like a cheese wire through the bush country on the hill. They took the horses slowly and gave them time to find their footing on the rocky ground. The rains had washed away soil from the hillside and revealed a myriad of pebbles and rough stones. Wayne recently had cattle in this paddock, so most of the remaining grass was eaten close to the ground and this enabled Lauren and Olivia to better see the obstacles before them. As usual, Lauren marked any sites of fence damage, but this time she also marked any saplings that grew on this side of the firebreak so that Wayne could cut them down. Proceeding thus, they covered the entire west fence line before they broke for morning tea at a fallen log in the shade of an ancient eucalypt.

The day was already hot, the sky cloudless and the aroma of eucalyptus wafted from fallen leaves, baked by the sun. A currawong warbled in the distance above the thrum of cicadas. They tied the horses to nearby shrubs and left them to munch on a patch of dry grass while they settled on the log for some chewy Anzac biscuits and iced tea.

As is common out bush, they were soon joined by a growing multitude of flies. Olivia incessantly waved them away from her face and could only imagine how many rode on the back of her shirt. Once again, Lauren was not thus troubled. There were no flies on her clothes, no pesky flies circled her face and none troubled the food—at least not until Olivia touched it. Olivia was annoyed with herself for not applying insect repellent before she left home. Clearly, Lauren had done so. But why did the flies stay away from the food? Nobody applied insect repellent to food; at least, it didn't taste as though it was so treated. Maybe it was all connected? Her stomach twinged again. She had to say something soon, before she lost her nerve.

Lauren swallowed a mouthful of biscuit. "Did your family enjoy the barbeque?"

Olivia hastily swallowed a mouthful that wasn't quite ready and it grated her throat. She flushed down some iced tea to head off a spluttery cough. "Very much. Thank you again for inviting us."

"You're welcome. I think Daphne and Elise discovered they had much in common."

Olivia nodded and added, "Much more than Daphne was expecting."

"Much more than Elise was expecting too!"

Olivia tried unsuccessfully to stifle a chuckle as she imagined Elise whining about having to entertain Daphne as much as Daphne had whined about having to attend the barbeque at all. "I reckon my dad was surprised that Wayne was such a good bloke too."

Damn! She was back to making small talk and her nerve began to fade.

"Yep!" Lauren sipped from her cup. "Wayne was surprised Art was less hostile than he was expecting. I guess once you get farmers talking about lucerne, the other differences don't matter so much."

"Well, my dad was way less hostile and much better behaved than I was expecting."

Lauren spluttered her drink and laughed out loud. "Parents can be so embarrassing sometimes."

"Really embarrassing!" Olivia blurted out before she remembered that Lauren was a parent too.

"Don't worry, when I was a teen, I thought my parents were the most embarrassing people on earth. My kids think I embarrass them on purpose and I'm certain that when they have teenage kids one day, those kids will feel the same. It comes with the territory of being a teenager."

"I don't think you're embarrassing." In her mind Olivia added, "*mysterious and weird maybe but not embarrassing*", though the words were never uttered — another sign of her depleting gumption.

Lauren cast her a piqued glance at first, then her face brightened. "Well, thank you. I'll take that as a compliment. While we're talking about parents, your mother seemed to enjoy the day."

"Yep. I think she's still trying to extract some recipes from James." Olivia waved some flies from her face. "Can't blame her, the food was really good. She loved seeing the house too. It's nothing like other houses in the district. Actually, it's not like any house I've seen anywhere. It's really amazing."

Lauren beamed at the compliment. "Thanks. I really like how it's turned out."

Olivia took another biscuit. She stared at the ground and noticed an ant carrying off a biscuit crumb as she tried to find words. Even though Olivia found conversation with Lauren easy, she had a sense that Lauren could be formidable when crossed and she was worried about how Lauren would take her questions. What if she was wrong? What if all she achieved was to offend Lauren and lose a great riding partner? Would she be confined to riding in the house paddock for the rest of the holidays? Would she never get to ride in the Kilkivan Horse Ride?

Lauren frowned. "Is everything OK? Is something bothering you that I can help with?"

It was now or never. Olivia took a deep breath and finally her curiosity overpowered her self doubt. She had planned a carefully considered question, but her body tensed up and her heart beat faster and all the clever words melted away. "Can you read minds?" she blurted out, then recoiled and berated herself internally for being so blunt and tactless.

Challenge

"Jeez, mate! Nice house," Elton said as soon as Javier opened the front door. "Guess you've been slumming it at my place?"

Javier stepped aside and gestured for Elton to enter. "Nah, I think of this place more as a gilded cage." Javier closed the door and followed Elton into the lounge room. "This is Charlie." He gestured toward the kitchen.

"You must be Elton," Charlie said as she cut a glazed chocolate mud cake into slices. "I thought you two might get hungry." She placed a slice onto a plate and slid it along the kitchen island in Elton's direction.

Elton stepped up to claim it. "Thanks."

Charlie had two more plates at the ready.

"'Scuse me a minute." Javier suddenly needed to visit the bathroom. He took the time to wash his hands and enjoy the peace and quiet. The muffled sound of friendly banter meant Charlie and Elton were getting along. The reverie was broken by loud yelling. "Oh crap! Dad's home." Javier bolted for the kitchen.

"Who the hell is this?" Andrew's face was purple as he stormed toward Charlie.

Javier leapt between them. "He's a mate from soccer, come over to watch a movie."

"Likely bloody story." Andrew pulled up inches from Javier. He moved to go around him; Javier blocked his path.

"More likely you're seeing this prick behind my back and you've got Javier covering for you." He made another unsuccessful attempt to circle past Javier. "Bloody whore."

Elton sat statue still, ice pale. His fork, with a piece of cake skewered on it, was held in mid-air.

Javier inhaled deeply and focussed his mind. "He's my mate from soccer, Dad, and you need to go back to work."

Andrew's face became a lighter shade of purple. He glared at Charlie.

"You need to go back to work, Dad," Javier repeated, calm now and motionless.

Andrew switched his gaze to Javier. "I should be getting back to work."

Javier's shoulders relaxed. "Yes, Dad, you need to get back to work."

Andrew turned, took his car keys from his pocket and made for the door. "The prick better be gone by the time I get home," he said, closing the door behind him.

"Yes, Dad," Javier called after him. He heaved a sigh and turned to Elton. "Sorry about that, mate. Now you know why I don't invite people home."

"Me either," Charlie whispered.

"You alright?" Javier realised Charlie still had a knife in her hand. He felt a pang in his gut as it dawned on him what might have happened.

"I think so," she replied. "After all, it could have been worse."

Javier rolled his eyes. She still didn't realise the danger. "So, where's my piece of cake then?"

Charlie placed a fork on the laden plate and pushed it toward Javier. A loud cry sounded from a distant room. "All that noise has woken Henry. Excuse me." Charlie dashed off to soothe the child.

"That was bloody awesome, mate!" Elton finally placed the piece of cake in his mouth and waved the fork about.

Javier stared at him, incredulous.

"Sorry, I know you don't like swearing and I can see why." Elton waved his fork toward Javier. "That was still bloody awesome though." He paused a moment, thoughtful. "Are you a Jedi or something? I mean that was a real 'these aren't the droids you're looking for' moment."

Javier just shrugged. "I just do what works." He sliced a piece of cake off with his fork.

"Maybe I was wrong about you, mate." Elton sliced off another bite-size piece of cake. "Maybe you're not just a selfish, entitled jerk. Maybe you're the hero secretly protecting Charlie and Henry." Elton put the cake in his mouth. "Girls love heroes, mate. Reckon that Olivia girl would too."

Javier wallowed in guilt. He didn't want to be a hero. Still, if it helped him get Olivia ... "So, what movie shall we watch?" He tilted his head toward the TV.

"Look at the size of that freakin' screen!"

Javier was glad Elton was so easily distracted. He popped the forkful of cake into his mouth and relished the soft chocolate sensation. Charlie sure baked a luscious chocolate mud cake.

"Can't blame your dad though." Elton walked reverently toward the screen. "I mean Charlie is pretty hot. I reckon I'd be a bit jealous too if she was my wife "

"Jealousy doesn't justify assault, mate."

"You're right, Javier. It doesn't." He sat and gazed at the screen in awe, even though it wasn't switched on yet.

Risk

Lauren reached for another biscuit and stopped mid-reach. She held her cup of iced tea firmly between both hands and gazed quizzically at Olivia. "What makes you think that?"

Lauren's fingers were white on her cup. She held it very firmly indeed; had it not been a strong enamel mug, it might have been crushed to splinters in her hands. Olivia resolved to choose her words carefully, but her heart pounded in her chest and she struggled to string the words together.

"Well," she began, as she tried to buy herself thinking time. "During the entire barbeque, you barely said a word to Elise, James and Wayne, yet you all acted as if you were talking to each other. I mean, Wayne and James were talking to you about things, but you barely answered them and you and Elise barely spoke at all. You just looked at each other sometimes as if you had said something."

Olivia stopped talking. She had blurted out far too much information already. She worried she might explode with suspense waiting for Lauren to respond, but Lauren just sat there and gripped her cup. The small furrow in Lauren's brow suggested she was considering Olivia's revelation carefully, but to Olivia's intense frustration it felt like minutes passed before Lauren finally drew breath to speak.

"The answer to your question is yes and no. We keep to ourselves and rarely have social functions at our home in case someone notices." Lauren still gripped the cup tight. "It sounds like Wayne and James did a good job at camouflage, but Elise and I let the side down. We'll have to do better next time."

Olivia stared at Lauren in stunned silence. Would this be like a scene from one of the thriller movies that her dad liked to watch? After all, the two of them were alone in isolated bushland with no witnesses beyond two horses, now busily eating grass. Still, she had told her parents where she was going, maybe that would be protection enough?

Lauren relaxed, chuckled and loosened her grip on the cup. "Don't worry, I don't dispose of people to keep our secret."

Olivia tried to smile, but she was still tense and it felt as awkward as it probably looked. She was somewhat reassured, but had Lauren just read her mind or did she deduce what she was probably thinking from the pale, scared expression on her face?

"Do you think any other members of your family noticed?"

"I don't think so." Olivia was confident about that. "They don't pay attention to that sort of thing. After all, it's not something you expect around here … or anywhere else for that matter."

"Indeed." Lauren released one hand, put her elbow on her knee and rested her head on the closed fist. "So, you're the only one who suspects. What shall we do with you?" Lauren flashed Olivia a mischievous grin that partially neutralised Olivia's alarm at the question.

"Well, you know I won't tell anyone." Olivia tried to sound reassuring. "I'm very discreet."

"That does appear to be the case." Lauren sat her cup on the log beside her. "Not that anyone would believe you anyway. After all, it is practically impossible to produce evidence."

"I guess so." Olivia realised that any attempt to expose Lauren's secret could easily backfire. Perhaps Lauren had years of experience managing such situations; surely Olivia was not the first to notice.

"Good." Lauren seemed satisfied. "Now we can pack up here and get onto the next stretch of fence line."

A short while later, they rode along the northern fence line of the same paddock. They ambled past a mob of kangaroos lazing in the shade. A few of them popped their heads up in alert curiosity, but Olivia barely noticed. She followed a little behind, deep in thought, pondering the implications of her discovery. Lauren busied herself with marking the fence and saplings as if content to give Olivia processing time.

Eventually Olivia egged Vanilla up beside Aztec. "I was just thinking." Olivia broke the silence.

"Yes?" Lauren replied as the two horses walked casually, side by side.

"Could you...?" Olivia started, tense and uncertain. "I mean, would you please teach me?"

Lauren pulled Aztec to an abrupt halt. Vanilla walked a few steps more before Olivia too pulled up.

"Really?!"

"Uh huh. I mean, please"

"Look," Lauren began. "I appreciate the excellent manners, but I don't think you've really thought through the implications of your request."

"Yes, I have. Just then, while we were walking."

"So, you want me to teach you a skill that will make you feel socially awkward for the rest of your life. A skill that will make people feel somewhat ill at ease around you even though they can't quite put a finger on why. All this so you can gain an unfair advantage over people." Lauren's eyes fixed on Olivia, expectant of a response.

"Well, not exactly," Olivia mumbled, caught out.

Lauren's stern expression softened as Olivia faltered. "I'll make you a deal. I'm not planning to ride again for five days. That gives you time to think this through. If you really want me to teach you, you'll need to give me a good reason why you want to learn."

"That's fair." Olivia was certain she could think of ample reasons in five days.

"And you'll also have to watch *The Karate Kid* movie," Lauren added. "The first one or the newer remake, doesn't matter which, as long as you watch one of them."

Olivia was puzzled. "Why?"

"Hopefully, that will become clearer after you've watched the movie."

Olivia pondered for a moment. "Do you know how … I mean, have you ever actually taught anyone else how to do it?"

"Both my kids and Wayne and James." With that, Lauren urged Aztec forward. "Now can we talk about something else? This is getting dull. I'm planning on running some goats on the place. What do you think?"

"Goats! What kind of goats?" Olivia urged Vanilla forward to keep up.

When The Student Is Ready

It was a long five days.

Olivia found the first *Karate Kid* movie in her dad's DVD collection, and as the remake was now rather old (for a movie), it was easy and cheap to access from a streaming service. She watched the original on the family TV and the other on her laptop while cloistered in her bedroom. The movies were a welcome distraction from unsuccessfully trying not to think about Javier. After each viewing, Olivia went for a walk, or did some chores, or just sat around brooding and pondering. Deep in her own thoughts, she didn't notice her parents hovering about more, even though they repeatedly asked if she was OK. Olivia gave a standard response, "fine thanks", and resumed what she was doing. She cheerfully participated in other activities and conversations with her family, but this part of her life, she kept closed off.

When the day of the next ride with Lauren finally arrived, Olivia rose early. She was too excited to sleep any longer than necessary. She scoffed down the fried eggs and toast that Sheree had prepared for her and downed a glass of orange juice in only two gulps in her haste to be on her way.

"I'm going riding with Lauren." Olivia raced out the door toward the horse yard.

* * *

"Beautiful day for it," Lauren said as soon as Olivia was within hearing range.

"Sure is." Olivia hadn't paid attention before, but the azure sky was cloudless. A currawong warbled from the thick vegetation of the creek bed and a flock of galahs scavenging breakfast in the nearby pasture took flight; a pink and grey flurry of feathers, screeches and squawks as they disappeared over fields of lush green lucerne and tall, dry pasture dotted with lazy, munching cows. A warm breeze gently ruffled the grasses and leaves and the temperature at this hour heralded another hot day.

They plied their way to the western field that was the target of the day's inspection and chatted on the way about how their respective families had celebrated the new year. Art had taken the family to Goomeri in the afternoon. At Sheree's insistence, they had stopped in for afternoon tea at the Goomeri bakery then headed to the Showgrounds to watch the finals of the rodeo. Art had whooped and cheered at the thrills and spills of the competition. Olivia had watched on, largely in silence, too concerned for the animals and injured competitors to enjoy the events.

Sheree had alternated between cheering riders and gazing with concern at Olivia. Arriving in the afternoon, after the worst of the day's heat, was a smart move as it left them energetic enough to enjoy the music and dancing that followed. The fireworks at midnight were modest, but much appreciated by the crowd. Daphne had returned to the city for work and Sheree tried to video call her at midnight to include her in the festivities, but Daphne wouldn't pick up the call and simply texted 'Happy New Year' half an hour after midnight—she had her own life now.

Lauren described her family's more subdued celebrations. They had played a family table tennis tournament and a pool tournament, all the while consuming delicious food and drinks that James had spent two days preparing. At midnight they had all paused to watch the Sydney fireworks on the large screen TV and toast in the new year.

"After all," Lauren declared. "It just doesn't feel like a new year unless I've seen Sydney Harbour and the bridge exploding in fireworks to a soundtrack that becomes more unfamiliar with every passing year."

"Really?" Olivia smirked at the thought. "I find the soundtrack gets more familiar each year. Not so many of those old-time tracks that no one has heard of."

Lauren didn't respond other than raising an eyebrow as she held open the gate to the western paddock. A shiny new fence sparkled in the sun.

"Wow!" Olivia took in the sight. "What kind of fence is that?"

"An exclusion fence. Part of my crazy idea to run goats on the place."

"It's really tall." It was too, nearly two metres tall with two strands of barbed wire at the top and an interlock mesh below, with progressively smaller spacing as it approached the ground where it disappeared.

"The mesh runs about half a metre under the ground on the outside." Lauren pointed at the plant-free band of earth along the outside of the fence.

"Well, that should keep the dogs out."

"I hope so. It cost enough. The tricky part is making sure all the kangaroos and feral deer are on the outside before we close off the fence for this paddock. Otherwise, it just becomes a very protected breeding ground for interlopers. The gate will be impressive too, two metres tall with a concrete runner embedded in the ground below and motion-activated light to scare off any dogs that might think about breaching it during the night."

Olivia marvelled at the engineering of the fence as they made their way along it. She wondered what her dad might say about it. In fact, it gave her a safe topic to talk to her parents about when she got home from the ride. She figured that after a few dismissive comments about the "bloody waste of money" he would watch closely to see if it actually protected the livestock against the ever-increasing population of feral dogs in the area.

Feeling awkward about how to broach the subject, Olivia blurted out, "I watched the Karate Kid movie!"

Lauren kept Aztec casually pacing forward and seemed totally calm and relaxed as she turned to Olivia and asked, "Which one?"

"Both of them." Olivia was confident her homework was thoroughly completed.

"How many times?"

"Lost count." Olivia was a little sheepish now. Would Lauren think she was too obsessive and not want to teach her?

"Impressive. Are you always this thorough?"

"Only when something is important to me."

"I notice you're just a tad persistent too."

Olivia tilted her head in dismay. "Only when something is important to me." She wondered if all hope of being taught was ebbing away.

Lauren glanced back at Olivia. "So, did you come up with a good reason why I should teach you?"

"Actually," Olivia began, more cautious now. "I think only you can answer that question. I can only tell you why I want to learn."

"Fascinating." Lauren flashed a raised-eyebrow glance. "Go on."

"Well, after watching the movies, I thought it would be good to learn it for self-defence. I mean if someone intended to hurt you and you knew about it in advance, you could take action to protect yourself."

Olivia paused to gauge Lauren's reaction, but there wasn't one, so she continued. "Then I thought it could also be used offensively. I mean, you could mess with people's heads and get them to do what you wanted them to do. If your intentions were good, it could work out OK. If they weren't, or if you just got used to messing with people it could get horrible for them."

Still no reaction from Lauren, so she took a deep breath and pressed on. "Then I thought, hang on, it's a communication skill. I mean, thousands of years ago, our ancestors just communicated using gestures and grunts. They got by, but I bet there were a lot of misunderstood conversations that probably ended brutally. When they developed spoken language and they could communicate more clearly, with fewer misunderstandings, it helped them to work together better. They even developed writing and reading so that messages could be effectively sent over long distances and even through time. I mean, we're still able to read ancient stories and poems today."

Lauren pursed her lips and tilted her head.

Olivia took it as a sign to continue. "So now we've developed smart phones and we can communicate with anyone and get information from anywhere in the world. There are even apps that can translate so language isn't a barrier. Our privacy has been broken down too, with computers being able to monitor our calls and conversations. But what if we've had the capacity to do this all along? I mean, send information and messages to each other over vast distances without the aid of a device? What if this is just the next step in our evolution? I think it would be kinda like karate and kung fu; if everyone is taught how to do it, then no one is particularly advantaged or disadvantaged. They all learn to respect each other and exercise self-discipline in how they use the skills. So, I want to learn it because I think it's important for our evolution and hope that one day, we can teach everyone."

"I see," Lauren said. "But before we change the world, what about people treating you differently because they sense something different about you?"

"That's kinda like martial arts too," Olivia said. "I mean, when people who have been picked on learn martial arts, they become more confident in their ability to defend themselves and this changes how they carry themselves and how they behave, so people treat them differently. It's not necessarily a bad thing."

There was a brief pause. Olivia added, "Though I reckon being telepathic could probably have gotten you burned at the stake a couple hundred years ago."

"Probably." Lauren gazed off into the distance as if lost in a faraway memory.

"Fortunately, we live in more tolerant times."

"Fortunately for both of us," Lauren said with a wry grin.

"Does that mean you'll teach me?" Olivia almost shouted with excitement.

"Very well."

"Awesome! When do we start?"

"After we've had something to eat. See if you can find us a good spot for morning tea."

Olivia fought to contain her excitement and scanned the area for a suitable spot. She spied a patch of shade cast by an old eucalypt some distance in from the fence. "Will that do?"

"Excellent," replied Lauren. They turned the horses to make for the shade.

* * *

Replete on cake and iced tea and with the horses casually munching grass nearby, Olivia and Lauren sat quietly on the ground, relaxed in the warmth of the summer day. Despite spraying herself thoroughly with insect repellent before leaving home this time, Olivia was still annoyed by the occasional persistent fly. They also sat near an ant trail and an orderly parade of meat ants marched to and from the nearby nest. Meat ants had a nasty bite, so Olivia brushed a few stray, exploring ants from the top of her boot. She noticed that Lauren was not only completely unperturbed by flies again, but the ant trail had developed a distinct curve around Lauren as if to give her a wide berth. Lauren must have used a superior insect repellent and Olivia resolved to ask the brand sometime. For the moment though, she had more pressing things on her mind.

"So, can we start now?" Olivia interrupted the sounds of nature around them, the rustle of leaves in the breeze, the strum of cicadas and the distant bellow of a cow.

"Very well." Lauren averted her gaze from the far creek and focussed on Olivia. "What else did you glean from the Karate Kid movies? Having watched them so often, I'm sure not much got past you."

Olivia grinned at the sarcastic compliment. "Well, I noticed there was lots of self-discipline involved and, in the beginning, there was lots of excruciating, meaningless repetition. I'm wondering what the mental equivalent is of painting the fence or picking up the jacket?"

Bemused, Lauren said, "So, you have some idea of what you are in for?"

Olivia gave a sheepish nod and hoped it wouldn't be too tedious.

"OK," Lauren said. "I propose that we continue to ride twice each week. During each ride, I'll give you an exercise to practise and a point or question to ponder and we'll see how you've gone at the next ride. Sound OK?"

"Sounds like fun." Olivia's voice had the wavering uncertainty of someone unconvinced.

"Maybe." Lauren plucked a stalk of dry grass and rolled it between her fingers. "So, this week we're going to start exercises to teach you how to relax."

"The mental equivalent of painting the fence?"

"Exactly! Do they teach, what do they call it now? Ah, yes, mindfulness. Do they teach mindfulness at your school?"

"They tried in Year Eight, but most of us didn't really see the point." Olivia quickly added, "But I think I'm beginning to, now."

"Good. Now sit comfortably upright."

Olivia sat bolt upright and began to wrestle with her legs.

"What are you doing?"

"Trying ... to ... ugh ... get into the ... lotus position," Olivia mumbled as she tried to get the foot of each crossed leg to sit on the opposite thigh. Wearing tight jeans and riding boots wasn't helping.

"What are you doing that for?"

"It's supposed to be the best position to sit in for meditation." Olivia puffed and gave her left foot one last heave into position.

"Yes," Lauren said. "An excellent position if you want to focus on the annoying pain that is developing in your ankles and butt."

Tension was indeed building at both those sites and Olivia untangled her legs.

"Now, like I said, sit comfortably upright."

Olivia experimented and found she was most comfortable sitting with her legs casually crossed.

"Better." Lauren beamed approval. "At home you could practise sitting in a chair, on a cushion, on your bed, on the edge of your bed, whatever is comfortable."

Olivia was impatient to get to the good bit. "OK."

"Best to sit upright though. That way, if you find yourself so relaxed that you fall asleep, you'll at least wake up when you fall over!"

Olivia chuckled at the thought.

"Now, you can keep your eyes open a little if you want to, but if you find it distracting, then best to close them."

Olivia closed her eyes and became instantly aware of the sounds around her. A breeze rustled the leaves and grasses, a bird chirped, cicadas sang, one of the horses farted—that made her smile. Lauren's voice was also clearer and easier to focus on.

"Good. Now you're aware of the sounds around you."

Olivia unsuccessfully tried to hold back a grin.

"We're going to start by practising relaxation."

"But I'm already really relaxed." Olivia frowned in frustration. "Can't we just move on to the next step?"

There was no response, so Olivia opened her eyes. Lauren gazed at her expectantly.

"What?"

Lauren lifted an eyebrow and continued gazing directly at Olivia.

"Oh, I remember." Olivia's shoulders slumped in defeat. "We're patiently and repetitively painting the fence."

Lauren smiled and Olivia closed her eyes again.

"Now, notice your breaths. Each time you inhale you take in life-giving oxygen and each time you exhale, you release waste gasses back into the atmosphere."

Olivia became more aware of the sensation of breathing as Lauren spoke.

"So, we're going to use your breaths to get rid of tension that you don't need. Now, notice any tension in your feet, then gently escort it slowly up to your lungs and exhale it with the next breath."

Olivia imagined the tension as a kind of grey smoke. She imagined it flowing up to her lungs and out into the air when she exhaled.

"Good. Now do the same with the tension in your legs, then your hands, then your arms, then your abdomen, then your head, then your neck and finally expel the last remnants of tension in your chest and just breathe."

Olivia did as instructed. When the task was completed, her body seemed barely there; her consciousness alone sat within the sounds of gentle rustling and the cicadas and the birds and the horses.

"Great!" Lauren's voice broke her reverie. "Let's go home."

Olivia didn't really want to open her eyes, she just wanted to stay where she was, feeling relaxed and peaceful. She forced herself to open her eyes.

Lauren packed up the food containers and cups. "And you thought you were relaxed before."

"Clearly mistaken." Olivia squirmed to her feet, though her body still felt like jelly. She helped Lauren pack the remaining items into the saddle bag. They mounted up and headed for the creek crossing.

"Is that what I have to practise over the next few days?" Olivia asked as they ambled along.

"Indeed, and the more you practise, the more proficient you will become."

Lauren urged Aztec to a canter and Olivia and Vanilla followed, so they arrived at the creek crossing well before noon.

"You'll be home in time for lunch." Lauren held the gate open for Olivia to pass.

As the gate swung closed behind her, Olivia turned back toward Lauren. "What is it I'm supposed to ponder till our next ride?"

Lauren's expression became sombre. "What would be the properties of a universal language?" She wheeled Aztec in the direction of home and called back, "See you in a few days!"

Olivia waited until Lauren had ridden off some distance before she steered Vanilla through the creek crossing and made for home. She began pondering immediately.

Confiscated

Olivia was still elated when she arrived at the house. Lauren had agreed to teach her; there was something to practise and a homework task. As she brushed Vanilla and stuffed lucerne hay into Vanilla's feeder, she made plans for the evening. First, she would have her regular online catch up with Mel, then she would practise.

At dinner, Sheree and Art discussed the weather and day's activities on the farm in the usual manner, but every time there was a pause in the conversation, one or the other gazed at Olivia with concern. Olivia dismissed it as parental weirdness. She was too busy pondering Lauren's question to give it any more thought or to add to the conversation.

After the meal, Olivia helped clear the dishes to the kitchen, where Sheree loaded the dishwasher. Art appeared in the doorway and moved side to side to block her attempts to pass. Finally, she stood in front of him, glaring and annoyed. "What?"

"We need to talk to you about something, Possum," Art said, his brow furrowed with concern.

Sheree moved up behind her, drying her hands on a tea towel.

"Yes, dear," Sheree said in response to Olivia's confused expression. "You'd better sit down." Sheree gestured to the chairs around the small table in the breakfast nook.

Sheree and Art glanced furtively at each other as they all nervously took their seats.

"What's the matter?" Olivia was curious to discover what could make her parents behave this way. "Has someone died or something?"

Those words made her parents look even more distressed. Maybe Grandma had fallen or had a stroke or something.

Eventually, Sheree composed herself. "We've been very worried about you lately, Livvie," she said. "You've been brooding and reclusive since the start of the holidays."

"The only time you seem yourself is when you go riding," her father piped in.

"We're very worried about you," Sheree continued. "Is there something or someone bothering you?"

Her parents glanced at each other supportively then fixed their expectant gaze at Olivia.

No way Olivia was going to tell them about Lauren, her discoveries and her lessons. That would ruin everything. She wasn't going to tell them about Mel and Javier either. Her love life, or lack thereof, was none of their business. "Nothing's wrong."

Her parents nodded at each other as if vindicated.

"We thought you'd say that," Art finally said.

"We've done some research." Sheree placed her hands on the table and leaned toward Olivia. "Your behaviour and everything fits the profile."

"You spend evenings alone in your room on your computer." Art presented his evidence.

"Brooding about all day." Sheree joined in.

"You avoid conversations and questions."

"Eating less."

"You've been watching self-defence movies over and over."

"It all fits!" Sheree declared.

"Fits what exactly?" Olivia felt outnumbered and confused.

"You're obviously being hyper-bullied!" Art said.

Olivia was even more confused. "What?"

"He means cyber-bullied, dear." Sheree cast Art a glance that said, "thanks for your contribution" and "get it right" at the same time. "The evidence is clear."

Olivia was incredulous. "What are you talking about?" She glanced from one parent to another seeing only a wall of steely resolve. "I'm not being cyber-bullied!"

"That's what the website said you'd say." Art glanced at Sheree with concerned vindication.

Olivia was helpless. Was every protest to be taken as further evidence of this fiction?

Sheree lowered her voice and spoke softly "We're worried you may harm yourself."

"What!" Olivia protested, even if it was futile. "I have no intention of suicide if that's what you're worried about."

The mere mention of the word caused both her parents to go suddenly pale.

Sheree leaned over and whispered to Art. "See, dear, I told you she's been thinking about it."

Olivia slumped her shoulders in defeat. Everything she said, every explanation, every protest would be taken as further evidence of her precarious mental state.

"We can't just sit by and do nothing, Possum," Art said.

"No, we can't," Sheree agreed. "So, as you're unwilling to own up to the problem, we've decided to take the advice on the website and confiscate your phone and computer."

"What!" Olivia jumped to her feet. "That's ridiculous!" She took her phone from her pocket and held it close like a vulnerable pet.

Art stood up and faced her. "Hand it over, Possum."

"Either hand it over or give us the access codes so that we can check the phone and computer for ourselves." Sheree was not to be deflected.

No way Olivia was going to let her parents trawl through her private conversations and photos. "But how will I arrange to go riding with Lauren?"

Sheree stood up and held out her hand for the phone. "When you get a text from Lauren, I'll supervise your reply then I'll take the phone back."

"But what about when I'm out riding, how will I get in touch with you if there is a problem?" Olivia clutched at straws.

Sheree flicked her hand forward again for the phone to be handed over. "Firstly, you've already shown that the danger spots on the farm have no phone reception. Second, you are only allowed to ride with Lauren and she is fully capable of helping you in such situations. So, you don't need the phone."

Olivia reluctantly moved the phone forward and her mother quickly snatched it.

"Now the computer." Art held out his hand. "Go get it and hand it over."

"How am I supposed to keep in touch with Mel?" Tears started to well in Olivia's eyes at the injustice of it all. "She's expecting me to video call in a few minutes." Worse still, if Javier should call or text or email, she would miss it. What if he thought her disinterested and took up with some other girl instead? The thin thread of hope that Javier might contact her was being cut and it felt like they were stabbing her in the heart. How dare they? Yet, she dare not speak of it. Her defence crumbled.

"Either hand over the access code or hand over the computer." Sheree firmly clutched the phone.

Art followed Olivia to her room. She unplugged her laptop from its charger and picked it up from her bedside drawer unit; Art promptly snatched it from her grasp and made off with it. She hoped Mel wouldn't think she was being snubbed and that Javier would persist, if he messaged at all.

"We're only doing this for your own good," Art said, reaching the doorway with the device.

"Bullshit!" Olivia slammed the door behind him.

She threw herself onto the bed and sobbed until the hurt and anger had subsided a little. It took a while. The pangs of injustice and frustration smouldered as she showered and changed into pyjamas.

"No way I'm going out there to say goodnight," she muttered. She braced the chair from her desk under the door handle in protest. She did not want to be disturbed.

Reluctant hero

Elton's words echoed around in Javier's head for days. Was he really another entitled, selfish, private school jerk? He really liked Olivia, but he hardly knew her. Would she like him if she knew how much of a mess his family was? Could she really like him for him? Would she run for the hills if she knew his secret? Maybe she could like him if he was a hero. Elton was right, there were two people he cared about who needed a hero right now.

Andrew regularly made snide comments about Charlie having secret affairs and how Henry probably wasn't even his. He likened Charlie to Javier's mum and declared that all women were the same and not to be trusted.

"If I was Charlie," Javier mused in front of the bathroom mirror one evening, "Dad's behaviour would be enough to drive me into the arms of another man for protection and comfort." It was a testament to her devotion to family that she hadn't. That was an epiphany. "Note to self: be kind to women so you don't drive them off to seek another man."

On Friday evenings, Andrew went to the pub after work, so Javier made a point of staying home. The later his father came home, the more drunk and violent he would be. It was Friday night, late, and Andrew wasn't home yet. Charlie and Javier sat in silence in the living room. They tried to find a TV show or movie to distract them, but nothing held their attention. Sometimes they just stared at each other; Charlie looked scared and Javier tried to look calm and reassuring.

Javier jolted at the sound of keys fumbling in the door. "Don't worry Charlie. It will be OK."

Charlie sprang to her feet. She didn't look convinced. The door burst open and Andrew staggered in. The smell of alcohol reached Javier around the same time as the obscenities he muttered.

"Freakin' bloody whore!" He staggered toward Charlie. "How many pricks have you been entertaining today?"

Javier's muscles tensed. Andrew was more difficult to manage when he was drunk.

"I want a DNA test," Andrew said, his speech slurred. "Do you hear me? I want a freakin' DNA test!"

Andrew approached Charlie and Javier stood and moved between them. "Settle down, Dad. You're drunk. You don't know what you're doing."

"I know exactly what I'm bloody doing." He made to move around Javier. "I'm going to punish that bitch for tricking me into raising some other bastard's kid."

Andrew lunged forward and tried to push Javier sideways to get to Charlie.

Javier raised his arm and deflected the push sideways. Andrew tried to follow up with a punch and Javier deflected it with his other arm. He hooked his leg behind Andrew's ankle and stepped forward. Off balance, Andrew fell backward and landed with a soft thud on the plush floor rug. He made to get up but ran out of energy and will. The alcohol took over and his head slumped sideways.

"Is he OK?" Charlie edged forward, her eyes wide with concern.

This bloke was about to assault her in a drunken, ignorant rage and she was worried whether he was OK? Javier's mum was right; Charlie was complicit in her own demise.

"Yeah." Javier stepped back from Andrew's splayed form. "He's fallen asleep. You may want to get him a blanket."

Charlie disappeared and returned with a throw rug. She placed it over Andrew and stepped away.

"You need to move Henry into your room tonight and lock the door."

"But what if he wakes up and wants to come to bed?"

"For Henry's sake, don't let him in. He won't be anywhere close to safe until morning."

Charlie stared at Andrew who was snoring and farting on the floor.

"Do you understand me, Charlie?"

"Sure." Charlie turned toward Javier. "Nice moves. Where did you learn to do that?"

"Mum insisted I do jujitsu as a kid."

"Cool." Charlie headed for Henry's cot and carried the sleeping child into her room. "Goodnight, Javier, and thanks again." She closed the door behind her.

The lock clicked and Javier's muscles relaxed. "I always thought Mum wanted us to learn jujitsu to protect us from strangers," he mumbled to himself as he made for the bathroom to shower. "Now I see she wanted us to be able to protect ourselves from Dad."

The strategies Javier used to protect Charlie and Henry were working for now. With each success, his confidence and strength grew. Yet the problem escalated and, with his new perspective, he dreaded not being there when the situation eventually came to a head.

Javier lay in his bed on edge that night and waited for what would be unleashed when Andrew woke. Fortunately, Andrew didn't wake till mid-morning when he demanded something for his headache and put himself to bed for the rest of the day.

Lesson Two

Olivia forced herself to interrupt her burning resentment with episodes of practice. The resentment subsided a little more with each session. Without the distraction of devices, Olivia found she had much more time to practice, so, practice she did.

True to her word, Sheree kept her phone charged and had passed it to Olivia when Lauren texted. Olivia confirmed the ride time and Sheree promptly snatched back the phone. This treatment flared up the outrage. How dare her mother treat her like a criminal when she had done nothing wrong? Before the ride, Olivia scribbled some notes on a piece of paper and tucked it carefully into her jeans pocket so it wouldn't be seen. She was thankful her parents hadn't escalated to body searches.

* * *

Lauren and Olivia rode toward the latest section of shiny new boundary fence. Eventually Lauren broke the silence. "Is something wrong?"

"My parents think I'm being cyber-bullied."

"Fascinating," Lauren said. "Are you?"

"No." The horses paced a few steps further. "Do you believe me?"

"Yes, Olivia. Yes, I believe you."

"Thanks, Lauren. It's nice to know someone does. For the last few days, I felt like I was going insane. I mean, they've confiscated my phone and my computer so now I can't keep in touch with my friend Mel and all our texts have to go past Mum. It's so unfair!"

"Yes, it is." Lauren pulled up Aztec and looked Olivia in the eye. "But there's no law that says life has to be fair. Besides, misguided as their efforts may be, they are only doing it because they care about you."

Olivia humphed and sneered.

"Indeed, it's my observation that how we handle the unfair is not only character-building but character-revealing. So, how are you handling it?"

"Keeping to my room mostly—and practising."

"So, when the world is handing you lemons?"

"I guess I'm making lemonade," Olivia said then added, "That's such a cliché."

They eventually found a sheltered spot for morning tea. Ice clunked into the cups as Lauren poured the beverage from the flask.

"I thought lemonade on ice would be good on such a hot day." Lauren winked at Olivia.

They laughed at the serendipity of it and munched on their snacks. Olivia soon wondered though, if it really was serendipity.

"Could I ask a favour?" Olivia pleaded with her eyes. She remembered herself and added, "Please?"

"What do you have in mind?"

Olivia pulled the paper from her pocket. "Without my computer or phone, I can't keep up my regular chats with my friend, Mel, over the holidays." She held the paper toward Lauren. "This is her email address. Could you please let her know what's happened? So that she doesn't think I'm snubbing her."

"So, you want me to collude with you against your parents' wishes?"

How could she expect another adult to take her side against her parents? What was she thinking? She closed her hand around the paper.

Lauren winked again and held out her hand. "I'm in!"

Olivia's expression brightened. She passed the paper across.

Lauren glanced at the writing. "That looks legible enough." She stowed the paper in a breast pocket and buttoned the flap to keep it secure.

Olivia was relieved to have at least one ally.

Lauren opened a plastic container and offered Olivia a shortbread biscuit. "Given that you've had lots of time to ponder, what are your criteria for a universal language?"

Olivia took a biscuit, cleared her mouth and took a deep breath. "The question was more difficult than I thought. I eventually made progress by analysing what would make a language less than universal and worked backward from that."

Lauren raised an eyebrow and sipped her drink. Olivia took that as a sign to continue.

"It can't be in any particular language. I mean English seems like a universal language because it is used in so many countries, but not everyone in the world speaks English. In fact, there are probably more speakers of Chinese and Hindi than there are of English."

Lauren waved her biscuit in the air as a signal for Olivia to continue.

"Then I figured that it couldn't be spoken. I mean, what if someone was deaf? It wouldn't be universal if deaf people were excluded. It couldn't be written or visual either because that would exclude blind people. I guess it could be tactile, like Braille, but that would be cumbersome to transmit and again it requires some sort of word or symbol-based language."

"So…?"

"So, I eventually figured that only direct thought transfer from consciousness to consciousness without using words could be truly universal."

"Impressive!" Lauren downed the last swill of her drink. "Now let's see how good you are at painting the fence." She gazed at Olivia expectantly.

Olivia set her biscuit and cup on the upturned container lid, sat cross-legged on the rug and systematically relaxed. She had practised it so often that it only took her a minute or so to get into a fully relaxed state.

"That's very good, Olivia. You've practised well." Before Olivia could break the relaxation and open her eyes, Lauren continued. "Now, let's move on to picking up the jacket."

Olivia opened one eye: Lauren lounged on the rug, she wore a smug grin and held another biscuit.

"I want you to focus on the breaths and only the breaths. Focus on inhaling, nice and slow, and experience the sensation of air entering your airways and lungs."

Olivia slowly inhaled. She had never paid attention to inhaling before. Cool air moved in her nose, there was gentle pressure on her larynx and her lungs smoothly inflated. Suddenly it was more like inhaling a cool, thin liquid than air.

"Good. Now exhale slowly and focus on experiencing the entire exhalation."

Olivia had held the breath for most of Lauren's instruction and was relieved to release it. Her lungs shrank down and the chest wall with them. This time it didn't feel cool; it was like a thin warm liquid flowed effortlessly out through her nose.

"Excellent!" Lauren adjusted to a more comfortable lounging position. "That's the first part. Now continue to repeat that."

Olivia did so immediately, breath in, breath out. Nice and slow, she experienced each one. She wondered what the second part was.

"You'll soon find that your mind gets bored focussing on the same thing over and over and thoughts will creep in."

"Like, what's the next part?" Olivia's eyes were still closed and she tried to focus only on breathing.

"Exactly," Lauren replied. "Now trying to force the thoughts away will take way too much thought energy. Besides, you'd end up focussing on stray thought expulsion instead of on breathing. So, you need to find a way to gently send each thought on its way. You could try using an invisible, magic mind broom to gently sweep each one out of your head. Or you could pop each one onto an invisible passing train that will carry it away. While you practise this week, pick a method that works for you. Start with practising for short periods then gradually increase it as you get better at staying focussed without stray thoughts."

Olivia continued to breathe slowly and deeply.

"Enough for now, let's get moving."

Olivia slowly opened her eyes. Not only did she feel completely relaxed, but her head was unusually clear, as if the attic of her mind was cleared of cobwebs. She hovered a while in the moment before she got to her feet and helped Lauren gather up their things and load the saddle bags.

* * *

Vanilla was unusually calm on the walk back to the creek. Normally Aztec was ridiculously calm on their walks while Vanilla fidgeted and Olivia repeatedly pulled her back in line. Now Vanilla was different. Now she was nearly as calm as Aztec.

"Something wrong?" Lauren asked as Olivia tipped her head sideways at Vanilla for the third time.

"I don't know. Vanilla seems unusually quiet all of a sudden. I'm worried she might be unwell or something."

Lauren chuckled and glanced at Olivia. "It's been my observation that horses tend to take on the mood of their rider."

"So, if I'm feeling calmer?"

"Vanilla will be feeling calmer." Lauren maintained a steady pace. "And seeing as we're supposed to be training for the Kilkivan Horse Ride, what are the implications?"

"If I can keep calm and not be stressed during the ride, then Vanilla will be calm and not stressed during the ride?"

"Indeed." After a few more paces, Lauren added, "I see it every year. Riders who worry about their horse being stressed by the ride."

"Which makes the horse stressed on the ride?"

"You've got it."

"Which makes the rider even more stressed, then the horse gets even more stressed." Olivia could see how such a situation could escalate out of control.

"To add insult to injury, the horse ends up being labelled as 'high strung' and unsuitable for such events. Or even unsuitable for riding by young people as it's invariably the young people who get into such a pickle."

Lauren looked wistful, even sad, as if thinking about the poor horses condemned when their only crime was to be in tune with their riders.

"So, shall we canter the rest of the way?" Lauren broke the glum mood.

"Awesome!" Olivia's excitement was soon mirrored by a sudden spring in Vanilla's step. Now that she understood, the change in Vanilla didn't unnerve her in the slightest. She enjoyed the fun of being excited together.

Lauren and Aztec took off in an instant with Olivia and Vanilla hot on their heels. Olivia felt charged at the joy of it and Vanilla settled into a long, loping canter beneath her. When they reached the gate, both horses puffed through their nostrils and stepped about as if dancing with enjoyment.

Olivia passed through the gate that Lauren held open for her and turned Vanilla toward the creek crossing. She stopped abruptly and returned. "I almost forgot. What's to ponder this week?"

Lauren frowned. "Give some thought as to how people react when they hear voices in their head."

Olivia considered this a moment. That topic would be easy. Then she remembered something. "I've been meaning to ask. What brand of insect repellent do you use? It seems way more effective than mine."

"I don't use insect repellent." Before Olivia could consider that, Lauren added, "That reminds me, next time we can chat about the side effects."

"What side effects?"

"Sometimes when people practise mindfulness, they get side effects: clearer concentration, more vivid dreams. Happy to chat about any that you notice at our next ride."

"Sure." Olivia turned Vanilla for home, already trying to fathom how Lauren could have a built-in insect repellent and whether that could possibly have something to do with side effects.

Crazy

"Don't fidget." Sheree picked up a magazine from the coffee table.

"This is so unnecessary." Olivia would have pulled out her phone at this point and checked in with her social media apps or texted friends to disconnect from what was happening and allay the awkwardness, but her phone was still officially confiscated. It was in her mother's handbag, presumably to have on hand as evidence. "I don't see why I have to talk to a psychologist. I'm fine. I just need my phone back so I can keep in touch with my friends. How would you feel if Dad confiscated your phone?"

Sheree glanced at Art, her brows furrowed and her expression a warning to not even think it. She turned back to Olivia, all politeness under the watchful eyes of the receptionist. "Don't be like that. We're still worried about you." She took a magazine from the table and aimlessly flipped through the pages.

Olivia turned to her father for support.

"Don't worry Possum," Art said. "This won't take long. At least I hope not. I've gotta move the mob of cattle from the flats paddock to the hill paddock this arvo. Want to give me a hand? It'll be good riding practice."

"Sure." Olivia sighed and slumped in the chair. She was outgunned.

"Dr Bell's running a bit late." The receptionist peered over the reception counter. Her platinum blonde hair with dark roots was pulled up tight into a high ponytail that swished about when she moved her head. "Shouldn't be long now." The girl was not much older than Olivia.

The telephone rang and diverted the receptionist's attention. A door beside the reception desk opened and first to emerge was a boy, no more than five years old. He was cheerful and bounced at the end of his mother's arm, but his mother was not so cheerful. The frown lines between her brows were so furrowed that Olivia was sure they'd remain even when the woman smiled.

"I'll see you again next week," said a female voice from inside the room. "Becky will organise the time for you."

"Thank you." The woman proceeded to the reception desk and waited for Becky to finish the phone call.

Eventually a woman emerged from the doorway and approached them. She was older than Becky but younger than Sheree and her vivid, auburn, tightly curly hair bounced about in a short bob held back with a thin green silk scarf. She was not what Olivia expected a psychologist to look like. Sheree's eyes widened; this was not what Sheree had expected either. Art just beamed, the way he always did when he saw an attractive woman.

"Mrs McKinnon?" The woman approached with her hand outstretched. "I'm Dr Margaret Bell." She shook Sheree's hand firmly but slowly. "Mr McKinnon." She greeted Art with a handshake too.

"Dr Bell." Art still grinned and Sheree frowned at him.

"And you must be Olivia," Dr Bell said without reaching out to shake hands.

"Let me guess, you've heard a lot about me." Olivia caught her mother's disapproving glare in the corner of her eye.

"Not as much as you think and not as much as I'd like to." Dr Bell responded with the ease of someone who had been through this scenario many times before. "Please, come through."

Like the waiting room, Dr Bell's office was decorated in a style of Hamptons-meets-French Country. The walls were a muted grey and any furniture item that could be painted distressed white, was. The floors were a grey hardwood and the soft furnishings were tan leather. A tall bookcase beside the window was filled to capacity and on the wall behind the desk hung a watercolour painting of a rural landscape reminiscent of Kilkivan. On the opposite wall hung a bevy of framed certificates. Relics of farming, like once useful butter churns, were now just ornaments strategically placed on shelves and a low table.

"Please, sit down." Dr Bell gestured to four chairs on one side of the desk as she settled herself into the swivelling office chair on the other. Sheree and Art took the chairs closest to the door and Olivia the one closest to the window. This left an empty chair in between and triggered another glare from her mother.

"So, how can I help you?"

"We're worried our daughter is being cyber-bullied." Sheree gestured toward Olivia as if she were "Exhibit A" in the case.

Dr Bell's expression was all sympathy. "That is concerning indeed. What makes you think so?" She glanced at Olivia and smiled with half her face so that only Olivia could see.

Sheree began to recite a list of everything unusual Olivia had done for the last month. She went on to cite the website she had used to assess all these observations and described how she had reached the incontrovertible conclusion that Olivia was a cyber-bullying victim. "We hear about kids on farms committing suicide without warning because they were cyber-bullied and we don't want our Olivia to be one of those," Sheree said in righteous conclusion.

"That would be grave indeed and we certainly wouldn't want that." Dr Bell turned to Art. "Mr McKinnon, do you share your wife's concerns?"

Olivia turned away and gazed out the window. If they were going to talk about her as if she wasn't in the room, she was justified in zoning out.

"Well, Dr Bell, I certainly wouldn't want anything bad to happen to our Possum here. But I didn't think she looked upset until we took away her phone."

Olivia cringed. Her father had called her Possum in front of a respectable professional. How humiliating! She glared at him.

"You took away her phone?" Dr Bell glanced toward Olivia with concern.

"And her laptop," Art added.

"And we stopped access to the family computer," Sheree said, as if it were some great accomplishment. "We had to make sure there was no way that they could get to her."

"I see. So did Olivia have any way to communicate with her friends, the ones who would support rather than bully her?"

Art looked to Sheree who shook her head sheepishly.

Dr Bell typed a note into her computer. "Do you have any other children?"

"Another daughter, but she is away at university now," Sheree replied.

"Well, cyber-bullying can be very serious indeed and is not to be taken lightly."

Sheree put her hand on Art's knee and gave him an "I told you so" nod. Art put his large paw of a hand over hers and gave her hand a reassuring squeeze. Sheree turned back to Dr Bell. "So, what is the next step?"

"At this point Mrs McKinnon, it is important that I speak with Olivia alone."

Sheree frowned and leaned forward. "I think it's important that my husband and I hear what Olivia has to say."

"Mrs McKinnon, years of training and experience tell me that Olivia isn't going to say anything important while you are in the room," Dr Bell said in an utterly professional manner. She cast a subtle half-grin in Olivia's direction that almost looked like a wink.

Olivia was moved beyond humiliation to anger. How could her parents treat her like this? She glared at her mother then gazed back out of the window. It was difficult to tell whose side Dr Bell was on and she would reserve judgement.

"Olivia! Be more respectful," Sheree hissed under her breath.

"May I suggest a stroll. There's a lovely park just down the street with a cafe on the corner." Dr Bell got up, walked briskly to the door and held it open, a signal for them to leave. Sheree gathered up her bag and they made their way out. Dr Bell closed the door behind them and leaned on it until the latch clicked shut.

Dr Bell heaved a sigh. "Well, Olivia." She pushed herself off the door toward Olivia. "What would you like to talk about?"

Olivia shrugged. She just wanted to be out of there but Dr Bell's sudden change in demeanour caught her by surprise.

"Look," Dr Bell continued. "I have to address your parents' concerns; they are paying my fee. It's also clear that they really do care about you. But there's always at least three sides to every story and I'm keen to hear yours." She walked toward her desk, but stopped short, grabbed one of the vacant chairs, turned it to face Olivia and planted herself in it. "So, Olivia, what would you like to tell me?"

Olivia sat expressionless and gazed toward a bookshelf, silent.

Dr Bell sat motionless, patient, attentive, expectant. Olivia got the impression that Dr Bell had years of experience at outlasting the silence of reluctant teenagers.

"The more you give me to work with, the sooner we can get your phone back."

"Actually, it doesn't bother me anymore. I'm doing fine without it now."

"Well, that's not something I hear from people your age. I'm fascinated. Do explain." Dr Bell sat with her hands still and calm in her lap, her attention focussed entirely on Olivia.

"Well, I missed it at first, but then I found other things to occupy my time and I don't miss it so much now." Olivia tested the waters with a morsel of information to see how Dr Bell would react.

"Aren't you upset at not being able to communicate with your friends?"

"My best friend Mel is on holiday in Singapore with her family. They go every year. I was worried she would think I was not speaking with her, or injured or something, so I asked Lauren to email her and let her know her my phone was confiscated."

"Who is Lauren?"

Oh crap! Olivia was determined to be discreet and not mention Lauren, then in the first minute: blah! She mentioned Lauren's name. A bad case of verbal diarrhoea. She would have to think fast and be more alert. "Um. Lauren is our neighbour. I go riding with her once or twice a week. Mum and Dad don't like me riding alone since I came off my horse."

"I see. And Lauren is around your age?"

"More like around your age." Why was the whole conversation suddenly about Lauren? Olivia shifted about in her chair, uncomfortable and she bet Dr Bell noticed. After all, she was trained to notice such things.

"Your mum says you've been very moody since the start of the holidays." Dr Bell stopped at that, looked at Olivia and awaited an explanation.

"It's a boy issue. None of their business."

"Oh, I see." Dr Bell tried to conceal a grin. "You don't feel comfortable talking to your parents about boy issues?"

Olivia glared at Dr Bell as if she was from some sort of alien culture and shook her head.

"Is there someone you do feel comfortable confiding in? Your best friend maybe?"

"No. She's part of the problem."

"Sounds complicated. Look, I'm just trying to understand your support network. Everyone needs someone they can talk to about the complicated stuff. Who do you feel you could talk to?"

"I'm sure I could talk to Lauren about it. But I haven't yet. The matter is pretty much on hold till the end of the holidays, especially as I can't communicate with Mel." Somehow the conversation was back to Lauren, again.

Dr Bell seemed satisfied with the answer, though, and moved swiftly to the next question. "So why were you watching the Karate Kid movies over and over?"

Olivia was relieved at the change in subject. She thought out her response carefully this time. Saying that Lauren asked her to was not a good idea. "Well, school was pretty stressful last semester and it's supposed to get worse next year. I read somewhere that meditation and mental self-discipline could help, so I watched the movies for inspiration. When Mum took away all my devices, I couldn't research it further, so I tried to get as much out of the movies as I could and spent a lot of time in my room trying to practise meditation." The story was mostly true, so Olivia didn't feel too bad about it. She was getting the hang of diversion.

"I'm impressed. Lots of studies have shown that meditation is a great way to manage stress. That was a good choice." Dr Bell's countenance was sincere. "So, how's it been going?"

"Oh fine. I'm much more relaxed and focussed now." Which was the truth, just not all of the truth.

"You know I have to ask, don't you? Have you been cyber-bullied, or the subject of any other form of bullying for that matter?"

"No," Olivia said firmly, then added, "I'm too ordinary to be a target."

Now that the line of communication was open, Dr Bell fired more questions. "How would you say you feel most days?"

"Fine." Olivia stonewalled and Dr Bell patiently waited for more. "Not miserable if that's what you want to know. If it wasn't for my parents trying hard to ruin my holiday, I reckon I'd be pretty happy."

Dr Bell looked at Olivia as if considering an odd specimen, then frowned. "Do you feel powerless when it comes to dealing with your parents? Or your friends?"

Olivia retracted in her chair, blindsided by the question.

"What about your sister? Does she stand up to your parents?"

Olivia's attention was diverted. "Daphne stands up to them all the time. They can't get her to do anything they want. She tells them where to get off all the time."

"I see." Dr Bell's expression softened. "I hope you don't get the impression I want you to be more like Daphne. Loud bluster is often an illusion of power and crumbles when tested. True power comes from understanding yourself and developing your skills and talents. I'd like you to consider that."

Olivia tightened her lips and gave Dr Bell a nod. She would think about it later.

Dr Bell asked a few more questions that sounded like they were from some sort of checklist then got up and walked to her side of the desk. "Thank you for talking with me, Olivia. It was most helpful. Just for the record, I think you're a normal, well-adjusted teenager and I intend to tell your parents as much." She sat and turned to her computer. "I expect your parents stayed in the waiting room the whole time." She gave Olivia a knowing grin. "Would you mind swapping places with them? I need to allay their concerns and negotiate for the return of your devices."

Sure enough, Olivia found her parents sitting expectantly in the waiting room. "She wants to talk to you."

Her parents shared a concerned glance and almost bolted to the door while Olivia made herself comfortable in a chair. She looked forward to seeing the distress on her mother's face when Dr Bell was finished with her.

* * *

The car drive home was a long one.

"We're sorry, dear," Sheree said, multiple times. She fumbled through her bag for Olivia's phone and handed it over. "You should have told us the truth."

"I did. Only you wouldn't listen." Olivia checked the charge level. There was enough on the phone to see them home.

"That's not true, dear."

"Yes, it is," Art corrected. "She kept telling us she wasn't being bullied, but you wouldn't listen."

Like a summer thunderstorm rolling in, an argument brewed. Olivia fumbled in her bag for earbuds and wired herself for sound. Her playlist was a welcome old friend for the remainder of the trip while her parents sustained their argument until they pulled up at the house.

Olivia claimed her computer and strode directly to her room, determined to catch up with friends and social media, but when she got there, she didn't feel like it. She did a focus practice instead and felt much better.

Lessons Three and Four

When Olivia finally checked her devices later that evening there was no trace of communication from Javier. Her heart sank. Clearly, he wasn't yearning for her as much as she was yearning for him. Grief welled up, grief at losing something she never had. Olivia sought distraction; thankfully, Mel had sent emails, so she replied to those.

It felt good to organise the next ride with Lauren without her mother acting as "phone police". With ample practice, Olivia had become proficient at all the exercises to date. Lauren was right; her dreams were more vivid and in colour. In quiet moments, she pondered Lauren's homework task, but was frustrated that the teaching process was slow. Despite all her practice and contemplation, the lessons so far had nothing to do with sending or receiving a single thought. She watched the original Karate Kid movie one more time to remind herself to be patient, diligent and persistent.

Olivia briefed Lauren on the encounter with the psychologist as they rode along a section of new fence. She omitted to mention that Lauren's name had repeatedly come up. If Lauren thought she was indiscreet at this stage of the game, she may have refused to teach her further.

Eventually they settled in for morning tea, perched on a log in the shade of a grand gum tree.

Lauren held a plastic container of biscuits toward Olivia, then promptly withdrew it. Her face went suddenly expressionless. "Stay very still. Don't move a muscle."

"What?" Olivia stayed motionless but her eyes scanned about. Her heart skipped a beat when she caught sight of the long, fat, brown snake as it quietly slithered toward them through the grass.

"Don't move," Lauren repeated, her voice calm and firm. "If you don't move, you're not a threat. It's OK to talk though, snakes don't hear sound through air very well."

"I'm not a threat? Me? One of the most venomous snakes on the planet is slithering toward us and I'm the threat?" Olivia thought. She was a farm girl and she knew about snakes, but the last time she saw one this close, its head was shattered by a shotgun blast and her father had draped the still-twitching carcass over a fence as warning to her and Daphne to be careful.

"This is a good time to see how well you have practised, Olivia." Lauren didn't flinch. "Let's see if you can relax and focus with a bit of a distraction?"

Olivia fought the urge to leap and run. "You're kidding me?"

"Nope. Think of it as a practical pop quiz."

Olivia glared at Lauren, incredulous. She began the relaxation routine but couldn't bring herself to close her eyes. The tingle of adrenaline in her body slowly waned. Even Olivia was surprised at how relaxed she felt despite the approaching reptile.

"Very good. Now focus."

Olivia resisted the urge to turn and look toward the sound of Lauren's voice. Her gaze was still fixed on the snake. She focussed and cleared her mind of all thoughts. It was surreal; a deadly snake approached her feet, yet she felt completely calm. The snake slithered quietly over the tops of her boots. The weight of its body pressed the leather down onto her toes and its smooth scales glinted in the sunlight, yet her mind was clear.

The snake gave Lauren's boots a wide berth and slithered quietly into a hole in the earth by the end of the log.

"Nice work, Olivia." Lauren put the container onto the log between them as the last of the snake's tail disappeared from sight. "The snake acted as though you were part of the log and didn't sense any fear from you. You have practised well."

Ordinarily Olivia would have heaved a sigh of relief and relaxed, but she was already relaxed. She let that realisation and other thoughts churn in her head. "So, how come the snake went around your boots instead of over them?" Olivia took a biscuit and the offered drink.

"Because I asked it to." Lauren took a biscuit for herself.

"Is that why the ants and flies...?"

"Yep." Lauren took a bite of the biscuit.

The graphic reminder of what she was here to learn renewed Olivia's determination to stick with the program. She took a bite of the biscuit. Her eyebrows raised, then lowered into a frown as she considered the confection. "Different. Yummy, but different."

"Glad you like it. James calls them lavender butter cookies. They're one of my favourites. They smell like lavender, but because lavender has little taste, they taste like butter cookies." Lauren took another bite.

Olivia sniffed the biscuit and took in the floral lavender aroma, then bit off another piece and savoured the sweet buttery crumbliness that melted in her mouth.

"So, what are your thoughts about hearing voices in your head?" Lauren topped up the drinks.

Olivia swallowed and eyed another biscuit. "Most people associate hearing voices in your head with going crazy."

"They do indeed." Lauren sipped her drink and pushed the biscuit container toward Olivia, encouraging her to take another.

Olivia just held her drink in her hand and frowned a little, trying to crystallise her ponderings into cohesive conversation. "I reckon I'd be startled, especially if it sounded like someone else's voice. I'd want it to go away and try to convince myself I wasn't going nuts."

"That's pretty much what most people do and it effectively shuts down the transmission. So effectively, in fact, that it becomes subconscious and most people never hear these transmissions at all."

"I guess that's why most people never hear voices in their heads."

"Yep." Lauren sipped her drink. "It's unacceptable in most human cultures."

"Plus, if you were using words, it wouldn't be a universal language. It would be even weirder to hear words in your head in a foreign language."

"Exactly."

"So, is it possible to think without using words?" Olivia gulped down the rest of her drink in one long draught. The floral sweetness of the elderflower cordial was a perfect complement to the biscuits and felt too fancy a refreshment for a goat paddock.

"Yes, with practise." Lauren glanced at her and started to pack up for the ride back.

Olivia rolled her eyes. "But what exactly do you practise?"

"Normally when you think, you hear your own voice in your head right?"

"Right." Olivia handed Lauren her empty cup.

"It's like a long script of words, words, words."

"Uh-huh." Olivia tried to follow where this was going.

"So, get calm, focus and empty your head of thoughts like you practised, then think of something without using any words. You may want to start with the image of an object, like a candle for example. Once you've mastered that, try thinking wordlessly about doing something with the object."

"Like lighting the candle or snuffing it out?"

Lauren secured the clasps on the saddle bag. "Try to work your way up for longer and longer periods until you can spend most of a day thinking without words."

"OK." Olivia took up Vanilla's reins. "I'll give it a go."

* * *

The ride home was uneventful. Olivia tacked down Vanilla and made directly for her room, keen to get started. She knew the process well now; relax, focus, clear the mind. She tried to think of the curtain in front of her, but the word popped straight into her head. This was more challenging than she expected. She remembered the process of brushing away thoughts. Each time the word curtain popped into her head, she would brush it gently away until all that was left was the image and idea of the curtain. She repeatedly tried to hold just the idea for as long as possible.

Olivia practised four or five times a day. Since the consultation with the psychologist, her confused parents said nothing and just let her be.

Within a day she mastered holding the idea of an object. Two days later she was able to think of simple activities, like opening the fridge, without thinking of a single word. By the day of her next ride with Lauren, she could quietly do her activities and chores around the house for up to fifteen minutes without thinking of a single word. She enthusiastically communicated this to Lauren only minutes into their next ride. She was keen for the next lesson.

"You have practised well, Olivia." Lauren led them along the creek to check if anything needed to be removed or prepared for the forthcoming summer torrents.

"Actually, it's rather fun when you get the knack of it."

"Indeed." Lauren cast Olivia a quizzical glance. "Most people your age have different ideas of what is fun."

"I know." Olivia watched the ground ahead while Lauren scanned the creek. "I just don't see the fun in getting drunk, spending more money than I have buying clothes I'll rarely wear, or trying to impress boys I don't like."

Lauren raised an eyebrow but said nothing.

"So, what's the next step?" Olivia was impatient to move forward and maintain the momentum. She had already moved beyond what most people achieved and she was spurred on by the thrill of being a pioneer. "What do I need to practise next?"

"Would you like to learn how to transmit a thought?"

Olivia jolted upright with excitement and Vanilla pranced beneath her. "Really? I'm up to that bit? I'd love to." She worked to calm Vanilla so she could concentrate on Lauren's words.

"Like the last exercise, this one is tricky to master, but the more you practise, the easier it will get."

"OK." Olivia had settled Vanilla to a smooth stride.

"Start with the usual routine; relax, focus and clear words from your mind."

Olivia hung off every word. "Uh-huh."

"Next, try to think of three things concurrently, each without using words. The first is the thought you wish to send, the second is the person you want to send the thought to and the third is imagining the thought being sent to them, rather like passing a note in class but directly to their mind."

"OK?" Olivia found the idea challenging and expected the task to be even more so.

"You might want to start with a simple thought like an itchy nose. You can tell if it's been successfully sent when the recipient scratches their nose." Lauren's wink and wry grin hinted at the fun Olivia could have with this. "Try not to bombard your parents though. You'll find pets can be helpful training partners." Lauren pulled up Aztec and turned to Olivia. "Keep in mind, most animals are proficient in the Universal Language and they'll know what you're up to. It adds an extra level of challenge and entertainment."

"So, if I send someone the idea of doing something, they won't be able to help themselves?"

Lauren moved to walk on, but pulled up Aztec instead, her tone now sombre. "Do you act on every idea that pops into your head?"

Olivia thought about this. "No. If the idea to eat mustard popped into my head, I wouldn't do it. I loathe mustard."

"That's called a filter and our minds are full of them. As we discussed earlier, there are cultural filters."

"Like the one that stops us from hearing voices in our head?"

"Yes, exactly. There are also other filters, like self-protection filters that try to stop us from injuring ourselves and scruples filters that try to stop us from injuring others."

"So, for a transmitted thought to get through to someone or to get them to act, it has to get past all their filters?"

"Indeed." Lauren loosened the reins. "Oh, and if someone is focussing intently on something else, that tends to delay or block them receiving the thought too."

"At that rate, I'd be surprised if anything gets through at all."

"You'll probably be more surprised at how much does get through to some people." Lauren walked Aztec on.

Olivia pondered the new information in silence for a while. She took both reins in one hand to scratch a persistent itch on the side of her nose. "Can people tell who sent them the thought?"

"Could you?"

Olivia was confused. What did Lauren mean by that? Had Lauren sent her thoughts over recent weeks? Perhaps it was something more immediate. She tried to recall any unusual thoughts over the last few minutes and scratched that annoying itch again. Olivia's eyes widened as she realised Lauren had sent her the itch. She gasped, amazed.

Lauren laughed and rode on. "When thoughts pop into our heads, we usually can't tell where they come from. We assume they are all our own and process them through our filters accordingly."

The mysterious itch was gone.

Lauren changed the subject and asked about Olivia's week and her friends, now she was back in contact, but Olivia was distracted. Her thoughts drifted back to the task to be practised and the implications of what Lauren had said. She persuaded Lauren to cut the ride short so she could get home and start to practise immediately. Olivia was so focussed on the lesson she failed to notice Aztec had no saddlebags that day.

Lauren released the gate at the creek and it clicked shut behind Olivia. "By the way, if you want to broadcast a message, you simply imagine sending it to everybody at the same time."

"OK." Olivia wasn't really interested; she wanted to master sending a single, directed message first. She could always learn the rest later.

* * *

Sheree intercepted Olivia as she marched through the house to her room. "Is everything OK, dear? You've been alone in your room a lot lately."

"All good, Mum." Olivia grabbed an apple on her way past the kitchen. "Just getting lots of meditation practice in before school goes back." Only a couple weeks of the summer holiday remained.

"Alright then," Sheree called after her. "But you may want to ease up on the riding over the next week or so. The cyclone that flattened part of Fiji last week is heading toward the Queensland coast. First cyclone of the season they reckon. Forecast to make landfall on Friday as a category four."

"OK." Olivia closed the door of her room. They were far enough inland to miss the brunt of cyclones, but she hoped the accompanying rain wouldn't interfere with her next ride with Lauren. She settled, sitting on her bed and immediately began to practise. Who could think of cyclones when there were such skills to be mastered?

It was trickier than she expected. Even when Olivia thought she had mastered the skill, she had no way of knowing whether she was successful, at least while she was alone in her room. The next morning, she tried to send an itchy nose to her mother over breakfast. Sheree suddenly scratched the side of her nose and Olivia fought to restrain her surprise and excitement. Had it worked or was it merely coincidence? She calmed herself down and started again. This time she tried to send an itchy nose to her father. Art sliced a fried egg, put a portion in his mouth, put down his knife and scratched his nose. Wow! Two out of two. This was a lot less like coincidence and the triumph felt good.

When breakfast and the required small talk with her parents was complete, Olivia headed outside to see what she could transmit to chickens.

Her parents seemed happy she was spending more time out of her room during the week. Within a day she could ask the chickens to come to her and she soon achieved the same with the dog. The farm cat was more of a challenge. It sat contentedly soaking up sun on the verandah. When Olivia tried to transmit a thought to come to her, the cat suddenly sat up, eyes wide, and stared at her as if she had transformed into an alien creature. Olivia sensed a sensation of surprise, disdain and hunger as the cat got up and made for its food bowl, where it sat expectantly until Olivia walked away. Olivia concluded that cats were difficult to transmit to and wondered if the cat had actually transmitted a message to her.

She spent that afternoon pondering cats and their filters. The weather report on the evening news showed the rainbow swirl graphic of the cyclone still bearing toward Queensland. It gained energy over the water and became bigger, stronger and more dangerous.

Respite

Time dripped by until the week of the real estate conference. Andrew made regular snide remarks about Charlie not being trustworthy in his absence. "At least Javier will be here to supervise you." He sneered. "That's better than nothing."

Charlie and Javier conspired not to tell Andrew that Javier was to spend the week with his mum. To be sure that the neighbours wouldn't mention it, they agreed that Charlie would drive Javier to a distant location for the transfer to his mum's car. This was especially necessary as Andrew had forbidden Charlie from ever speaking to Javier's mum. He painted her as some kind of evil witch to be avoided at all costs.

"I don't like going behind Andrew's back," Charlie said as they discussed the plan over lunch.

Javier rolled his eyes and took a deep breath, ready to launch into an explanation of why it was necessary.

"But all of this clandestine stuff is rather thrilling." She grinned at Javier's suddenly raised eyebrows. "Heaven knows, there's not been much thrill in my life lately."

Javier was speechless. Unable to devise a coherent response, he ate his lunch.

On the Sunday morning, Charlie drove Andrew to the local airport with Henry in tow. On her return, she parked the car inside the garage and closed the door. Charlie attended to Henry's nappy and snack while Javier loaded his luggage into the car. With Henry safely reinserted into the baby seat, Javier and Charlie climbed in.

"No good," Charlie said as Javier fastened his seatbelt.

"What?"

"The neighbours will see you in the car on the way out."

"But not on the way back?"

"Exactly." Charlie glanced back to check Henry, who happily played with a set of large, plastic keys. "You need to get down on the floor. At least until we're clear of the suburb."

Javier tried to move forward but was restrained by the seat belt. He unclipped it, slid forward and did his best to fold his tall frame into the footwell.

"That's much better." Charlie flicked the switch to open the garage door. "I'll take Henry to the supermarket on the way back and grab a few bags of groceries."

"So it looks like a shopping trip?"

"I'm enjoying this cloak and dagger stuff more than I expected," Charlie said with a smile, reversing the car out of the driveway.

* * *

During the drive, Javier unfolded himself and, like a great, lanky snake, he slithered up into the seat and clicked his seatbelt in place.

Henry held the now slimy keys to one side and observed the process, entranced. "'Gain! 'Gain!" Henry clapped his hands and jingled the keys.

"Next time, mate." Javier handed Henry a cloth book. "Look, Henry. This one has cows. Can you find the cows?"

Javier's mum was waiting, leaning against her car in the deserted school car park. Charlie pulled into the drop-off bay some distance in front.

"Sorry about the walk, Javier, but I'm going to keep my promise to Andrew and not talk to your mum."

"That's OK, Charlie." Javier cast her a reassuring glance. "I know Mum understands."

Javier unloaded his luggage onto the kerb. "Thanks, Charlie," he said as he closed the rear door. He waved to Henry as he walked to Charlie's open window. "Take this opportunity to look after yourself, OK?"

Charlie tilted her head and raised an eyebrow; this was not a phrase typical of Javier. Understanding dawned on her face and she smiled. "You too, Javier." Charlie gave Javier's mum a nod of acknowledgement as she pulled out and drove away.

Javier's mum raised her hand in response and climbed into her car. The diesel engine growled to life and she moved the sleek, iridium silver SUV up beside Javier's luggage and pressed the button to open the rear door.

"Hi, Mum," Javier said as his mother got out of the car and walked toward him. He moved in to give his mother a warm hug. "It's so good to see you."

She held him for a few moments. "Good to see you too, Javier." She stepped back and helped Javier load his bags into the rear of the car. "You look like you really need this break."

"Like you wouldn't believe." Javier positioned the last item and tapped the button to close the rear door.

"Would you like to drive?"

"Hell, yeah." Javier ferreted the P plates from the glove box and affixed them to the car. He climbed into the driver's seat, pulled up the screen menu and selected his name. The seat moved into position. "It remembers me." He winked at his mum.

"Thought you could use the practice," she said as Javier pulled the car away from the curb. "I don't expect you're getting much at your dad's."

Javier felt more relaxed and free than he had done in weeks. "Let's get as far away from this town as possible."

"Yes, let's."

* * *

By the time they pulled in at Gympie for a relief and refreshment stop, Javier had briefed his mum on most of the goings on in Andrew's household.

"He just keeps treating her worse and worse." Javier sipped on a coffee and launched into a slab of apple slice. "I don't get it, Mum. She stays. No matter how bad he treats her, she stays." Javier loaded his fork with a chunk of the apple slice. "Is that what you did?" He popped the confection into his mouth and awaited a reply.

"Charlie is probably reminding herself that marriage is a life-long commitment."

"Yeah. She mentioned that."

"I bet Andrew is doing his best to convince her that all the problems are her fault."

"Now that you mention it..."

"So, she's on a treadmill of trying to make it work. The harder she tries, the worse Andrew treats her."

"Then she tries even harder?"

"Exactly."

"How did you get off the treadmill, Mum?"

"I didn't."

Javier raised an eyebrow; that was unexpected.

"I was pushed." Javier's mum took a sip of her tea. "They do a lovely chai latte here."

Javier was determined to draw her back to the topic at hand. "You were pushed?"

"Yes. You and your sister were little, so maybe you don't remember. I had to go away for a while." She took another sip and savoured it. "Once I was off the treadmill, I could see clearly. Once I was off it, I was never going back."

"How do we get Charlie off the treadmill before someone gets hurt?" Javier scraped the last crumbs off the plate onto his fork.

"Someone has already been hurt."

"You know what I mean, before someone gets…"

"Killed?"

Javier stared at his mother. "He wouldn't, would he?"

"I don't know." She gulped the last of her tea. "Let's discuss strategy in the car." She looked around the cafe. "Fewer ears there."

When they cleared the town, Javier glanced toward his mum. "What if she was pushed?" He tensed his grip on the steering wheel. "What if I kidnapped Charlie and Henry and brought them out here?"

"In her current state of mind, she'd go right back to him."

"Yeah, reckon she would." Javier watched the road attentively while his mind ticked through options.

Javier's mum broke the silence. "The trick might be to get her thinking about something more important to her than her own safety."

"Henry?"

"Henry."

"So, every time there is an incident, I should remind her that next time it could be Henry who gets hurt?"

"Yes. You could also hint that Andrew might not be the best role model for Henry. I mean, would you want Henry to grow up and treat women the way Andrew treats her?"

"That's a good point, Mum."

"I'm full of good points," she said with a grin. "So, enough of the sombre stuff. Shall we explore your playlist?"

"I thought you'd never ask."

The sun hung low in the sky when they shuddered over the cattle grid onto the farm driveway. Javier's mum wound down the window. "I just love the gloaming and the smell of the fields."

"It's good to be home."

"It's good to have you home." She smiled at him and patted his shoulder. "By the way, I have to go to the coast tomorrow for the day. I didn't think you'd mind."

"That's fine, Mum." Javier flashed a wicked grin. "I'll probably be sick of you by then."

She poked him in the ribs and they were still jovial as they pulled up to the house.

Torrents

Olivia's phone pinged and she checked the message.

Called away to the Sunshine Coast. Will ride again in a few days ☺

Disappointed and restless for a ride, Olivia donned her riding clothes anyway and prepared to confront her mother on her way out of the house. She stowed her phone and a handkerchief in her pockets. She could hear the feint burbling of the TV in the living room; it was rarely on this late in the morning, so Olivia edged toward the living room to satisfy her curiosity.

Sheree was perched, attentive, on the edge of the couch, clutching a cup of tea.

A fresh-faced reporter appeared on the TV screen with a serious frown on his cherubic face.

Cyclone Nigel made landfall just north of Bundaberg. After flattening the local community, it is petering out as it moves inland. The southern tail of the storm brought a deluge of rain to the coast south of Bundaberg and further inland.

Palm trees with shredded foliage stood pitifully behind the reporter and the street was littered with debris.

Olivia knew it. Wave after wave of rain had fallen on the McKinnon farm during the night. By now the skies had cleared and the morning air was warm and humid. Paths and dirt roads on the farm were prone to becoming slippery mud after such rain. She would have to be careful.

With her mother fixated by the news reports, Olivia crept from the house unchallenged and tacked up Vanilla. She resolved to ride just to the creek and back. That should be safe enough, even in these conditions. She convinced herself that Vanilla needed the exercise and the horse was keen to go.

Vanilla's hooves slipped on the muddy track, so Olivia steered her onto the short grass on the side until they reached the creek. Two days before, the creek bed had been parched and rocky, with the gnarled trunks of bottlebrush bushes that leaned in the direction of past water flows. Now it was transformed: a torrent of surging, roaring, brown water that bashed and eddied low around the bushes and tree branches.

Olivia surveyed the scene. She could probably still safely cross the creek on Vanilla at the ford now, but with all the rain that had fallen in the catchment, the water level was likely to rise and the return crossing may not be possible until the flow subsided. Olivia's ride with Lauren would have been cancelled even if Lauren wasn't away. She was about to turn Vanilla for home when she spied a cow pacing restlessly by the water's edge.

Olivia guided her horse toward where the cow bellowed frantically. She pulled Vanilla up and strained to see through the tangled branches. Over the low roar of the water she heard the desperate high-pitched bleating of a calf.

Olivia dismounted, secured the reins to her saddle and silently asked Vanilla to stay put—an act that would have been alien only weeks ago and now seemed perfectly natural. She carefully made her way to the water's edge, close to the sound, until she could see the calf. Its legs entangled in branches, it thrashed frantically, trying to free itself and keep its head above the water. The cows in this paddock were her dad's best breeding stock, the culmination of decades of careful selection. She cursed her father under her breath for not putting them in a safer paddock for calving.

Gauging by the height of the surge on the familiar tree trunks, Olivia estimated the water was still only knee deep. There was a discernible path from tree to tree to reach the stranded animal. Get in, free the calf and get out before the water rose further. It looked feasible. She sent the cow a thought of reassurance and the beast calmed a little. The cow watched intently as Olivia made the attempt.

Water gushed into her boots on the first steps. Olivia adjusted to the sensation and worked her way from one tree or bush to the next, bracing herself against the upstream face of each trunk as surety against the relentless tug of the water. The brown water reeked of mud. This was not going to be as quick as she had hoped.

Olivia reached the calf as it began to tire. It bleated and struggled vigorously at her approach. The poor animal assumed she was a predator and railed against its perceived dismal fate. As the calf's cries intensified, so did the anxiety of its mother. The cow paced and bellowed with even more vigour as the calf began to slump. Olivia was no longer calm enough to send thoughts of reassurance.

She reached the calf in time to hold its head above the water. Olivia braced herself against the trunk of a bottlebrush tree, held the calf's head up with one hand and ran her other hand, under the water, down the calf's legs to assess the degree of entanglement. One foreleg was caught in the fork of a branch and the water had pushed a small log crosswise in front of the fork securely entrapping the calf's foot.

From her braced position against the trunk, Olivia placed both feet on the log and heaved against it with all the force she could muster. The calf's foot popped out and the wet, struggling animal slipped from her grasp to be swept further downstream. Olivia's right boot slipped on the sodden bark sending her leg into the fork and the mighty force of the water shoved the log toward her and trapped her foot in the exact same manner as the calf had been trapped, painfully tight around her ankle. "Oh crap!"

The calf dragged itself from the water a short way downstream and the cow was instantly upon it, attending and nuzzling it. The two walked off together to re-join the herd.

"Thanks for your help and concern!" Olivia shouted, but sarcasm was futile.

She braced against the log with her free foot and tried to push it forward, but the force of one leg alone was no match for the sheer power of the water. She tried to slip her foot free, but the branches gripped her ankle so tightly that she could not even wiggle it, let alone try to slide her boot off to escape. To her horror, Olivia realised that the water level was steadily rising. It was now waist deep. She pulled her phone from her top pocket, thankful that she had invested in a water and bump proof cover, only to find there were zero bars. She was deep in a signal black spot. "Oh crap!"

The situation was clearly dire. She secured her phone back into her pocket.

"Help! Help!" she yelled at the top of her voice, but there was no one to hear her. Even if someone was near, her voice was overwhelmed by the crescendo roar of the ever-rising water. Yelling was futile, struggling was futile. There was only one more thing she could think of to do. One feeble thread of hope.

She knew the process so well now it was almost routine. Braced against the tree trunk Olivia calmed herself, focussed, wordlessly visualised her current situation and allowed herself to feel her panic and her desperate need for help. Then she broadcast it as intensely as she could muster. Not sure if it would work—she hadn't practised broadcasting before—she attempted the broadcast three more times. Calmer now, she resolved to conserve her energy and just work on keeping her head above the rising water. She hoped beyond hope the water would stop rising before her face submerged.

Perhaps she would drown. She wondered if it would be painful and she thought about how distressed her parents would be at her passing. She wanted to tell them she was sorry. Sorry for risking her own life for a calf, sorry for causing them such pain. But there would be no opportunity. Her brief life would end without ever having ridden the Kilkivan Horse Ride and without seeing Javier again, without finding out if he really liked her. The desolate idea of not seeing Javier again ached in her heart. She would fight to stay alive, to see him again.

The merciless water rose and precious time eked away.

Water pummelled the base of her neck and Olivia held her arms in a blocking position in front of her face to deflect the debris the torrent thrust in her direction. The water sucked out her body heat. She was cold, wet and felt so alone. This was a dismal way to die.

Rescue

Did she imagine it? Was that movement on the creek bank to her right? Olivia looked again, straining to see between the branches while still trying to block debris and keep her face above water. A dark brown limb moved beyond the tree branches. Not the black leg of a cow, but the brown, long, slender leg of a horse. On the chance that the horse had a rider, Olivia mustered as much of her remaining breath as she could and shouted, "Help! Help! Help!"

Someone dismounted. Olivia could make out brown boots, denim jeans and a royal blue work shirt. He had his back to the creek.

She shouted again, "Help! Help!"

A rope was rapidly secured to the saddle and two lengths were passed over a fallen tree trunk. The man tied one end around his chest, just below his arms, secured the other around his waist and marched into the torrent toward her. Someone had come to her rescue. Her tears of relief were erased by a splash of brown water gushing over her face. It got into her nose and mouth and tasted like mud. Olivia coughed and spluttered.

Her rescuer passed through a beam of light piercing the canopy and his golden locks glinted in the sun as his lithe frame ploughed through the water, from tree to tree, toward her. Olivia would recognise that hair, that physique, that movement anywhere. There was no mistaking Javier Evans. Her gut spasmed and the blood drained from her face. The humiliation of it. Rescued—cold, wet, muddy and grimy—by the Adonis, Javier Evans. She wanted to sink below the water and let herself drown, but another brown wave swept over her face and she spluttered and struggled to breathe. If she survived this, there would be time for embarrassment later.

A drenched Javier was soon upon her, his face contorted in a desperate look of concern. He braced himself on the tree trunk beside hers. Without a word, he untied the rope around his waist and proceeded to tie it around Olivia's chest, high under the armpits. He struggled against the torrent, held his breath and briefly disappeared beneath the water as he ran his hand first down one of her legs, then the other, seeking the cause of the entrapment. At any other time, this would have moved Olivia beyond words, but all she could do was struggle for each breath as the water washed over her face in waves. Javier's sodden face emerged and he gave something a potent kick. One side of the branch fork fell away. Javier pulled her toward him and her foot slipped free of the pressing log. She worried that the strong current would wash her away, but Javier held the rope secure and it tightened around her chest and held her near him.

Javier hauled her toward him and the expression on his face changed from gritty determination to recognition, to an impish grin. She wanted to hide from those intense brown eyes but there was nothing to be done except let Javier place a strong arm around her torso and draw her to him.

"Hold on!" Javier shouted above the roar of the water.

Olivia placed her arms tightly around his neck. The ropes around them tightened and hauled them toward the fallen tree trunk that kept both their heads above the water, most of the time. When Javier's feet finally found solid ground, he hauled a limp, exhausted Olivia out of the surging water and deposited her on the creek bank before he collapsed down beside her.

He took a deep breath, half rolled to face her and held out his hand. "Hi. I'm Javier. Nice to meet you."

Shivering, Olivia feebly took and shook his wet hand. "Olivia."

"Are you OK?"

"I think so."

Javier's furrowed frown eased. "So, what possessed you to go swimming in the creek?"

"Rescued a calf."

"Uh-huh. The calf's life was clearly more valuable than yours then?" Javier shook his head in disbelief.

"I wasn't expecting to get stuck."

"Clearly." Javier smirked and stood up. He untied the rope from around his chest. "May I?" He pointed to the rope around Olivia.

"I'll do it." Olivia was determined to regain some semblance of dignity. Lying wet and brown on a muddy creek bank beside the boy that she had secretly admired from afar for years was too embarrassing for words. Her shivering fingers struggled with the unfamiliar and tight knot. Her hands fell to her side in defeat and she nodded assent.

Javier's capable hands quickly untied the knot and gently drew the rope from around her. He looped both lengths of rope and hooked them on the saddle of a tall bay gelding waiting patiently higher up the creek bank. "Probably best if you come to our place and dry off a bit, then I'll drive you home."

Olivia hauled herself into a sitting position. She was weak and her skin hurt where the pummelling debris in the torrent had found its mark. Tomorrow she would be covered in bruises. She hoped Javier wouldn't see them. "OK." She didn't have a lot of other options.

Javier gestured to Vanilla, grazing serene on the other side of the creek. "Can you send your horse home?"

"I think so." Olivia fought to still the shivering, relax her depleted muscles and calm herself. She concentrated and sent the thought. Vanilla looked up, regarded her a moment, then walked off in the direction of home.

"Your parents will be worried when your horse arrives home without you. Do you still have a phone on you, or do you need to use mine?" Javier pulled a phone from a pouch on the side of the saddle.

Olivia wrested her phone from her wet shirt pocket. It sprang to life. The waterproof protective cover had not let her down. She texted her mother, 'Fell in the creek. I'm OK. Getting a lift home.'

That should do it. When they were higher on the creek bank, there would be enough signal for the message to send. "So where exactly do you live?"

Javier returned his phone to its pouch. "Over there," Javier said and pointed at the house with the sloping roof.

"That's Lauren's place."

"Yeah. Lauren's my mum."

Olivia gaped, stunned. She struggled to wrap her head around the idea that she had spent much of the school holidays with the mother of the boy she so wanted to meet. She remembered Lauren had said she taught both her children the Universal Language. "So, you picked up my broadcast message?"

"Loud and clear." Javier walked back to her and reached out a hand to help Olivia up the embankment. "Mum's been teaching you then?"

Olivia was still weak and unsteady. Javier put his arm around her waist and drew her close to him for support. She melted onto him and not just from muscle fatigue. She managed a feeble nod.

"Lucky for both of us that she did," he whispered as he guided her toward his horse. He leaned her up against the horse's hindquarters. "Don't worry. Max is quiet. He won't drop you. Reckon you can balance there a moment?"

"Yeah." Olivia let Max's powerful muscles take her weight as Javier mounted.

"So Lauren's last name is Evans then?"

"No. Mum changed hers back to Kendle after the divorce."

Javier reached down for Olivia's arm and hauled her gently but firmly up behind him. He placed her hands around his taut waist. "Hold on."

Olivia didn't need to be told twice. She tightened her grip, drew herself close to his back and buried her face just behind his shoulder. Through the soggy shirt, she felt his warmth and smelled the scent of him through the odour of muddy water. She wondered if it was a wonderful type of cologne or whether it was eau de Javier. Either way Olivia was in soggy, exhausted heaven for the duration of the ride.

* * *

James and Wayne were waiting at the door to receive them.

"What happened?" James asked, all concern.

"Got herself trapped in the flooded creek." Javier pulled his horse up just in front of them.

Wayne caught Olivia as she slid down from the horse. He passed her to James, then led Max to the horse yard while James and Javier helped Olivia inside.

"I'd say a shower, some clean dry clothes and a nice cup of tea are in order," James said as they parked the still weak Olivia on a kitchen stool. James disappeared for a few minutes and returned with an armful of clothes. "Some of Elise's things. I'm sure she won't mind in the circumstances."

"Thanks." Olivia stepped up from the stool to take the bundle and wobbled a little.

Javier instantly leapt forward and supported her arm. "Allow me to escort you to the guest bathroom."

"OK." Sometimes being weak and wobbly had its advantages. Holding the bundle of clothes close to her with one arm and with Javier supporting the other, Olivia was duly and happily escorted.

"You are also in need of a shower Javier," James called after them.

Awkward panic twinged Olivia's gut.

Javier must have sensed it. "Don't worry," he said with a wink as he deposited Olivia at the bathroom door. "This house has more than one bathroom."

Olivia leaned against the door handle, relieved and watched Javier lope back toward the kitchen. She pressed down on the handle and swung inward with the door. The bathroom was as amazing as the rest of the house. It was huge by Olivia's standards, bigger than her bedroom at home. The walls were covered in tiles that imitated a pale timber and the floor was covered in sand-coloured tiles that surrounded a central mosaic of two circling fish. A clean, fresh towel, bathmat and face washer were neatly folded on the edge of the basin.

The warm water soothed Olivia's skin, flushed the mud and debris from her hair and began the process of invigorating her. The day was like a weird dream. She had faced death in a flooded creek, been rescued by the divine Javier Evans (of all people) and she was now showering in the most palatial bathroom she had ever seen in real life— and in Javier's house of all places. It had to be real; even Olivia couldn't dream up such a day.

The clothes were an adequate fit, if not quite her style. She donned loose-fitting, calf-length linen drawstring pants and a boat neck black T-shirt with a diagonal peacock design. The top repeatedly slipped off one shoulder no matter how hard Olivia tried to balance it evenly.

She found a comb on a shelf by the mirror and set to work on her wet, tangled hair and eventually fastening it in a loose ponytail at the nape of her neck. Olivia folded up her wet clothes, stacked them on her boots and proceeded, barefoot and carrying the bundle, back toward the kitchen.

Javier was posed like a model from a country outfitter's catalogue: on a kitchen stool, clad in clean, dry, sand-coloured shorts, a pale blue, body-hugging T-shirt and canvas shoes. His still wet hair was combed away from his face and the familiar curls formed sequentially as his hair dried.

He turned to Olivia, looked her up and down, fixed on her eyes and smiled. "Feeling better?"

Olivia had to pause a moment; she had forgotten to breathe. "Much."

Javier seemed pleased.

"I'll get you a bag for those," James said on seeing the bundle of wet clothes. He disappeared from the kitchen and soon reappeared with a plastic carry bag. He helped Olivia stash her items then took the bag and parked it near the front door.

The round breakfast table near the expansive window was replete with some slices of cake, a few sweet buns, a pot of hot tea and settings for two.

"I hope there is something here you like." James poured the tea. "I suspect you two have much to discuss, so I'll leave you to it." With that, James disappeared in the direction of the laundry.

Javier gestured toward the table. "Please."

Olivia selected a seat and Javier sat in the seat beside her.

"Oh, and for the record, I do like sushi."

Olivia cringed with embarassment. She remembered the note she had imagined sending to Javier, realising it had got through.

"You're blushing."

"Sorry. I had no idea at the time that you'd actually receive that message."

"Saw the note loud and clear. Your imagination has very clear handwriting."

Olivia cringed again. "I had no idea I was using the Universal Language at the time. I didn't even know it existed."

"Most people don't. They have no idea when they are sending a targeted message, no idea when they are broadcasting and no idea when they are receiving a message either. Most people simply assume that any idea or feeling that pops into their head is their own."

"Let me guess, if someone acts on an idea they've had and inadvertently sent, they just assume it's coincidence."

"Yep. Unless they're in love. Then they assume it's kismet, or evidence of some divine connection."

"Which it is in a way." Olivia added some sugar to her tea. "I mean, it's beyond their level of perception and understanding so it would seem like magic at the very least."

"And divinity for the religiously inclined."

They chuckled together at the thought and Olivia glanced into Javier's eyes just for a moment. That's all it took for a surge of warmth to well in her core. Awkward and silent, she selected a sweet bun, took a bite and placed it down on her plate. Javier was being chivalrous and polite but he couldn't possibly be interested in her romantically? Surely he wouldn't stoop to having a girlfriend in the year below him and even if he did, Mel was a far better match. They'd look great together. Olivia resigned herself to being unworthy of him.

"Don't you like it?" Javier looked concerned and began to assess the platter for other options for her.

"It's delicious."

"I thought you'd be hungry after your ordeal."

Olivia was hungry. Ravenous. However, it had taken only one mouthful of the bun for her to realise that it wasn't food she was hungry for. Javier's proximity, company and conversation were infinitely more satisfying. No way was she going to tell him that. She carefully controlled her thoughts. "I am. I just like to eat slowly."

"Hope you don't mind but I don't." Javier selected an enticing slice of cake and placed it politely on his plate. He grinned and added another two, plus a bun. "Just for starters." He winked at Olivia.

Olivia's core had turned to mush. At this point, he could choose to discuss the local sewage plant and she would still be enthralled. She pulled her thoughts together, resolved not to get her hopes up and decided to satisfy her curiosity. "So, do you use the Universal Language at school to bewitch all the girls?"

Javier snickered and swallowed. "It doesn't work that way."

"How does it work?"

"When a thought pops into your head, you don't usually analyse where it came from do you?"

"Well, not until recently."

"Exactly. Most people just weigh up the thought against their value system, their feelings and their personal objectives. If it fits, they accept it and decide whether or not to act on it. If it doesn't, they dismiss it and move on."

"So?"

"So, I can't actually bewitch anyone who isn't most of the way there already."

"But you can pick up what they think about you if they're inadvertently transmitting."

"Like you for instance?"

Olivia knew she was blushing again but did her best to look expectant of a more informative response.

"Look, to me it feels like both options are cheating and I don't find relationships built on cheating very satisfying. So, I tend not to bother with them at all."

"Which is why you don't have a girlfriend?"

"Which is why I don't have a girlfriend."

"That makes sense." Olivia took another mouthful and washed it down with some tea.

Javier polished off the bun. "So why don't you have a boyfriend?"

"How do you know I don't?"

Javier cast her a sceptical sideways gaze that bored into her eyes.

All Olivia's pretence evaporated. There was clearly no deceiving Javier. "Usual story. I don't like any of the guys who seem interested in me and the guys that I'm interested in don't seem to like me."

"Which category do I fit in?"

Olivia took a deep breath and searched for words to deflect the question. But what would happen if, for once, she could brave up and be honest? "I have you in an entirely different category."

"Really?"

OK, he didn't look like he was going to bite her head off. Maybe it would be safe to confess.

"And what category is that?"

"The 'Out of my League' category." There, it was said.

Javier was about to raise a cup to his mouth. He put it down and began to laugh. It was a warm hearty laugh that

Olivia found oddly soothing. "So, tell me how you came to spend time with my mum?"

Olivia related the whole tale. Javier listened intently and punctuated the conversation with questions and insightful comments like, "Now you know why we don't invite many people over."

After more than an hour of comparing their perspectives on the last few months, the conversation lapsed into a brief silence.

"If you don't mind me asking," Olivia ventured, trying to gauge Javier's response. "Why is it you spend so little time here? Do you prefer to live with your dad?"

Javier frowned. His expression was pained. He sat upright in his chair and folded his arms in front of him. "Not at all. The farm is great and I'd much rather be here. Even more so after today." He smirked and cast a sideways glance at Olivia. "I play a lot of sport and I need to be in town for the games."

"They're mostly on weekends?"

"Exactly." The muscles in Javier's arms tensed. "Also, my dad has remarried and ... no, forget I mentioned it."

Olivia waited to see if there was more. She sensed there was something about his dad's family he didn't want to talk about. She was in no position to press the point, so she took advantage of the situation to simply gaze at his face. To Olivia it was perfect.

"Well, we'd better get you home."

* * *

When the shiny silver SUV with P plates attached pulled up near the McKinnon home, it was quickly surrounded by

Sheree and Art. Both raced to Olivia as she and Javier alighted from the car.

"Are you OK, Possum?"

Olivia winced and sighed at the words. "I'm fine, Dad."

Being called Possum in front of Javier was embarrassing. Perhaps not as embarrassing as bringing home the man of her dreams to find her mother had hung all her underwear on the clothesline for him to see. She glanced toward the clothesline near the orchard and her stomach plunged. Perhaps if she didn't say anything he wouldn't notice that it was her underwear on the line.

A glance in the other direction saw Vanilla munching hay in the house paddock, content.

"Vanilla made it home OK?" she asked, to deflect attention away from the clothesline.

"Vanilla is fine, dear," Sheree replied.

Javier walked up to Art. "Javier Evans. I believe you know my mother, Lauren." He held out his hand and Art shook it firmly as if testing Javier's grip.

"Art McKinnon." Art stepped back and glared at Javier. "So, what happened?"

"I got stuck in the creek trying to rescue a calf and Javier managed to pull me out before I drowned."

Art's expression changed from one of suspicion to one of surprise. "Really?"

"Really, Dad." Olivia glanced toward Javier with a smile. "If he hadn't come riding by, I'd be dead by now."

Art stepped forward to give Javier another, more vigorous handshake and patted him on the back with his other hand. "Thank you, Javier. Thank you for saving our little Possum."

Olivia cringed again on hearing her nickname.

"Yes, thank you." Sheree stepped forward and enveloped Javier in a hug. "Would you like to come in for a cuppa?"

"Thanks, Mrs McKinnon." Javier stepped back. "I'd better be getting back home. Another time maybe?"

"Sure," Sheree said. "I'm looking forward to it."

Olivia wondered, was Sheree's disappointed expression caused by the declined hospitality or by the lost opportunity to find out more about Javier's family?

Javier walked to Olivia and placed his hands on her shoulders. Her muscles relaxed under the warmth.

"So, you're OK now?"

"I'm fine now. Thank you."

"Good. I'll be in touch."

He looked into her eyes and smiled. That's all it took to turn Olivia's stomach to soup as Javier strode to the SUV.

The McKinnons waved as the vehicle disappeared down the driveway.

"Nice young man," Art said as he watched the vehicle exit the farm gate. He turned to Olivia. "Why the blazes did you go into a flooded creek to retrieve a calf? It's only a bloody calf. How many times have I warned you about flooded creeks?"

"What on earth possessed you to let our best breeding stock calve in a paddock with a flooding creek in it?"

Art stood dumbfounded and his shoulders slumped. "I'm so glad you're alive, Possum."

"What's that you're wearing?" Sheree looked Olivia up and down.

"They lent me some of Elise's clothes. Mine are in here." Olivia raised the plastic bag by her side.

"Well, let's get you inside and get those clothes in the wash. You can tell us the rest over lunch."

Olivia wasn't the slightest bit hungry. "Sure." There was clearly much more that her parents wanted to know and even more that she was determined to conceal.

Keeping it Real

Javier's head was a jumble as he drove back to the farm. It was like pieces of a jigsaw falling into place, only he didn't like the picture.

When he finally walked through the door, the house was deserted. He slid open the glass patio door to the pool area and found James and Wayne having lunch under the wisteria arbour. No longer in flower, the vine's foliage created dense shade from the midday sun. Javier sauntered over and planted himself on an empty chair.

"You're back already." James tore a piece off a crisp, crusty roll and dipped the bread into the sauce smeared on his half empty plate.

Wayne looked up. "Javier." He was a man of few words.

"So, tell me, Wayne." Javier grabbed a bread roll from the basket at the centre of the table and tore off a piece. "When I dashed from the house this morning in urgent need of my horse, how is it that Max was already saddled and waiting?"

Wayne swallowed and cleared his throat. "Thought you might want a ride this morning."

"And you, James ..." Javier turned to face him and watched as he put a forkful of salad into his mouth. "How is it you just happened to have fresh cakes baked and ready and a table set for two when I brought Olivia back to the house?"

James swallowed hard and looked Javier in the eye. "I thought you might like a nice morning tea and I set a second place just in case you brought a friend."

"I see." Javier glared at each in turn.

The two men looked up and in unison said, "Your mum."

At exactly the same time, Javier said, "My mum."

James and Wayne grinned.

Javier shook his head. "I should have known."

The sound of a car door slamming at the front of the house stymied any further conversation. Javier strode inside, folded his arms and leaned against the kitchen island with direct line of sight to the front door. As soon as Lauren closed the door behind her, he let fly. "How could you?"

"Good to see you too, Javier." Lauren moved into the living room and placed her bags on the floor by the sofa. "How could I what?"

"How could you teach Olivia the Universal Language?" Javier moved his hands to his pockets. "How could you when you knew I liked her?"

"Did I know?" Lauren leaned against the sofa. "When did you tell me? I can't recall."

"Don't tell me you didn't detect it. You deliberately taught her to undermine my chances with her."

"Has it undermined your chances, Javier?" Lauren stood calm and cool, one hand resting on the sofa and the other holding her car keys. Occasionally she twirled the key ring around her finger. "Has she told you she wants nothing to do with you?"

"No, not yet." Javier looked away so he could gather his thoughts.

Olivia seemed interested in him, but she didn't know how messed up things were with his father. She might not want to be associated with that; she might tell him to "bugger off" and leave her alone.

"You were hoping perhaps for a power imbalance? You get to eavesdrop on her thoughts and plant ideas in her head, while she remains oblivious?" Lauren twirled her keys again. "Even if you told her nothing, she would have subconsciously sensed you were hiding something. Eventually her suspicions would have grown to paranoia and driven a wedge between you. I've seen it happen, more than once."

"Still." Javier was deffused by the logic and tried to rustle up some more indignation. "You could have told me you were teaching her."

"Why?" Lauren tilted her head sideways. "You didn't mention she was important to you. She was a neighbour in need of a riding companion. When she detected our ability, she asked me to teach her, so I did."

"It's still not fair."

"Fair to whom?" Lauren scooped up her bags again and walked toward the stairs. "You forget, Javier. If I hadn't taught her the Universal Language, she would be dead now and this would be a very different conversation."

"So, what are you going to do? Try and teach everyone the Universal Language?"

Lauren slowly ascended the stairs. "Why not? Maybe it's time for our species to take the next evolutionary step?"

Javier stood there and sulked. His mother always had a counter argument to every point he raised and he hated it when she was right. "Thank you!" he called out as Lauren reached the top step.

"For what?" Lauren paused at the top landing.

"For helping me save Olivia's life."

"You're welcome." Lauren beamed and disappeared into the depths of the mezzanine studio.

Javier's frown soon faded and he took himself to his room, shut the door behind him and sat on the bed. Through the window a small mob of kangaroos lounged in the nearby field, clustered in the shade of a leaning gum tree to escape the midday sun. He lay on his bed, in the cool of the air-conditioning, hands behind his head, and he scrutinised the events of the morning.

That evening, when the house was quiet, Javier sat, tense, on the edge of his bed. He took his phone from his pocket, pulled up Olivia's number and pressed it to make the call.

Ride After the Flood

The heat of the day was still only a promise when Olivia tacked up Vanilla. It had taken a couple of days for the bruises to be less sore, though they were still very visible, and Olivia was keen to ride again.

Art pulled up at the house in the dusty farm ute. He'd been out baling lucerne since before dawn, while the air was cool and tolerable and he was taking a break for morning tea before heading back to the tractor. If he got the lucerne in that paddock tightly wound up into large round bales before the forecast evening storm, it would withstand a soaking downpour and dry quickly the next morning, ready to be carted. If not, it would only be good for silage.

Art got out of the vehicle and slammed the door shut. "Off riding again, Possum?" he said with a grin and tilt of his hat, before he turned toward the house.

"Yeah, Dad," Olivia kept walking. "Thought we'd try and squeeze one in before the storms arrive."

"Take care." Art strode toward the house.

"I will."

Olivia set about tacking up Vanilla. She sent a thought, Vanilla exhaled and Olivia tightened the girth one more notch. She sent a thank you and followed it with a hug and a pat.

Using the Universal Language had become routine and almost effortless now. Olivia's face broke into a Mona Lisa smile of quiet satisfaction at the thought. She opened the yard gate, walked back to Vanilla, unwound the reins from the fence and led Vanilla to the mounting block. She flipped the reins over Vanilla's neck, stepped onto the block, placed a foot in the stirrup and launched herself into the saddle. Vanilla stood stock still until her rider was safely settled in her seat.

Vanilla needed little prompting. At the first hint of urging, Vanilla made for the open gate and the track toward the creek.

The subdued flow in the creek bed now merely tickled at Vanilla's knees as it flowed on through shadows and between bottlebrush trunks. Olivia's riding partner waited patiently on the far side.

"Hello Olivia."

"Hi, Javier." He looked magnificent, sitting tall on the majestic, bay thoroughbred gelding. "Hi Max."

The horse moved his head up and down in a nodding motion and tugged against Javier's hold on the reins.

"I see," Javier said, feigning indignation. "You've come all this way to converse with my horse."

Olivia returned a cheeky grin. "Well, my dad says I should always acknowledge those who are doing all the work."

Javier raised a mischievous eyebrow and chuckled. "Well then. Good morning, Vanilla."

Vanilla quickened her pace and made directly for Max and his rider.

"So where shall we ride today?" Olivia asked as Vanilla pulled herself up beside their companions.

"I was planning to ride along the creek toward the front gate. It's a scenic ride with lots of shady spots to retreat from the heat, but Wayne insists that we check out the hill paddock, where the goats have just been taken off and investigate anything unusual in their wake." He sighed as if disappointed he had not arranged a more enjoyable outing.

Max carried no saddle bags so there would be no refreshments either, not that she minded. In Javier's proximity it was difficult to think of mundane things like food and water. "No worries. I'm used to the routine. I've been riding with your mum for months remember." She flashed him a reassuring smile.

Javier's mood brightened and they turned the horses toward the hill paddock.

The goats had been thorough. The grass was like a closely clipped lawn and the trees and bushes were denuded of leaves and twigs to the height of a man's shoulder. The paddock looked like a rural estate and the slopes of the hillock that gave the paddock its name were clustered with small, erect eucalyptus trees.

Olivia caught a glimpse of something white among the trees and pulled up Vanilla. "What's that?"

"What?" Javier pulled Max up beside them and looked in the same direction.

"That." Olivia pointed at a wisp of something white wafting in the slight breeze.

"It's getting warm, I'd rather head for the shade of the creek." Javier cast a glance at the inviting snake of green foliage in the distance. "Still, Wayne did say to check out anything unusual." He turned Max toward the hillock and Olivia turned Vanilla to follow.

Not until they penetrated halfway through the trees on the slope could they make out the cause of the movement.

"Well, look at that." Javier glanced at Olivia and urged Max to quicken his pace up the hill.

"Wow!" Olivia took in the sight and signalled Vanilla to keep up. "It's lovely. Did you organise this?"

"I wish I had." Javier pulled Max up by a fallen log and tied the reins to a shaded branch that protruded up from it.

Olivia did the same and moved to Javier's side as they beheld the sight. A white, canvas marquee sat atop the hillock and white crepe paper streamers, tied at each corner, caught the breeze. A round, ornate, white table was planted at the centre of the shade cast by the marquee and two matching chairs stood beside. On the ground by the table sat a wicker picnic basket and a blue plastic esky. They walked slowly toward the vision.

"Do you think your mother...?"

Javier was distant for a moment. "No. It wasn't Mum."

These distant gazes were no longer bothersome to Olivia. Javier was using the Universal Language to interrogate his family.

Javier chuffed and leaned back with a grin.

"James?"

Javier tilted his head. "Conspiracy actually."

"James certainly has this much class." Olivia waved her hand over the setting.

"And Wayne has the ute to get it all here." Javier moved behind one of the chairs and placed his hands on the back of it. "Do take a seat. After all, you must be weary from the long ride," Javier said in a feigned British accent.

"Thank you, kind sir." Olivia feigned an accent too. They giggled together at the absurdity of all this in the middle of a goat paddock in the middle of nowhere in particular.

Olivia opened the picnic basket and found a tablecloth neatly folded atop the contents. She shook it out and placed it on the table. Javier retrieved a tall, chilled bottle from the esky and placed it on the cloth. Olivia gave it a double glance.

"Don't worry, any plans I may have had to get you drunk were thwarted. It's sparkling grape juice."

"Oh well, some other time." Olivia retrieved two glasses from the basket and placed them beside the bottle.

Javier regarded her with one eyebrow raised and relaxed at her impish grin.

As Javier poured the drinks, Olivia retrieved a plate of cut sandwiches and a platter of cake from the basket, followed by serving plates, cloth napkins and cutlery. "James was very thorough. He thought of everything."

They took up their glasses.

"To James and Wayne for being so thoughtful." Olivia raised her glass.

"To us." Javier raised his glass to clink hers. "As was clearly their intention."

Olivia blushed at the thought.

They talked about school, their career plans and their friends. They relived the flood from each other's perspective and by the time all the food and drink were consumed, they had still not run out of conversation. Olivia sent a "thank you" thought to James and Wayne for the enchanting morning tea. Together Olivia and Javier bundled the debris back into the basket and esky.

"We should take the horses down to the creek," Olivia suggested. "They're hungry and thirsty too."

The horses fidgeted. "Good idea."

"Shall we take down the marquee or something?"

"No. I reckon Wayne and James will collect it all shortly." He stood slowly and made his way toward Olivia's chair.

Standing beside her, he held out his hand. Olivia placed her hand in his and stood. He gently pulled her toward him. Inches away, she felt his warmth. She inhaled the mixed scent of Javier, cake and horses. His breath was warm on her face and her heart pounded. She raised her face toward him and his warm, strong lips met hers. Something melted deep inside her. Her knees felt weak. Before she could worry about whether her knees would hold, she forgot about them—and everything else. In that moment, there was only Javier.

"Wow," was all she could manage to say when their lips finally parted.

Javier smiled a warm, satisfied smile she had not seen before. Had she done that? She placed her hand around his neck and drew his face toward hers one more time.

"We should go now." Javier finally drew breath. "Or we'll have an audience." He tilted his head toward the paddock where the farm ute wound its way toward the hill.

"Good idea." Olivia wriggled herself free and unwrapped Vanilla's reins. The fallen log made an excellent mounting block.

Javier did the same and the pair made their way toward the creek. Javier finally spoke, "Seeing as we get along so well and haven't run out of things to talk about, may I call you most evenings?"

Olivia struggled to believe what was happening. The unattainable Javier had not only kissed her in a way that she could happily be kissed until the end of time, but he wanted to spend more time talking with her. She tried to be cool, despite the rush of feelings. "Sure, I'm looking forward to it."

Vanilla pulled herself up, probably confused at the signals she was getting from her rider.

Javier walked Max in slow circles around them. "Perhaps we could spend more time together whenever I'm here?"

Olivia wrestled to organise her thoughts and feelings, with limited success. Javier was only talking about spending time together away from the public eye. Maybe he was uncomfortable about being seen with her, especially at school. She was determined not to spoil the moment by reading too much into it. It was way too soon to do that. Time, conversation and the Universal Language would eventually tell her what she wanted to know. "I'd really like that."

Javier moved Max in close. He leaned over and kissed Olivia on the forehead. She marvelled at how such a manoeuvre could be accomplished on horseback.

"Excellent," he whispered and turned Max back toward the creek.

They walked the horses into still water, protected by a fallen bush, and let them drink. Javier spied a shady embankment, where they dismounted and let the horses graze on the soft grass. The pair kissed and talked until the horses became restless. Thunder clouds rolled and swelled on the west horizon when Javier escorted Olivia back to the gate and the creek crossing.

"You're a much more enjoyable riding companion than your mother." Olivia began to walk Vanilla down into the creek. She glanced back at the confused expression on Javier's face.

"Thanks, I guess." He waved as she crossed the creek. "Call you tonight?"

"Counting on it," Olivia called back as Javier, still stationary on the bank, disappeared from view behind foliage.

* * *

A smile persisted on Olivia's face and her parents tried to figure out why. She wondered if there was a matching smile on Javier's face and how many seconds it would take Lauren, James and Wayne to detect the reason behind it. Perhaps living in a household where everyone used the Universal Language made him more practised at controlling and concealing his thoughts.

Around eight Olivia's phone pinged.

Let me know when it's OK to call ☺.
☺ 👍

Olivia sprang into action. She showered, superficially caught up on only the most essential socials and settled onto her bed with pillows stacked so she could sit upright.

Ready 👍.

She waited.

Maybe she had taken too long; he could have fallen asleep by now. Maybe he was already frustrated because she kept him waiting. Maybe he wouldn't call.

Her phone rang and she answered it on the first ring. "Hi Javier."

"Hi Olivia. How was your afternoon?"

"You know, one of those exciting afternoons you have when a storm hits and the only place that's not wet, muddy or subject to torrents of rain is indoors."

"Glad to hear it. At least you didn't feel the need to go swimming in the creek this time."

Olivia huffed as she remembered the humiliating rescue. "This is going to become a running joke, isn't it?"

"Absolutely. Your chances of forgetting the incident are..."

"Zero."

"Or Buckley's."

Olivia sighed but said nothing.

"You'll be pleased to know that James and Wayne are delighted we enjoyed their morning tea."

"Did they manage to get it all stowed back at the house before the storm hit?"

"Yes and no. The first raindrops hit just as they got back to the house with all the gear on the ute, so Wayne drove the loaded ute straight into the hay shed. They went inside while the storm raged and went out to unpack it later."

"Good. After doing such a great job of making our day delightful, I'd hate to think that they ended up in a soggy mess as a result." The line was silent. "So, can we ride again tomorrow?" In the twenty-first century, Olivia wasn't about to sit meekly and wait for Javier to keep asking her out. The silence on the line threw her. Maybe Javier was not of like mind?

"Much as I'd like to, Mum's sending me back to town tomorrow morning." Javier's voice sounded dejected at the thought.

"Is she trying to stop us spending time together?"

"No. It's not that. She's really quite ... supportive."

Olivia sat quietly and waited for Javier to find the words, hoping he wasn't having second thoughts.

"You see, my dad is at a conference and he gets back tomorrow evening."

"But school doesn't go back for another week and a bit. Surely your dad can spare you for a few more days?"

"It's not my dad we're worried about. It's Charlie and Henry."

"Charlie and Henry?"

Javier slowly explained the whole sordid situation while Olivia peppered the explanation with questions.

"So, you've been spending extra time at your dad's place to protect your stepmum and brother?"

"Uh-huh."

"That's a very noble thing to do."

"You think?"

"Absolutely. Between rescuing damsels in distress from certain doom in floodwater and protecting your stepmum and brother, you're a real-life hero." The line was silent again but she thought she could sense a smile. "From now on I'll be checking to see if you are secretly wearing a superhero outfit under your shirt."

"Nah. It's too bloody hot for that. There's only so much sweltering heat even a superhero can take."

Olivia giggled at the thought. They chatted for over an hour and eventually stopped, not because they had run out of things to talk about, but because they were dozing off.

"Chat again tomorrow night?" Javier's voice was muffled and slurred by weariness.

"Yes please," Olivia mumbled back slowly. "Let me know how things go with your dad."

"Mmm, goodnight, Olivia."

"Goodnight, Javier."

Swooshing, bumping noises signalled Javier fumbling with his phone and he ended the call. Olivia barely had enough coordination to place her phone on its charger before she too was asleep.

Mel Update

Guilt gnawed away at Olivia. Somehow Javier did prefer her over the amazing Mel and Olivia felt compelled to break it to her, yet she avoided doing so at every opportunity. Any distraction would do; she even offered to help her mother with extra housework.

One evening, after Javier returned to town, she set about vacuuming the entire house; she carefully timed the task to finish just as Javier was due to call, so there was simply no time to contact Mel. She plied the noisy machine over the beige woollen carpet as Dr Bell's words echoed in her head, "Do you feel powerless...?" Olivia dared ask herself why she was avoiding Mel and the answer struck like a hammer blow. She switched off the vacuum, slid down the hallway wall and sat pale and silent on the clean carpet.

The stairs creaked and Sheree appeared. "Have you finished, dear? I'd like to catch up on some telly."

"Sure." Olivia had lost all zest for the task.

Sheree stepped over Olivia's legs enroute to the living room.

"Mum."

Sheree had the TV remote in hand. "Yes, dear."

"Do you think I'm powerless?"

"Not at all." Sheree pressed buttons and looked at the TV. "What on earth makes you think that?" She planted herself on the sofa as the TV lit up the room. "Oh, Livvie," Sheree said, her eyes fixated on the screen, and Olivia's question apparently forgotten. "My friend, Alison, is coming over for afternoon tea tomorrow. I told her it's OK to bring her kids. You'll look after them while we catch up, won't you dear?"

Olivia waited for her mother to request confirmation, for at least a small hint that Olivia had a say in the matter, but Sheree remained fixated on the screen. She was determined not to be as powerless with her friends as she seemed to be at home. Olivia texted Mel to see if she was available for a video call, stowed away the vacuum cleaner and made for her room.

A familiar face materialised on the computer screen. "It's so good to see you, Mel. It feels like ages."

Mel looked like a model. Her face was made up—classy, not overdone—and it emphasised her stunning eyes. "Hello, Livvie." She leaned back from the camera and revealed a teal silk top embroidered with a peacock design on the left side and a white bolero jacket. "Can't talk long, my parents have invited another family over for dinner and I'm supposed to help entertain them. Their kids go to Oxford, so it will be a chance to suss out that university for next year."

A door opened in the background and Mrs Lawrence's head poked through. She muttered something in Mandarin.

"I'm chatting with Olivia, Mum." Mel turned toward her mother. Her hair was carefully bunched into an updo, held in place by a pearl-encrusted pin. "I won't be long."

Mrs Lawrence stepped into the room and burst into a wide smile that encompassed her entire face. "Hello Olivia!" She waved at the screen. "I hope you have good holiday."

Olivia waved back. "Hello Mrs Lawrence. It's fine, thanks." Such a useful word, fine, it concealed so much.

Mrs Lawrence said something in Mandarin and Mel replied in Mandarin. Mel rolled her eyes as she turned back to the screen. Mrs Lawrence shut the door behind her as she left.

Olivia would have to be quick. She took deep breaths to help build her nerve, but her efforts were eroded by the thought she might be ruining a lovely evening for Mel. "There's something I have to tell you, Mel."

"Oh, I have so much to tell you too." Mel fastened a string of luminous large pearls around her neck. "There is so much happening here. We'll have so much to talk about when we get back to school."

"Really, Mel," Olivia pleaded. "I need you to listen."

A knock sounded on Mel's door. "I really have to go now, Livvie." Mel glanced at the door and back to the screen. "If it's really important, I'd prefer you told me face to face. You can tell me on the first day of school." Mel glanced down at her keyboard. "Miss you."

"It's about Javier."

Too late. Mel disappeared from the screen mid-sentence.

"I'm seeing Javier," Olivia said to the blank screen. She pressed the laptop closed. "Just thought you ought to know."

Back to the Maelstrom

After breakfast Javier tossed his luggage into the back of Lauren's SUV. It landed with a thud. He took his leave of James and Wayne, who were still gloating over the successful surprise they had executed in the hill paddock the previous day.

Wayne pulled a white streamer from his pocket, passed it discreetly to Javier as they shook hands and whispered, "A memento."

"Thanks, mate." Javier plunged the streamer into a front pocket of his jeans.

Lauren smiled and waved to them. "See you this arvo. Text if there's anything else you need me to pick up in town." She tossed the car keys to Javier and he affixed the rear P plate.

Lauren affixed another to the inside of the windscreen. "I do enjoy having a driver sometimes. I get a much better view of the scenery this way."

For the first part of the journey, Lauren surveyed the landscape and they discussed what the local landowners were doing with their properties. They critiqued the quality of roadside maintenance by the council, the condition of the roads and who was responsible. Javier appreciated the distraction. He didn't want to think about what awaited at his destination any sooner than necessary.

After a brief stopover in Gympie for morning tea, the second part of the journey was spent discussing contingency plans for all the scenarios they conceived might play out over the coming few weeks.

Javier was adamant that Lauren's projected worst-case scenarios were unnecessary speculation. He expected things would go on as they had done till now. The only difference was that now he had a powerful impetus to spend more time on the farm. For Olivia, he could stick it out a while longer. For her he could be a hero.

When they pulled into the school car park, Charlie was already waiting. Her vehicle was parked in the shade of a poinciana tree with all the doors open.

"Looks like Henry is asleep," Lauren said as Javier pulled their vehicle in nearby.

"Better not beep the horn then, hey?" Javier turned off the ignition and flicked the switch to open the cargo bay.

"Best not." Lauren turned to him her brows furrowed. "She looks terrified, Javier."

Javier peered under the sun shield. "Yeah ... yeah, she does, Mum." He tried to look confident and reassuring.

"Never underestimate a woman's gut feeling." Lauren placed a hand on the door latch.

"Or her ability to be emotional and irrational in a crisis." Javier also placed a hand on the door latch.

"Now, now, Javier," Lauren said as they emerged from the car simultaneously. "Women don't have a monopoly on that one."

Javier flashed Lauren a grin and turned to Charlie, who was leaning on the side of her vehicle beside the open rear passenger door. Inside, Henry sat slumped in the car seat: head to one side, eyes closed, mouth open and drooling profusely.

"Hey Charlie," Javier said in hushed tones, so as not to wake the sleeping toddler.

"Good to see you, Javier." Charlie's mouth smiled but her eyes didn't. "Lauren." She tilted her head to acknowledge Javier's mother.

"Charlie." Lauren raised an eyebrow at the unexpected communication.

Javier transferred his luggage from Lauren's vehicle to Charlie's. He sauntered over to Lauren and gave her a hug. "See you, Mum."

"See you soon. Keep in touch."

"I will." Javier released his hold and turned toward Charlie.

Charlie closed the car doors as silently as she could. After each one she paused and peered in the window, tense with apprehension lest Henry wake and demanded attention. Javier perched his tall frame on the front passenger seat and gently pulled the door closed. He sat as quiet as he could manage and turned to check Henry. Henry's tongue popped in and out and his fingers twitched, but his eyes remained closed.

Charlie tilted her head to acknowledge Lauren before she stepped into the driver's seat and gently closed the door.

Lauren removed the P plates from her vehicle as Charlie's SUV pulled out of the car park. She gave Javier one final wave, with the plates in hand, before she disappeared from view.

* * *

Javier and Charlie arrived at the house around lunchtime. Javier made directly for the fridge.

"Out of there," Charlie said with a serious frown. "I'll make you a sandwich if you change Henry."

"Deal." Javier lifted the toddler from Charlie's hip and made for the child's bedroom. When he emerged, two fat ham and salad sandwiches sat on a plate at the table and a much smaller version sat on another plate in front of Henry's highchair. Javier placed the animated child into the chair.

"Mmmm," Henry said, wide eyed, as he reached for the first sandwich.

Charlie poured drinks and placed them on the table.

"Aren't you having some lunch?" Javier took a sandwich in his hands and lined it up for the first bite.

"I ate while I was making yours."

Instead of sitting in the chair beside Henry, Charlie flitted about the room, restless. Compared to the tranquil ease of the farm, this house felt like a simmering pressure cooker. Thinking about riding horses with Olivia calmed Javier down and the calmn fuelled his appetite. Both sandwiches and the tall glass of water were promptly consumed.

Henry wasn't coping though. His mother was restless and unsettled and it was contagious. Halfway through his meal he threw the morsel of food in his hand onto the table.

"Aren't you hungry?" Charlie picked up the scrap with some paper towel and offered Henry his cup.

Henry took it, sipped a little and threw the cup. It clunked onto the table. Fortunately, it was a sealed cup, designed for moody toddlers and little was spilled.

Charlie grabbed another piece of paper towel and cleaned up the liquid. "Oh Henry, I really don't have time for this." Her face was strained and a frown deepened the furrows between her brows. "Your daddy's coming home this evening and I need some peace and quiet so I can cook a special dinner. Would you like a special dinner tonight, Henry?"

Henry shook his head and tried to wriggle free of the chair.

Javier sprang to his feet. "It's OK, Charlie. I'll take him to the beach." He lifted the pouting child free of the chair and wiped his face clean. "Now, let's go get some sunscreen on, little man."

"Thanks Javier."

* * *

The tension diminished as Javier pushed the stroller—loaded with Henry and a large carry bag—away from the house and Henry's mood brightened too. At the beach, Javier set up a small sun shelter where the sand was still moist from the receding tide. Waves broke gently onto the sand and playing children shouted and squealed in the distance. Clad in a rashie and swimmers, topped with a wide-brimmed hat, Henry resembled a brightly coloured mushroom. He was equipped with plastic shovels, a rainbow of coloured buckets and pots in assorted shapes and he set happily to work sculpting the sand. Javier sat beside him to watch and began to add a potful of sand here and a bucketful there. Henry clapped with delight as Javier dribbled peaks of wet sand to top the towers. By the time they were done, the structure was a fairy-tale castle, complete with moat. Henry played with the sand and water in the moat, trying to practise the sand dribbling technique.

"Time to go, mate." Javier packed away the implements and the sunshade.

By the time everything was stowed in the bag and the pram, a smiling Henry sat in the moat, covered in slushy sand. Javier picked up the child and carried him, squealing and giggling, to the water where he dipped him a few times in the breaking waves to rinse off the sand. He carried Henry up the beach and strapped him into the stroller.

On the walk home, Javier started a game.

"Bwoo ... bwoo!" Henry shouted and pointed every time he saw a blue car. Javier stopped the stroller and gave him a 'high five'. Henry sustained the game all the way to the house.

Coming in through the front door felt like entering an ice castle and not just because the air-conditioner was on. Charlie flustered about in the kitchen. The recipe was not going to plan. Henry was instantly grumpy and Javier's work was not yet done. He organised a snack for Henry and went to put him down for a nap. Henry was restless and disinclined to sleep so Javier sent him a nice, long, sleepiness thought and watched, bemused, as the child succumbed to his own heavy eyelids.

* * *

Javier peered out his window at the sound of a car door slamming. A taxi, bathed in the golden light of sunset, pulled out of the driveway. The front door opened and his father was greeted with a cheerful "Hello Andrew" from Charlie.

"Hello luv."

"How was the conference?"

"Good."

There were footsteps and the sounds of doors being opened and closed. His father checked every room of the house. Javier wondered why he would do that. He'd never done it before. The door to Henry's room opened and there was a prolonged silence before it closed. When the door to his room was finally pushed open, Javier swivelled his chair to face it. "Hi Dad."

"Hello Javier." Andrew lingered in the doorway. "Did she behave herself?" He gestured his head in the direction of the kitchen.

"Always does." Javier kept his face expressionless. "Charlie's a good mum."

Andrew sneered and left. Javier shook his head and swivelled back to his computer. There were more emails to attend to. Glass clinked on glass as his father pour himself a drink at the bar cabinet. Javier tried to send a message to stop drinking but the Universal Language could not penetrate the dulling effects of alcohol and the message had no effect. It was never a good sign when his father started to drink early. More clinking of glass as Andrew revisited the cabinet a few times more.

"Dinner's ready!" Charlie's voice carried through the house.

Burbling and cries signalled Henry was awake. Javier arrived in the corridor to see his father already at Henry's door. "It's OK, mate. I'll get him."

"Sure." Javier followed the delicious aromas to the kitchen. A pork roast stood triumphant on the kitchen bench and Charlie busied herself with serving plates and the side dishes.

Andrew emerged with Henry on his hip. "Hello mate." His face was close to Henry's. "Did you miss me?"

Henry considered him strangely and started to cry. Javier raced up, took Henry from his father and placed the sobbing toddler in his highchair at the table.

"Y'know there's a reason that boy doesn't like me, don't you?" Andrew glared at Charlie under his eyebrows.

Javier walked to his seat. "Because your breath smells of alcohol?"

"Iz because he's not mine y'know." His speech was already slightly slurred.

Javier planted himself on his usual dining chair. "I don't know what you're talking about."

Charlie placed the amply filled plates on the table; her expression was fixed between exasperation and fear.

"Bloody good conf'rence." Andrew shovelled a piece of pork into his mouth.

Javier and Charlie exchanged glances. Both knew better than to speak. Javier tried to send her a thought of reassurance, but her wall of fear was impenetrable.

"Call this cracklin'?" Andrew spat the morsel back onto his plate. "It's soggy as."

The room went silent, except for the crunching 'chit chit' of Henry gnawing avidly at his piece of crackling.

Andrew pushed the remaining vegetables to the side of his plate. "The carrots are raw."

Javier gently pierced one with his fork. His knife glided through it and he put the carrot, still glistening with butter in his mouth. His expression revealed how perfect it was, but Charlie was too stymied by fear to notice.

"The spuds are frigg'n burnt." Andrew plonked the cutlery down and shoved the plate away. "Couldn't cook to save ya bloody life, could ya?"

Charlie sat frozen. She dared not move, not dared not speak.

"I think it's delicious," Javier said between mouthfuls. "Looks like Henry does too." He gestured his knife toward the toddler happily munching with a piece of pork in one hand and a small carrot in the other.

"What would either of ya frigg'n know?" Andrew glared at each of them in turn. "Well, is there dessert? Please tell me there's somethin' edible in this place."

Charlie leapt to her feet and made for the kitchen. She gathered up two oven mitts and wrestled to put them on her trembling hands. She opened the oven door and released the aroma of fresh-baked apple pie. She pulled the shelf forward to reveal the golden dessert.

Javier saw her trembling hands move to lift the dish from the shelf. Mid-air, somewhere between the oven and the bench, the dish spilled between her shaking hands and crashed to the floor.

"Bitch!" Andrew flew across the kitchen toward her. He pushed her up against the wall, his hand around her throat. "Ya did that on purpose, didn't ya, bitch? The only potentially edible thing in this house and ya trashed it ta spite me. Didn't ya?" Andrew's face turned purple with rage.

Andrew pushed harder on Charlie's neck. Her feet left the floor, her breaths were squeaky rasps and her face turned blue.

Henry screamed.

"Dad!" Javier jumped to his feet and glared Andrew in the eye. "What are you doing? You could go to jail for this!"

Andrew glared at Charlie an instant longer, then pulled his hand away. Charlie dropped to the floor. Andrew slapped her across the face and kicked her in the leg. Charlie whimpered with each blow.

Javier wanted to rush to her immediately, but it was not safe.

"Shut that kid up!" Andrew turned his glare to the bawling Henry, whose hands were still full of food, now turned to mush.

"He's crying because he's scared." Javier moved slowly toward Henry. "When he stops being scared, he'll stop crying."

"So, you're all frigg'n 'gainst me?" Andrew stepped away from Charlie. "Happy to live off my money though aren't ya? Bunch of bloody parasites." He took another step back. "If ya don't shut that bloody kid up, I will." Andrew lunged toward Henry and raised his arm to strike the child.

Javier's arm blocked and deflected the blow.

Charlie had opened her eyes in time to see it, her mouth agape in horror.

Andrew swung a punch at Javier. Javier blocked that too and swept Andrews legs to the side. Andrew moved to take another swing, but his arm flailed in the air as he slid to the floor with a thud.

"So that's how it is?" Andrew said, as he army-crawled along the floor, away from the vigilant Javier.

"That's how it is." Javier's voice was stern.

Charlie closed her eyes.

"I'm going to the pub," Andrew said as he slowly pulled himself to his feet, using the couch for support.

"Anywhere out of the house works for me." Javier didn't budge. Not yet.

Andrew pulled his car keys from his pocket and they jangled in his hand. He walked, unsteady, toward the door. "I have no family." He walked out and slammed the door behind him.

Javier raced over to Charlie. "Are you OK?"

She opened her eyes. "Henry."

"Henry's fine." He closed his eyes at the sound of the boy's cries. "At least his lungs are working perfectly by the sound of it." He moved to help Charlie to a sitting position propped against the wall. "Are you OK here?"

Charlie nodded and whispered, "Henry."

Javier went and lifted Henry from his highchair. He wiped the tears and smeared food from his face and carried the child to where Charlie sat, then put him on the ground.

Henry tottered to his mother and wrapped his small, plump arms around as much of her as he could reach. "Mum."

"It's OK, Henry." She stroked his head. "It's OK now, thanks to Javier."

"You mean it's OK for now?" Javier sat himself on the floor beside them. "He'll be back. You know he'll be back."

Charlie nodded, weakly, and surveyed the mess on the floor.

"We must call the police."

"No." Charlie was emphatic. "It will only make him angrier, more dangerous."

"Charlie, it's getting worse each time. You can see that. It's not getting better, it's getting worse."

Charlie conceded a reluctant nod.

"This time he almost hit Henry. You saw that. Next time it could be worse."

Charlie wrapped an arm around Henry and pressed her face against the top of his head.

"You might be able to survive a hit from Andrew, but Henry?"

Charlie pushed her head back against the wall. Tears streamed down her cheeks. The whites of her eyes were blood-shot and red wheals were developing around her neck. "No police. Not yet. We'll leave."

"Now?"

"Not now. Tomorrow morning."

"But he'll be home before then." Javier pointed out. "Who knows how much damage he'll do?"

"He'll be too drunk to do anything but sleep when he gets home. He'll leave for work in the morning."

"That's our chance?"

"That's our chance." Charlie confirmed. "We can get away then, calmly, without scaring Henry."

"You've been giving this some thought while I was away?"

"Yeah." Tears streamed down Charlie's cheeks.

"Good on you. You're doing the right thing."

Charlie nodded feebly but looked unconvinced.

Javier salvaged some pie from the dish and placed it in a large bowl. He topped it with some ice cream and found three spoons. The three of them sat on the kitchen floor and ate the luscious pie until they felt better and the bowl was scraped clean.

Javier took Henry off for a bath and settled him to bed for the night. When he returned to the kitchen, Charlie was on her feet, cleaning up the last of the debris that had been dinner.

She packed the leftover meat and some bread, cheese and fruit into containers. "For tomorrow."

"Sure." He took his mum's advice and didn't tell her she wouldn't be needing the food. He had everything planned. Once they were out of the house, they would all be OK. They would all be safe. He would see to it.

"I'm going to bed now." Javier moved toward his room. "Let me know if you need anything."

Charlie managed a feeble smile. "Thanks Javier, for everything."

"No worries. See you in the morning."

"Sleep well," Charlie called after him as he reached his door.

"You too."

This was no time for sleep, at least not yet. Javier sent his mum a few thought messages illustrating the events of the evening and texted to say they'd be leaving in the morning. Her reply piqued him.

☺ 👍 Meet you in Gympie at the following address.

The address was unfamiliar. He replied:

He wasn't sure what his mother was up to, but he was learning to trust her judgement. He hoped Charlie would be able to do the same.

While waiting for his father to return home, Javier backed up the contents of his computer to a portable hard drive and into the cloud. He pulled a large suitcase from his wardrobe and began to fill it with some clothes, the hard drive and some personal items, then stowed it back in its place. He backed up his phone to the cloud, just in case.

"*At least there's one upside to all of this,*" he thought; he'd get to spend some more time with Olivia.

Javier amused himself on his computer until the front door opened. He swivelled his chair to face his door and waited, listening. There were bumps and groans as his father stumbled about in the half-dark. Andrew eventually stumbled to the master bedroom and went in. Javier listened for any commotion between his father and Charlie, but there was none, just the whoosh of a toilet flush in the ensuite.

He imagined Charlie lying there, too terrified to move, too terrified to open her eyes, feigning sleep, but too terrified to sleep. But he would need sleep. He would need to be alert for the long drive in the morning. When the house went silent, he crawled into bed and calmed his mind, like his mum had taught him, until he fell asleep. Charlie had said there wouldn't be any trouble during the night. He hoped she was right.

Flight

Javier and Charlie kept to their normal routines next morning but said very little and gave Andrew a wide berth. Andrew was hungover and grumpy. He made no effort to interact with Henry. He was still a time bomb. Javier could sense it and Charlie was tense, like a deer ready to run, so he knew she could sense it too. Still, Andrew was sober, so the time bomb was less likely to go off. They maintained the charade until Andrew's car left the driveway.

"He's gone," Charlie said. Her shoulders lowered a little from their rigid hunch.

"Not yet." Javier moved to where he could see the street through the curtain without being seen. "Wait ten minutes to be sure he doesn't come back for a spot check or because he forgot something. He's suspicious as hell." Javier checked his watch.

Charlie busied herself cleaning up Henry after his breakfast.

For Javier, the minutes eked past. "I think we're clear." He glanced at his watch one more time, then sprang into action. He raced to the bathroom and loaded his toiletries into a satchel, retrieved the suitcase and added the final items.

Suitcase in hand, he made for the garage. "Do you need help packing?" he called in the direction of Charlie's room.

"All good!" The voice came from the garage.

He arrived to see Charlie deposit the last bags in a pile beside the car.

"You have been giving this some thought. I'm impressed." Never before had he seen such steely determination on Charlie's face. Her courage shone through the bruises

"There eventually comes a point..." Charlie pushed the button on the remote key to open the cargo door. "...when enough is enough."

This was a new, stronger Charlie that he hadn't seen before. He wondered if she could hold this resolve for long enough.

"You OK to load up while I see to Henry?"

Javier stared at her. "Yes ma'am."

Charlie tossed him the key and disappeared back into the house. He loaded the bags into the cargo area with geometric precision. The car was packed and ready.

Javier went inside and found the kitchen to be tidy and clean. The dishwasher hummed and gurgled. An envelope sat on the middle of the counter. His first instinct was to snatch it up in case it contained details that would give away his plans, but he remembered Charlie did not know his plans. He sent the thought to Lauren and received reassurance in response. He let the envelope be.

Charlie gathered up Henry from where he played on the floor. "We're going for a drive to visit Grandma and Grandpa. That will be fun."

She smiled a wide, toothy smile and Henry beamed.

So that was her plan. As Charlie secured Henry in the car seat, Javier fitted his P plates to the vehicle.

"I'm driving," Charlie said as Javier walked toward the driver's seat.

"No, you're not. Besides, I have the key."

"It's my car."

"Technically it's Andrew's car and you're in no fit state."

Charlie reluctantly climbed into the front passenger seat and activated the garage door.

Javier manoeuvred the vehicle onto the street for the last time. His future was uncertain, but it felt wonderful, as if a load had been lifted from his shoulders and a momentous adventure was just beginning.

"We're going to my parents' house."

"No, we're not."

Charlie looked surprised but still intensely determined. "They're expecting us."

"Sorry Charlie." Javier tried to look apologetic, but he was determined too. "That's the first place he'll look for you and that will put all of us and your parents in danger."

Charlie's face transformed with realisation and fear.

"I know somewhere safer." He tried to send a thought of reassurance. "Please trust me."

Charlie cast a worried glance at Henry, burbling happily as he played with a cloth picture book. "OK."

"Good," Javier said as he steered the car toward the motorway, heading north. "Best phone your parents to let them know we won't be coming. Then power down your phone and remove the SIM. There's a tool in the cup holder."

Charlie looked quizzical.

"So he can't use your phone to track you."

Charlie glanced at Javier with a raised eyebrow and began to dial. "You've been planning for this too."

"Like you wouldn't believe." He flashed her a grin then focussed on driving.

* * *

"Why are we stopping here?" Charlie asked as they eventually pulled into the driveway of an auto repair shop in Gympie.

"You'll see." Javier didn't know either, but he wanted to sound confident.

An iridium silver SUV pulled into the driveway behind them and blocked their exit. Its rear hatch glided open.

Javier stepped out of his car, just before the driver of the other vehicle emerged. "Hi Mum." He gave Lauren a hug that somehow relieved much of his own tension. He didn't realise how tightly he'd been wound until he felt it start to dissipate. They pulled apart, their faces mirroring relief, and they exchanged happy thoughts. Javier felt compelled to transfer cargo between the vehicles. He nodded acknowledgement to his mother and set about the task.

Lauren moved toward the passenger door. "Hello Charlie."

Charlie emerged, looking confused. "Lauren."

"Don't worry, Charlie. I've survived Andrew with all kids alive and safe. That makes me well-equipped to help you do the same. Why do you think he didn't want you to get to know me?" Lauren's expression softened into reassurance and she offered her hand.

Charlie took it gingerly and they shook hands.

"I know what Andrew is capable of and I know how he operates. I need you to trust me. Can you do that?"

Charlie's brows furrowed. "You sound like Javier."

"It must be genetic." Lauren grinned and winked at Javier.

Javier knew that line. It was a great strategy to throw people off the scent of the Universal Language.

Lauren grabbed the day bag that Charlie had stowed on the back seat beside the now waking Henry. She placed it in the empty cargo area. "You might want to change Henry before you transfer him to the child seat in my car." She pulled a thick envelope from her back pocket and held it out, open, toward Charlie. "Phone and SIM please."

Charlie looked hesitant at first, then she relaxed. She deposited the phone and card and moved to extract Henry.

Javier transferred the P plates to his mother's vehicle. His mother's skills never ceased to amaze him. He would have to practise more if he wanted to achieve her level of proficiency.

By now a person Javier took to be the proprietor had emerged and made his way toward the vehicles. The man was clean-shaven with brown hair. His portly frame was ill-concealed by his maroon polo shirt embroidered with the business logo where a top left pocket would have been. Pinned above the logo was a shiny gold name badge with 'Glenn' embossed on it. His spotless polyester pants, clean hands and shiny shoes indicated Glenn did not work on the vehicles himself; he had a team for that. Javier concluded that Glenn owned the business and took care of customer relations. Glenn sauntered toward Lauren while eyeing the front car.

"Lauren." He beamed and shook her hand solidly, like an old buddy.

"Glenn." Lauren returned the smile, restrained.

"This the vehicle?"

"That's it."

Glenn walked around the car, peered inside and tilted his head to acknowledge Javier as he passed. When he walked past Charlie, his eyes flashed between her eyes and her neck. His eyebrows lifted and he looked away. He returned to Lauren. "Full strip search of the vehicle for devices and reassembly."

Charlie popped her head up in surprise. Javier gave her a reassuring nod.

"Yes." Lauren watched him with the hint of a smile. "By tomorrow afternoon. Can that be done for the agreed price?"

"Absolutely." Glenn relaxed and leaned on the car. "The team haven't had this much fun in ages."

Lauren retrieved a metal cash box from her car. "Put the devices in here and I'll collect them tomorrow with the car."

"No worries." Glenn took the box and tested the key in the lock.

With Javier driving, Lauren in the front passenger seat and Charlie and Henry in the back, they set out for Gympie Courthouse. They passed the old courthouse that looked just like the old town halls in American movies, complete with a lightning rod and cable. The new, modern courthouse was next door. In comparison, it looked stark and uninviting. The modern police station was perched on the street corner. No car spaces on the street were vacant, so Javier pulled up in a laneway around the corner.

Lauren opened her door. "Why don't you take Henry to the field near the hospital car park. You can both stretch your legs."

"I could use the walk." Javier glanced back at Charlie in the rear-view mirror. Her expression was pale and tense.

"Good." Lauren stepped out of the car. "Let's see if we can get you some more protection Charlie."

Charlie kissed Henry on the forehead and followed Lauren out of the car. Javier watched them disappear around the corner and pulled out of the laneway. The hospital car park was only a block away on the right. He pulled the vehicle into one of the many vacant spaces. The carpark sat atop a steep embankment that fell away to a green, mowed field, below which extended to a creek; delineated by tall trees.

As soon as Javier opened the door, he heard a distant wailing, shrieking sound. His imagination jumped to an image of suffering patients in the hospital, but the sound came from the direction of the creek. He extracted Henry from his car seat and locked the car. With a firm grip on Henry's soft little hand, Javier walked the slipping and sliding toddler down the embankment, then across the grass toward the creek.

The sound became louder as they approached; a cacophony of chatter calls. Javier crouched down to Henry's height and pointed at a myriad of dark objects dangling from the branches of trees like wriggling, gothic tree ornaments. "Look Henry. Fruit bats."

They moved closer and sat down on the grass to watch the mesmerising antics of the flying fox colony. "Froobat," Henry said and giggled and pointed toward the trees.

Henry was mesmerised by the bats for almost an hour, when Lauren and Charlie joined them.

"Froobat! Froobat!" Henry jumped about and pointed toward the creek; he eagerly shared the weird discovery with his mother.

"How did it go?" Javier asked when Lauren sat on the grass beside him.

"We went to the counter at the courthouse and I said Charlie would like to apply for a DVO. When I stepped aside, everyone came to life."

"Let me guess. The bruises on her neck and the red marks in her eyes." Javier lowered his chin and raised his eyebrows.

"Yep. That did it."

"They took lots of photos, then called a nice policewoman to escort us to the hospital for … what did they call it?" Lauren looked at the sky as she searched for the words. "Collection of evidence."

"How did that go?" Javier wanted the whole story.

"Based on the obvious lesions, an immediate order was granted and a warrant issued for Andrew's arrest on assault charges. That should slow him down for a couple of days."

"What do you mean, a couple of days?" Charlie weighed into the conversation, suddenly distressed again. "The officer said the DVO will keep him away for two weeks till the case goes to court."

"That didn't work last time, so it probably won't work this time either." Lauren leaned forward to face Charlie. "Don't worry, we'll be ready and you'll be somewhere safe."

"Last time?" Charlie glanced from Javier to Lauren. "Oh, that's right, you said you've already been through this."

"Yes." Lauren turned toward Charlie again. "My kids were a bit older than Henry is. Andrew was no less dangerous back then. He threatened to burn the house down with all of us in it if I went to the police or tried to leave."

Charlie went pale as she realised the game she was playing was even more dangerous than she had expected.

"You never told me that." Javier turned to face his mother.

"Not the sort of thing you tell little children."

"I'm not a little child anymore."

"True." Lauren glanced at him. "It seems we have much to talk about on the drive home."

When Javier pulled the car up to the farmhouse, it felt like returning to a sanctuary, and the feeling was reinforced by having now heard the details of his parents' separation. The years spent blaming his mother for the breakup had been a total waste of effort and he had a renewed admiration for her courage.

Lauren must have sensed his thoughts. As they walked toward the front door, she veered into him and whispered, "Never underestimate what a mother will do to protect her children."

James had a meal prepared and a highchair all set for Henry. It was an early night; all were too exhausted from the day to linger. Charlie used Wayne's phone to call her parents and let them know she was OK. They said Andrew had come by looking for her and Henry. He was highly emotional and more angry than sad. It had scared them. At first, he wouldn't believe that Charlie and Henry weren't there, but he eventually left when they threatened to call the police.

As soon as Charlie and Henry were settled, Javier called Olivia and related the events of the last few days. When Olivia ran out of questions, he fell asleep with Olivia's final words echoing in his head. "Goodnight, hero. Sleep well."

* * *

Charlie was more relaxed over breakfast the next day than Javier had ever seen her. James swung into a childcare mode that Javier never knew he had. He volunteered to tend Henry for the day. Charlie was uneasy at first, but Lauren reassured her. Henry seemed reluctant at first, but the offer of yummy food sealed the deal.

"James is an excellent cook." Javier placed a reassuring hand on Charlie's shoulder as he walked past her toward the door. "At the very least, Henry won't starve."

Javier drove Charlie and his mother back to Gympie. First stop was the police station. Charlie was now in a mind to give a statement and the officer was keen for Javier to do so too. Andrew had reported Charlie's car stolen and the officers cancelled the alert, marking it as part of a domestic violence property settlement case.

Lauren introduced Charlie to a family law solicitor called Gwen. She seemed like a female Dr Jekyll; she could switch from friendly to formidable and back again in an instant. Javier realised that could be a useful trait in a lawyer.

Property settlement proceedings were initiated, court orders were applied for and Charlie was advised that the domestic violence aspect meant that divorce could be accelerated if she wished. Charlie agreed to think about it. Next stop was the telephone store, where a new phone account with a new SIM was set up. The technicians at the store removed any software from Charlie's phone that Andrew could use to track her and suggested she not call Andrew from this phone so he wouldn't get the number. She was surprised how much tracking software there was, but even Javier was surprised at the number of bugging and tracking devices found in her car. Javier drove Charlie back to the farm in her car while she called the solicitor and said she wanted to proceed with the accelerated divorce. Javier was impressed. It seemed the revealed extent of Andrew's control over her life gave fuel to Charlie's resolve.

"I hope I'm not putting you and Lauren in danger," Charlie said, moments after she finished the call.

"Nothing Mum can't handle." Javier was fairly sure that was true. He changed the subject.

Sanctuary

The water in the creek was low and the rippling streak flowed gently over the rounded rocks at the crossing. Olivia urged Vanilla through and tried not to think of the previous torrents. Javier had been back on the farm for two days and she was keen to see him again. All around, the land was verdant, replenished. The fields of lucerne were a darker green than the pastures, which had grown so tall and fast in the hothouse conditions of summer that only the top half of each cow was visible.

Javier waited patiently for her on the far embankment. He watched her and smiled as she made her way through the ankle-deep water toward him. "Glad to see you can cross the creek without needing rescue."

"Nice to see you too, Javier." Olivia pulled Vanilla up close by. Max began to nod his head and Olivia grinned. "Still not letting me forget that flood incident?"

Javier glanced at Vanilla. The horse lifted her head to consider him, then relaxed.

Olivia patted the side of Vanilla's neck.

"Just glad you're still alive to chide about it." Javier's expression became sombre. "Sorry if it annoys you. I'll try to stop."

Olivia sent him a *"yes please"* thought.

Javier reciprocated with a thought of relief that promptly spread across his face.

"I'm looking forward to riding the creek banks." Olivia turned Vanilla in that direction.

"Sorry. Change of plans."

"What?" Olivia turned Vanilla back around. Max had not moved.

"Mum planned to take Charlie for a drive today and wanted me to come along." Javier tensed his lips and glanced at the ground. "I said I had plans to ride with you and didn't want to break them. Then she suggested I bring you along." Javier's eyes studied her face for a reaction.

Olivia would have preferred to ride alone with Javier; she wanted to find another secret creek-side location to pash some more. Yet, Javier seemed deflated and Olivia didn't want him to feel bad. "That could be fun."

Javier straightened in the saddle and his expression brightened.

"Besides, I'm curious to meet the woman you've been spending so much time with." Olivia smirked. "Lead on."

She spoke true. Javier had spent more time with Charlie over the last few days than with Olivia and a twinge of jealousy piqued her curiosity. She glimpsed a blush behind Javier's smile.

"Thanks." Javier turned Max toward the house. "Thanks for being a good sport about it."

Olivia pressed Vanilla to follow. "No worries."

* * *

Wayne waited for them near the horse yard. "I'll take care of these two." He took hold of the reins after they dismounted. "You two are expected inside."

Javier took Olivia's hand and led her toward the stables.

"The house is that way." Wayne gestured toward the obvious dwelling in the opposite direction.

Javier squeezed her hand. "Taking the long way," Javier called out as they disappeared into the shade of the first stable.

Olivia guessed what Javier was up to and had no intention of objecting. Once safely hidden from prying eyes, Javier drew her to him and cupped her cheek gently in his hand, his lips searching for hers. The warmth of his kiss shut out the world. Nothing existed but Javier, his warmth, his gentle kisses, the heady scent of him. She wrapped her arms about him and drew him even closer to her. His lithe muscles rippled under her fingertips.

"I missed you," Javier whispered in her ear when they finally broke for air.

Olivia's ear tingled. She struggled to think of something clever to say but all her thoughts were of Javier and the incredible sensation of being so close to him. "I missed you too" was all she could manage before his lips returned to hers and silenced any further conversation. The kisses eventually melted away into a tight hug.

"I just wanted to take a minute to remind you how I feel about you, in case we didn't get a chance later," Javier said while they were still entwined. "I hope you don't mind."

"Does it look like I mind?" Olivia gave him an extra squeeze.

His chest heaved against her arms as he sighed in her ear. "I guess not." Javier pulled away and looked into her eyes. "So how are you feeling? Are you up for this?"

Olivia was breathless and speechless with a warm glow somewhere in her middle that drove her to seek at least one more kiss. She restrained herself. "Up for anything as long as we're together." She wasn't exaggerating. With Javier close by, or better still, holding her hand, she could think of nothing but him. She certainly wasn't able to think about consequences so any anxiety was stymied at its heart.

Javier took her hand and they made for the house.

* * *

Javier nudged Olivia through the door first. Charlie stood up from the rug where she was playing with Henry on the floor, James looked up from packing food into a basket on the kitchen bench and Lauren came down the stairs carrying a cardboard shoebox.

Much to Olivia's relief, Javier broke the awkwardness by taking her hand. He drew her toward the centre of the room. "Olivia. This is Charlie."

Olivia stepped forward and shook Charlie's hand. A gentle, almost tentative grip. She took in Charlie's leggings and loose linen shirt. "Pleased to meet you." She also took in her sculptured features and blonde hair. The twinge of jealousy resurfaced and she hoped that Javier didn't prefer older women. Javier placed a reassuring hand on Olivia's shoulder.

Lauren looked bemused as she stepped away from the stairs. "I've found you some boots."

"Are you sure I'll need boots?" Charlie said.

Everyone in the room, including Olivia, nodded.

"Definitely," Javier replied. "Or you'll be spending a couple of days picking grass seeds out of your socks and shoes."

"Oh. OK then." Charlie walked to Lauren and took the box. "Thank you."

Javier continued the introductions. "And this is Henry." He gestured to the small boy sitting on the rug, clutching a wooden car in both hands and looking up at the activity around him.

Olivia crouched down on one knee. "Hello Henry. I'm pleased to meet you."

Henry responded with a wide grin. He held a wooden wheel toward her, then promptly pulled it away, drew it to his lips and bit down on it. He managed a grin around the wheel and burbled something unintelligible that resembled, "Lo."

"I guess that's a hello?" Olivia rose back to her feet and turned toward Javier.

"Yep." Javier took Olivia's hand and gave it a squeeze. "That's as good as it's going to get."

Minutes later, James loaded an esky and a picnic basket into the cargo area of Lauren's car. "Don't worry, Charlie. Henry will be fine."

"Thanks James." Charlie clambered into the front passenger seat. "I feel bad about foisting him on you so much."

"Don't." James walked back toward the door. "He's fun company and he likes my cooking."

Javier released Olivia's hand so that she could take a rear passenger seat. He walked around and took up the other rear seat. His hand found hers again as soon as the seatbelt was secured. It triggered another wave of bliss, so Olivia beamed at him and settled into it. Why fight a good thing?

Lauren took the wheel and steered the vehicle toward the driveway and an unknown destination.

* * *

For most of the fifteen-minute drive, Olivia and Javier gazed at each other, with occasional glances at the scenery. The fields and roads were familiar, until Lauren turned off the highway onto a dirt road that wound its way behind some gentle hills.

"I've driven past this road so many times and often wondered what was up here," Olivia whispered to Javier.

"Well, now we're both going to find out." Javier raised an eyebrow and looked out the window.

They both studied the scenery and the route and took in the novel landscape.

Lauren eventually braked and turned the car onto a well-mown and flattened verge, drawing to a stop in front of a metal gate. "Would you mind, Javier?"

Javier released Olivia's hand and went to open the gate. Once the vehicle passed through, he closed it and returned to his seat. "So, why are we here? There's nothing on this block." Javier looked at his mother via the rear-view mirror.

"Seems that way, doesn't it?" Lauren propelled the car forward past a small tree. A graded trail appeared before them and Lauren followed it. A mob of kangaroos lounged in the shade of a distant eucalypt. One of them stood to alert as the car passed by. "I bought this block a while ago to keep the bucks away from the does outside mating season. I thought about twenty kilometres away should do it."

The trail crossed a flat plain and approached a low hill. Off to the right was a dam where a small mob of shaggy, horned goats took a leisurely drink. The track rose upward and curved gently with the swell of the hill. Lauren stopped the vehicle at the top. Before them, the trail snaked to a second lower hill on which was perched a cottage and a smatter of outbuildings.

"How lovely," Charlie said. "It looks like something out of a picture book or painting."

Lauren's face broke into a smug, pleased smile.

"And conveniently out of sight of the road," Javier said.

"Exactly." Lauren drove onward. "I saw a cute Queenslander cottage in one of those house yards near Burpengary and fell in love with it. So I had it moved here and paid to have it renovated. I thought it would make a nice BnB. Only finished it last week. Now it is needed for a more urgent purpose." Lauren winked at Charlie.

"You mean?" Charlie froze, stunned.

"It's available for rent if you want it."

Charlie bobbed in her seat with excitement.

"So why didn't you mention this to us?" Javier asked.

Lauren glanced at him in the mirror with an eyebrow raised. "What would you have said?"

"I would have said it was a silly waste of money to buy a cottage on impulse and stick it in a paddock where no one could see it."

Lauren winked at the mirror. "Maybe that's why I didn't tell you."

Olivia grinned at the excellent repartee. It warmed her heart to witness it.

As they approached, Olivia made out a post and wire fence enclosing a yard around the house. It was one of those decorative ones where the twisted wire was painted and curved into arches at the top. The little front gate matched the fence. To the side was a carport with space for two cars. To the rear of the carport was a small shed. Part of the backyard had raised beds prepared for a veggie garden and to the side was a chook shed with an enclosed wire run, patiently awaiting occupants.

After they pulled into the carport, Lauren flicked the keys to Charlie. "Go take a look."

Charlie didn't need to be told twice. She leapt from the car and dashed to the front gate where she came to an abrupt stop. She placed her hands on the gate and just stared, as if trying to take it all in.

"I think she likes it." Olivia undid her seatbelt.

"I was hoping she would," Lauren said as she emerged from the car.

Javier and Olivia exited the car in unison. By the time the three had reached the front gate, Charlie had opened the front door. She let out a squeal of delight and disappeared inside.

"Seems to be going well so far." Lauren stepped onto the wooden verandah.

"This is fun," Olivia whispered to Javier as his hand found hers. Once inside, Olivia saw Charlie wafting from room to room, joyous, with tears streaming down her cheeks.

"I went with a French-farmhouse meets Queenslander-farmhouse style. You can change it if you like," Lauren said.

"It's perfect as it is." Charlie went to the kitchen sink and took in the view of the trail they had arrived by. "I can even see when someone is coming."

Javier's eyebrows lifted and he glanced toward his mother. She returned a smile. Javier's brows furrowed, puzzled. Olivia wished she could have detected the communication. Maybe if she worked some more on proficiency.

"Shall we unload the car and christen the kitchen?" Lauren gazed expectantly toward Javier.

Javier made for the door. "I'll get the gear."

"I'll help." Olivia followed.

"We could eat on the verandah," Charlie called out. "There's a table and chairs here."

* * *

"You and Henry can move in tomorrow if you like." Lauren took another sip of the juice that James had packed for them.

Charlie was suddenly solemn. "How can I afford the rent? I have no job." She paused partway through a cheese and cucumber sandwich.

"Weren't you a teacher before you married Dad?"

"Yes. I taught junior high school. Maths and science, believe it or not."

Lauren took a handful of grapes and placed them on her plate. "Lucky for you rural schools have difficulty attracting staff. Kilkivan school is in dire need of a relief teacher. Why don't you call in there tomorrow for a chat?"

Stunned and delighted, Charlie gazed toward the horizon as if beginning to wonder if it was all too perfect. Olivia knew it could be difficult for a city mouse to transition to country living. The expansive views and serenity could become a deathly silent black void by night.

Charlie scanned the landscape. "It seems very isolated here. I don't see any houses nearby."

"This place is well hidden. It will be difficult for Andrew to find you. You'll be safe here." Javier was right, but he missed the point.

"That hill over there." Lauren pointed to a distant rise. "What do you see on it?"

Charlie squinted to see. "A tower?"

"Yep." Lauren leaned back in her chair. "Line of sight to a mobile phone tower. You can be as connected as you want to be." Lauren turned her gaze to Javier. "I bet you thought I'd put the house at this site to keep it hidden. That just turned out to be a fringe benefit."

The furrow between Javier's brows told Olivia that he was only partially convinced.

214

Javier placed his hand on Olivia's. "Fancy a stroll to the creek down there?" He pointed to a snake of trees near the bottom of the hill.

"Absolutely." Olivia rose from the chair and they made their way to the steps. She craved time alone with Javier.

"Afternoon tea at four; James packed a cake," Lauren called after them.

"Four it is." Javier waved as he led Olivia toward the gate.

Warning Shot

The following night, Javier stuck to their routine. At 10 o'clock when he was ready for bed and everyone else had already turned in, he closed the door to his room, settled on the bed and phoned Olivia. The ring tone ended abruptly.

"Hi Javier." Her voice was jovial. "How was your day?"

Javier settled down onto the pillow. "Fine, I guess."

"You guess?"

"I spent most of the day driving people about and helping them move things."

"Charlie?"

"And Henry."

"So, how did it go?"

"We went into town and Charlie picked up some groceries and supplies. We delivered them to the cottage. I played with Henry at the cottage while Charlie went to the school. She got the job and starts Monday."

"That's awesome. What about Henry? While she's working, I mean. Are James and Lauren going to babysit?"

"The school has a childcare centre attached and Henry is now enrolled for whatever hours Charlie works."

"Excellent. So, when does she move in?"

"Already did. I helped her load up her car and she and Henry are spending their first night there tonight."

"That should be interesting."

"Oh, why?"

"City people totally underestimate how quiet nights can be in the country."

"And how dark, when it's cloudy."

"Exactly. I reckon she might need some company tomorrow."

"Maybe that's why Mum suggested James should go visit for the day."

"Probably. Reckon your mum is happy about the move. It's much easier to keep secrets if you can limit the size of the audience."

"Reckon so." The conversation paused. There were muffled sounds in the background.

"What's that noise?" Javier asked.

"The acoustics here are too good. Even with the doors closed, the conversation in any room can be heard from most other rooms. I have the TV on in my room to muffle out our conversations so my parents can't hear us."

Javier was satisfied that Olivia wasn't within earshot of her parents. His neck was getting stiff, so he rolled to one side.

"Shall we ride tomorrow?" Olivia's voice was hopeful.

"I want to…"

"But?"

"But Mum is particularly keen for me to do so. She suggested it three times and that's not counting the thought nudges."

"She sounds keen to be home alone tomorrow. I mean, she sent James off and he's always there, right?"

"Exactly."

"So, you want to stay and find out why?"

"Thanks for understanding. I thought you'd be miffed."

"I could be miffed." There was a pause. "I'll be less miffed if you tell me all about it tomorrow night and we do a creek ride the next day."

"Deal."

The conversation continued until interrupted by the muffled sound of banging on a distant wall and Olivia's parents calling for her to turn the TV volume down so they could sleep.

* * *

James left after breakfast to check on Charlie and Henry. Lauren assured him they had survived the night but would be happy for the company and conversation.

Javier sat, relaxed, opposite his mother at the breakfast table with an empty plate to one side and a cup of tea on the other. He scrolled through pages on his tablet device, not really interested in the contents; he was watching and waiting to see what happened next.

Lauren seemed tense after James left. "Are you sure you don't want to ride today?" Lauren looked at Javier with one eyebrow raised. "The weather is ideal."

"I'm happy to stay home today, Mum." Javier took up the cup of tea and leaned back in the chair. "We've arranged to ride tomorrow."

"The weather might not be as good then."

"We'll take our chances."

Lauren gazed out the window toward the distant fields. "Hmm."

"I get the impression you don't want me around here this morning."

"Good." Lauren turned to face him. "I'd hate to think I was losing my touch." She gave Javier a half smile and stood to return her cup and Javier's empty plate to the kitchen.

"Maybe it's something I could help with?"

The crockery and cutlery clattered among the other dishes by the sink. "I think not." Lauren leaned against the kitchen bench. "Actually, I'm more concerned for your safety."

"My safety?" Javier began to worry. It had been a long time since he had seen his mother look nervous. She usually took everything in her stride.

"I received a call from the police. Your father has been released on bail."

"And you think he'll come here?" Javier plonked the now empty cup onto the table and sat upright.

Lauren lowered her chin, her eyebrows lifted and her mouth tensed. "He's figured out that Charlie came here."

"But he'd be violating the DVO."

Lauren stared at Javier, expectantly.

"But that's not going to stop him, is it?"

"No." Lauren returned to the table and resumed her seat. "No. That's what makes him dangerous."

"I'm glad I stayed then. I can help protect you."

Lauren placed her hand on Javier's arm. "You were the one who organised Charlie's escape. I'm worried that you've become a target."

"I can look after myself."

"Maybe." Lauren gazed at Javier a while, then her expression changed to one of determined focus.

"You've got a plan, haven't you?" said Javier.

"Yes, Javier. I think I do." She withdrew her hand and her brow furrowed. "For it to work, you have to stay hidden. Can you do that?"

Javier nodded. "It involves the Universal Language too, right?"

"Of course." Lauren leaned forward toward Javier. "And your mobile phone and the local police."

"The local police?"

"Uh-huh." Lauren leaned back into the chair. "When they told me Andrew was released on bail, I warned them he would come straight here to find Charlie in defiance of the DVO. The nice sergeant said they would station an extra vehicle in Kilkivan for the day, just in case."

"I'd better make sure my phone is fully charged then." Javier took his cup to the kitchen, pulled the phone from his pocket and sighed on seeing the screen. "It'll charge faster if I plug it into my computer." Javier strode to his room with a new sense of purpose.

* * *

Just as he unplugged the fully charged phone, Javier felt compelled to join his mother in her upstairs study. He was not inclined to argue.

Lauren handed him a piece of paper. "Here's the number for the local police."

Javier entered the number on his phone.

"Now we need to find somewhere for you to hide, where you can hear what's going on but can't be seen." Lauren surveyed the room for a suitable nook.

"Why not just stay here?" Javier suggested. "I can hear what's going on and he won't see me as long as I stay at your desk or sit on one of the chairs."

"True." Lauren continued to look around. "But what if he decides to run about the place looking for Charlie, or you, and comes up the stairs?"

Javier recalled how his dad had room-checked his house on arrival lately. "Good point." Javier started to survey the room too.

"I've got it." Lauren made for a nearby door. "Follow me." She led Javier to the storeroom on the opposite side of the study area to the master suite. "It has a lockable door. It also has a vent that opens out over the kitchen so you can hear what is being said."

Javier entered, turned on the light and closed the door behind him. The lock was sound and the air musty. He couldn't see through the vent, it was too high up, but he clearly heard the churning of the dishwasher in the kitchen and he managed to perch comfortably on one of the cardboard boxes.

"Perfect." Javier emerged from the hiding spot.

Lauren's expression became sombre and she walked to the window. Javier joined her and saw the cloud of dust making its way along the road toward the property gate. "When he gets to the house yard, lock yourself in."

"Yes, Mum."

"Promise you won't emerge until he has left." Lauren stared intently at Javier until he promised. Satisfied, she made her way down the stairs and settled on a sofa facing the front door.

From where Javier stood at the study railing, he could turn and see the progress of the car through the window behind him. In front and below, he saw Lauren pull out her mobile phone, open the voice memo app and press record before she stowed the device in her breast pocket with the microphone end pointing upward. He liked the way his mother thought of everything and left little to chance.

At the sound of a car door slamming in the house yard, Javier secreted himself in the storeroom and locked the door.

The loud bashing on the front door was familiar. Javier imagined his mother going to open the door. The latch clicked open and his father's voice boomed into the house.

"Where the hell is she?"

"Hello, Andrew."

Javier was reassured; his mother's voice sounded cool and calm.

"Who is 'she'?" Lauren asked.

"Don't frigg with me, bitch. Where is she and that Judas son of yours?" Andrew's voice was even louder.

"She's not here. Also, if you think she is, you're breaching a DVO by being here."

"Stuff the DVO, I'm here to collect my wife and her bastard kid. They're not much, but they're mine."

"People are not property, Andrew. Haven't you figured that out yet?"

"They're here alright and I'm going to find 'em if I have to turn the place upside down."

A door latch clicked open and the door soon slammed shut again.

"No, Andrew, you won't."

"Oh shit. You can still do that?"

There was a pause. Javier figured Lauren was working on Andrew's mind. He felt compelled to call the police. He dialled the number.

"Kilkivan police."

"Hello, this is Javier out at Lauren…"

A woman's voice responded, "Hi Javier. I know who you are. Is Andrew there?"

"Yes."

"Are you safe?"

"Yes. I'm locked in a storeroom."

"Good. Stay there. I'm on my way."

The line went dead and Javier's attention returned to what he could hear through the vent.

"I told you never to come here."

"Just hand over my wife and the kid and I'll be on my way. You can keep Javier. I want nothing more to do with him."

Those words cut into Javier more than he would have expected. Andrew was still his dad and he still loved his dad, at least he ought to, but how could he reconcile Andrew's bad behaviour with the dad he was supposed to love? Weren't dads supposed to love their kids? Weren't they supposed to help and support them?

"That won't be happening, Andrew. Like I said, they're not here."

"Then tell me where they are and I'll be out of your hair."

"What? So, you can beat them and neglect them some more while you have affairs on the side?"

"They deserve it. She's been having an affair, too and he's not my kid. I have no flamin' idea who the father is."

"They don't deserve it, Andrew. He is your kid and I reckon a DNA test will prove it. It's the same pattern over and over, isn't it?"

"What do you mean?"

"You meet a nice girl; you fall in love and get married. Then your paranoia kicks in. You imagine her having affairs and conspiring to leave you. You begin to treat her as if she is and you escalate it until the only way she can stay safe is to flee. I'll bet you've decided that the girl you're having an affair with now is just the girl for you."

"She's a nice girl. She loves me. I can count on her."

"Until you decide you can't."

A surge of outrage welled in Javier's gut. His dad was having an affair behind Charlie's back. Charlie, who was so devoted to him and his child, had been betrayed like that? Any remaining respect Javier had for his father ebbed away.

"I don't need to listen to this bullshit."

"Yes, you do. You need to figure out that the only common denominator in all this is you. The reason why this keeps happening is because you don't think you're good enough."

"Shut the hell up."

"No. Why should I let you just go and torture another poor girl? The moment you've won the amazing girl, your insecurity sets in. You worry that she'll figure out you're not good enough and leave you for someone else. So, you start looking for the signs until you see them even when they're not there. You need to seek professional help, Andrew, before you do even more damage."

"You friggin' bitch!"

Something ceramic shattered and Javier made for the door. He had to help his mum. Before he could unlock it, a loud "aargh" came from downstairs, but it wasn't his mother's voice; it was his father's.

"I'll thank you to stop damaging my property."

Javier's hand froze on the handle. His mum sounded OK. He tried to figure out what was happening. It didn't make sense.

"Charlie and Henry are now under my protection, Andrew. Same terms and conditions. Don't even think about coming back here or going anywhere near them with malicious intent. Do you understand me?"

"You bitch."

"I didn't hear you. Do you understand me?"

Andrew hissed. "Yes."

"Good. Now it's time for you to leave."

Sirens sounded nearby. The police must have waited until they entered the house yard before switching them on.

"And that is your ride. Goodbye, Andrew."

"Oh shit!"

"Please don't visit again unless expressly invited. You know the rules."

Car doors slammed and relief washed over Javier. He sensed that he had permission to emerge. He reached the study railing; the scene was not what he expected. Lauren stood by the sofa as if she had just stood up. Andrew leaned against a wall in the entranceway, one hand clutching his groin. The ceramic fruit bowl from the entrance stand was shattered over the floor and two police officers were entering the front door.

"Andrew Evans?" the male officer asked as he surveyed the scene.

Andrew nodded, his brows furrowed, defiant to the end.

"You're under arrest for breach of bail and breach of a DVO. Are you going to come quietly or do I need to cuff you?"

"It's not me you need to arrest; it's her." He pointed toward Lauren, who still stood calmly by the sofa. "She's a witch. She assaulted me."

The officers stared at Andrew.

Eventually Andrew's shoulders slumped and his frown eased, defeated. "No cuffs needed."

The male officer took Andrew by the arm and led him to the waiting car. The female officer walked toward Lauren. "Are you OK?"

"Yes. I think so. I managed to keep my distance. Thanks for the helpful advice."

"Did you collect evidence?"

Lauren took out her phone, turned off the recording and held it up in nervous triumph. "I'm not sure if it recorded it all properly. I can bounce it to your device if you like."

The officer removed a tablet device from a large pocket and the pair worked together to effect the transfer.

"Thanks." The officer stowed the device back in her pocket when the transfer was complete. "We'll be in touch. Now, please excuse me, I need to go and ensure Andrew is appraised of his rights." She looked up and gave a cheerful wave in Javier's direction, then turned to leave.

Javier waved back and made his way down the stairs.

"What just happened?" Javier asked as he approached Lauren. "What I heard and what I saw don't make sense."

"Don't worry, Javier, I fired a warning shot." She moved toward Javier and gave him a hug.

"But..."

Lauren released him and patted his shoulder. "Don't worry about it. What's important is that you're OK. Besides, you'll have forgotten all the inconsistencies by this afternoon."

"No, I won't."

"Yes, you will."

And he did.

Let the Holiday End

The grass was tall after the summer rains and the track was damp from yesterday's storm. Only the tops of the cows were visible in the pastures, like black, bovine boats on a wafting green sea. Olivia enjoyed the smell of moist earth. She tried to steer Vanilla around the big puddles, but Vanilla delighted in splashing through them and powered onward, keen to meet with her equine buddy.

Olivia was not so keen. She had planned to ride with Javier every day for what remained of the summer holiday. Javier kept his word; they rode the day after Andrew's intrusion and they had both been looking forward to riding again today, but he called to say he was heading down to the Sunshine Coast early to prepare for the start of school the following week. Lauren had stepped up to ride today in his stead. This was not nearly as appealing and she wondered to what extent Lauren would detect it.

As Olivia approached the creek bank, Lauren arrived on the other side. Lauren waved and gestured for Olivia to join her.

There had been more rain and the creek flowed full. Not the torrent that had nearly killed her only weeks ago but, swirling enough to remind her and make her uneasy. As Olivia neared the water's edge, she moved to pull Vanilla to a halt, but the horse strode steadily forward without a break in pace. Panic twinged in Olivia's gut.

She glanced away from the swirling water flow and saw Lauren gazing at her with a warm, reassuring smile. The panic subsided and Olivia replaced it with hard determination. The water reached just over Vanilla's knees and Olivia rode her steadfast progress like a ship on the waves. She sighed with relief as Vanilla finally emerged from the water on the far bank.

"Hello, Olivia," Lauren said as Vanilla moved within earshot. Aztec nodded enthusiastically and Lauren let him have some rein.

Vanilla neighed in reply and pulled herself up beside Aztec. "Hello," Olivia replied. The horses exchanged a nuzzling greeting.

"I need to move the goats between paddocks this morning and could use some skilled assistance. Are you up for it?"

"Sure." Olivia turned Vanilla to stride beside Aztec toward the open gate. "Do you think I'll ever not be nervous about flowing creeks?"

"The more you confront them, the less troubling they will be." Lauren looked at Olivia as she spoke; the horses knew the way. "When I was a kid, I fell out of a tree I was climbing. The branch broke under me. As the ground loomed up, I contemplated imminent death only to suddenly stop centimetres above the ground. I was suspended by the back of my cardigan, caught on the broken branch. My fear of injury and death was soon replaced by humiliation. I was dangling and writhing helplessly in mid-air. My buddies laughed hard as they lifted me and unhooked my cardigan. I made sure the incident didn't stop me from climbing trees, but I developed a whole new respect for trees and heights. I always checked the integrity of any branch before I relied on it to bear my weight."

"Then I've sure developed a whole new respect for flowing creeks."

"Rightly so."

They rode through a paddock, where the grass tickled the horses' bellies, toward a gate at the corner. Lauren opened the gate using the rider's latch and they moved through into a paddock where the grass barely covered the horses' hooves. At the far end a scattered flock of goats grazed the stubble and nibbled at the trees and bushes, giving the trees a distinct umbrella shape.

Without a word spoken, Lauren rode Aztec directly toward the centre of the flock as Olivia and Vanilla strode off to one side. Lauren pulled up Aztec some distance away. Olivia and Vanilla circled behind the goats and slowly brought the scattered animals together into a single flock. Lauren turned Aztec and marched steadily toward the gate. The flock fell in behind Lauren and followed her. Olivia and Vanilla walked behind and made toward any animal that stopped for a snack, to remind them to pay attention and keep up. Lauren walked Aztec through the open gate; the flock followed and Olivia manoeuvred Vanilla to close the gate once the last goat had passed through. Lauren and Aztec paused to one side as the goats dispersed, only the tops of their white heads were visible in the pasture.

"That should feed them for a week," Lauren said as Olivia and Vanilla approached.

"It'll take that long for them to eat this down to a level where they can even see each other." Olivia smirked at the thought. "The Universal Language makes moving stock such a peaceful affair. No herding or darting about. Much less stressful for all."

"Indeed, it does." Lauren surveyed the landscape. "Shall we have morning tea by the creek?"

* * *

A goat bleated in the distance and a Currawong chortled in a nearby tree. Between mouthfuls of rosemary and orange cake and sips of iced tea, Olivia and Lauren chatted about the imminent resumption of school.

"Where will Javier stay this year?" Olivia asked before taking another bite. This cake was one of James's most delicious flavour experiments. "He can't very well stay with his dad anymore." She paused and considered for a moment. "We have space at our apartment; he could stay with us."

"I bet your parents would be thrilled with that arrangement. Especially given how close you two have become."

"You're right. They'd never agree to it."

"No need to worry. While I was on the coast recently, I made contact with Javier's friend Elton and arranged to drop by and chat with his parents. They have a spare room and can take Javier in as a boarder for the year. They wanted Javier to move in during the week before school so they can satisfy themselves that the arrangement would work and not be too distracting for either of the boys. After all, this is their final high school year and they need to focus on their grades."

"So that's why Javier left early this morning?"

"Yes." Lauren sipped her tea. "I'm sure he'll keep you posted on how it works out."

"It'll make it easier to get to and from soccer training and games."

"That too." Lauren looked off into the distance as if organising her thoughts. "I've noticed that you've become quite proficient at using the Universal Language."

"Thanks." Olivia beamed at the acknowledgement of her efforts. It had become second nature.

"Would you like to try the next step?"

"There's a next step?" Maybe riding with Lauren today wasn't so bad after all?

"Yes." Lauren clasped her cup in her hands. "Remember we talked about how people are programmed not to hear the voices of others in their head?"

"I remember."

"Would you like to have a go at pushing through that barrier?"

Olivia tried to imagine what it would be like hearing voices in her head. "Wouldn't that just make me schizophrenic or something?"

"Not if you learn to manage it—control what you hear and what you don't."

Olivia swallowed and stared at the ground. "It still seems risky. I mean, everything is working great just as it is, so why would I want to jeopardise it all by taking that step?"

"Because you never know when you might need it in a crisis." Lauren's tone sent a chill down Olivia's spine.

"OK then." Olivia helped herself to another piece of cake. "When do we start?"

"More a case of where rather than when."

Olivia raised an eyebrow; her curiosity was piqued.

"A great place to practise this is at the beach. I'm heading to the coast for a couple days this week to touch base with Javier and see how the accommodation arrangement is working out. I plan to overnight at a resort there. I've managed to book a two-bedroom suite. Would you like to join me?"

"Sure." Just the idea of seeing Javier again warmed her inside.

"Excellent." Lauren began to pack away the morning tea items. The enamel cups clattered as she loaded them into the saddlebag. "Shall we go and discuss it with your parents?"

"That should be fun." Olivia sealed the used serviettes into the empty cake container and handed it to Lauren. She smiled to herself; her parents didn't stand a chance.

To the Beach

They arrived on the coast in the early afternoon. Lauren turned her SUV into the hotel driveway and followed the green tunnel of arching branches. The shade opened out to reveal a pavilion set on white columns; it reached out from the building entrance to cover arriving cars. Lauren pulled the car up under the canopy.

"Want to come in?" Lauren stepped from the car.

Olivia was keen to walk about after the journey and get the blood circulating to her legs. "Sure."

Olivia heard the car lock ping behind her as she walked past the square pond with dancing fountains. The mighty glass doors parted before them, channelling them into the foyer. Olivia's eyes wandered over the marble tiled floors, the majestic potted palms, the plush sofas casually arranged to facilitate conversations and the vast, high ceiling, crisscrossed with wooden beams. Olivia stood just inside the door for a moment, breathless, and took it all in. She smiled to herself, considering what her ever-practical mother would say. Probably something like, "Imagine trying to clean the cobwebs off that ceiling".

Lauren marched directly to the reception counter and attended to the process as Olivia meandered slowly around the foyer. The palms were twice her height, but the tall ceilings dwarfed them. Even the sofas were chunky and oversized. She felt Lilliputian in the space.

"Imposing, isn't it?"

Lauren's voice from behind startled her. "It's grand alright." Olivia turned to follow Lauren to the car. "You seem to like places with high ceilings."

Lauren drew the corners of her mouth, raised her eyebrows and slowly tilted her head to one side. "Interesting observation. Perhaps I do."

Lauren drove them to their assigned parking place, where a valet waited to carry their bags to the room on the top floor of a three-storey block. When they found the door, Lauren pulled out a paper envelope with two plastic cards and handed one to Olivia. "This is yours, so you can come and go as you please." She gestured for Olivia to open the door.

Olivia held her card against the black panel above the door handle, the lock clicked, the light turned green and she pushed down the handle. The door opened into a spacious room. Olivia's eyes passed over the large wall-mounted TV, small kitchenette, the round table with four chairs and the large sofa. An open door to one side revealed a bedroom with a double bed and an ensuite, and a similar doorway on the other side led to a bedroom with two single beds and another ensuite.

"Will you be comfortable enough in there?" Lauren gestured to the room with the single beds as she walked into the other bedroom and dropped her handbag on the bed.

"Very comfortable," Olivia replied. "Thanks." She dropped her bag on the nearest bed and opened the sliding door onto the balcony. Their unit overlooked a small lake. People casually walked the path that circumscribed it and others paddled kayaks at one end. Near the other end was a sign, "Fish feeding at 10 am and 3 pm". To one side of the lake a large, curved swimming pool was being enjoyed by a few families. Beyond the lake was a row of trees and from that direction came the roar of distant surf.

Lauren emerged from her bedroom onto the far end of the balcony and took in the scene. "Javier will be arriving around five and having dinner with us. I've booked a table at the restaurant for six o'clock."

"Good." Olivia tried to conceal how much she was looking forward to seeing Javier despite knowing that Lauren probably sensed it anyway. Her insides warmed at the mere thought of him.

Lauren had a playful grin. "That gives us plenty of time to participate in the fish feeding in about half an hour. Are you up for it?"

"Sure am." Any distraction would do, or she risked curling up on the bed like a lovesick puppy and moping until five.

Being around Lauren was strange. She was Javier's mum, so sometimes it was like being around her mother-in-law. She was also a good teacher and confidante, so it was like being around her mentor. Lauren looked barely thirty, was sometimes playful and enjoyed having fun, so it was like being around a really cool girlfriend. Sometimes all these things mushed together and it just felt confusing.

They changed their outfits for loose short-sleeved shirts, shorts and thongs and made their way down to the lake. Lauren bought two bags of fish food from the young man in hotel uniform who cheerfully stood by the sign.

"Only feed them food from these bags," the young man cautioned as he collected money and handed out more bags. "Human food can make the fish sick, so we've sourced this special food for them."

Some children squealed with glee as the water surged and buffeted with jostling fish after each handful of pellets was cast. "Look Mum, that's a big one!"

"There's a black and white one, Dad!"

"There's so many!"

"My bag is empty. Can I have another one?"

"But the fish are still hungry!"

Lauren moved to the side of the crowd and Olivia followed. In the water, a handful of the largest fish followed beside them; one was nearly as long as her arm. Lauren stopped and began to distribute the pellets to each fish in turn. Olivia joined in. When they had run out of food, all but the largest fish returned to the main group to see if there were any stray morsels to be had. Lauren put her hand into the water and held it there. The large fish swam up to it, turned and rubbed the full length of its body against Lauren's hand before it swam away.

"Trying to be inconspicuous?" Olivia stood with her empty paper bag and a grin. "Not doing a very good job of it."

Lauren chuckled as she wiped her hand on her shorts. "He was a nice fish. We got along."

Olivia tried to look parental. "Uh huh."

"Fancy a stroll around the lake?"

They set off in the direction of the kayaks. Olivia glimpsed movement below the surface of the water. The large fish and a few companions swam beside them the entire time. Something anyone else could have noticed, but no one did.

* * *

Olivia emerged after changing into a light summer dress and tying up her hair ready for dinner. She checked her phone. Lauren was flicking through channels on the TV and settled on a news broadcast.

The two prisoners on the run from Goulburn gaol were seen at a fuel stop in Dubbo in western New South Wales. The public are advised not to approach these men. Anyone with information as to their whereabouts is asked to contact Crime Stoppers.

The blurry CCTV footage showed the men fuelling a small farm truck and walking back to the vehicle with arms full of snack foods and cans of drink. The banner at the bottom of the screen displayed the Crime Stoppers phone number.

Lauren looked at the images with the same expression Olivia's father wore when he was sent to deal with a snake in the chook pen.

Olivia took a closer look at the screen before the image flashed back to the newsreader moving on to the next item of news. "Those two still on the loose? I thought they would have caught them by now." She glanced toward Lauren. "At least they're still in New South Wales. Now that they've had a confirmed sighting, I reckon the police will recapture them before they get anywhere near Queensland."

"Let's hope so." Lauren glanced toward Olivia as if broken from a trance. She held out the remote. "Watch whatever you like."

Olivia turned the device in her hand. "Thanks." She flipped through a few channels. "Javier's late," she said without pausing her channel surf.

Lauren's phone chimed in her pocket. She retrieved it and considered the screen. "Not by much." Lauren pressed the answer button and shifted her gaze toward the balcony. "Hi Javier. Glad you could make it. Room 311. See you soon."

The restaurant served a seafood buffet that evening. Olivia loved seafood and Lauren encouraged her to avail herself of the offerings. Olivia took a large plate and piled it high with local prawns, Sydney rock oysters, chargrilled lobster tails, crumbed calamari and battered scallops. In the little space left on the plate, she carefully placed a spoonful of red cabbage coleslaw and dolloped some sauces around the plate rim. They were only staying for one night and she was determined to make the most of the opportunity.

Over the meal, Lauren updated Javier on how Charlie was doing and the goings on around the farm.

"How is staying at Elton's working out?" Olivia asked once the conversation and the pile of food on her plate depleted.

"Not bad actually." Javier placed his cutlery down and leaned back in his chair. "The whole situation is rigged, of course." He turned to face Lauren. "Isn't it?"

"I don't know what you mean." Lauren feigned nonchalance.

"I only get to stay there if I don't distract Elton from his studies, so now I'm bound to make an effort to game less and study more so that I look like a good role model and don't lead Elton astray."

Lauren grinned and popped a scallop in her mouth. "Oh really?"

"Don't act like you didn't plan this, Mum." Javier leaned toward Lauren. "I have to make a consistent effort to regulate my gaming and study hard just to make sure I can finish at the same school and stay with the soccer club." Javier leaned toward Oliva. "They've set a phone curfew for 10 o'clock and the acoustics in the house aren't great for privacy, so our evening conversations have been curtailed a bit."

"I guess we'll just have to catch up at school." Olivia placed a reassuring hand on Javier's arm. "Or any other chance we get."

Javier looked into Olivia's eyes and her stomach jiggled.

"I'm off to get seconds." Lauren folded her cloth napkin, placed it neatly on the table and made toward the buffet display.

Javier took Olivia's hand and warmly pressed it between his. "This is so frustrating." He looked into her eyes and all the seafood Olivia had eaten felt as though it was swimming again. "I was looking forward to seeing you and spending some time alone with you, but both mums reckon I can't stay here late this evening." He reached out and tucked a stray strand of hair behind Olivia's ear; it made her tingle. "I'll come back early tomorrow and we can spend the morning together. A morning walk on the beach may not be as romantic as a moonlight stroll, but it will have to do." He released her hand when Lauren returned to the table.

"Looking forward to it." Olivia grieved the missed opportunity of a moonlight walk on the beach, but there would be other nights and other beaches. For now, she would drink up every delicious moment she had with Javier and revel in how keen he was to spend time with her.

"Me too."

After dinner they walked Javier to his car. It was the silver SUV that Javier drove Olivia home in after the flood rescue.

"Your car?" Olivia asked, still holding Javier's hand.

Javier glanced at Lauren. "A gift from Mum on my seventeenth birthday. She's been keeping it on the farm for me until now. I learned to drive in this." He tapped the roof of the car as if patting a good horse.

Olivia tried to ignore Lauren standing nearby while she gave Javier a parting hug that he somehow transformed into a long, slow kiss. Still drunk from the kiss, she waved as the car headed down the resort driveway and watched until it was out of sight.

"Shall we change for a walk on the beach?" Lauren turned away from the disappearing car.

"Sure." Olivia's mood sank as the car disappeared.

* * *

The evening was warm and still. The crowds were gone, the beach was deserted and their path was lit by subtle moonlight. Olivia imagined how romantic it would have been to share this walk with Javier. Her reverie was interrupted by Lauren.

"This should do." Lauren stopped at the base of a dune near the top of the beach, pulled a blanket from her bag and laid it flat. "Ready?"

"I guess so." Olivia's heart wasn't really in it, especially with Javier gone. She sat on one side of the blanket. "What do I have to do?"

Lauren settled herself on the other. "Start by sitting comfortably."

Olivia experimented with a few positions. "Can I lie down? It's much more comfortable."

"After a meal like that, you'll be asleep in an instant."

"Good point." Olivia settled for sitting cross-legged. A cool breeze wafted on her face.

"Now, go through the steps: relax, focus and clear the mind."

Olivia closed her eyes and obeyed. As soon as her mind was clear, Lauren's calm voice interrupted.

"Focus only on the sound on the waves, one after another, and gently clear everything else. Then we'll see what happens."

Olivia focussed on the sound of the waves. It was a rolling, white noise that came at intervals, with a dull roar in the background. Suddenly she jerked forward, her eyes wide open.

"Tell me what happened."

Olivia gazed out to the waves as she gathered her thoughts. "There was the sound of the waves and the ocean, then there was the sound of a multitude of voices, all talking at once. I couldn't pick out anything specific and it startled me."

"I could tell. You looked like you'd been electrocuted." Lauren smiled, unperturbed, as if this was an everyday occurrence.

"What was it?"

"The white noise of the waves sounds a bit like a multitude of whispering voices, so when you focussed on that, it distracted your mind from maintaining the filter against hearing the voices of other people's thoughts in your head."

"So, I heard them? All at the same time?" Olivia gazed back out to sea as she tried to remember what she had heard. "Whose voices were they?"

"There's a lot of people around here." Lauren glanced toward the lights scattered like gemstones along the coast. "You heard the voice of everyone who was thinking using words and thinking of telling the whole world at the same time."

"Well, there were an awful lot of people doing that."

"Indeed. There would have been people wishing someone could fix this or do that. Others would be running a commentary on what was happening in the world and what they thought about it."

"Like yelling at the TV but in your head?"

"Exactly."

Olivia pulled her knees up and rested her chin on them. "I don't think I want to try it again. I don't want to go through life with a myriad voices in my head all the time."

"Are you hearing them now?"

"Well … no."

"Then you can control it."

Olivia considered that. The floodgate could be closed and her thoughts were still her own. "So, what do I do?"

"Start the process again and practise not being startled when you hear the voices. It may take a few goes. Try focussing on one voice. Like when you arrive at a party and there's music and everyone is talking at once. The noise could be overwhelming, but you focus on hearing only the voice of the person you are talking to. See how far you get."

Olivia resumed a cross-legged posture and started the process again. The voices began, she was startled and they stopped. She tried again and again and made incremental progress each time. She reached the point where she thought she could hear a single voice, then it evaporated into the cacophony. She was focussing again to try get it back when something touched her arm.

Olivia struggled to open her eyes. "What's happening?"

Lauren softly laughed and said, "You're so tired that you're toppling over." She stood up beside the blanket. "That means it's time to go."

"But I didn't finish."

"Don't worry, you did enough."

Olivia wobbled to her feet. The moon had shifted from near the horizon to high in the sky. "What time is it?"

"Let's say, you've been at it for a couple of hours." Lauren took up the blanket and began to fold it. "Your persistence is impressive."

* * *

Javier arrived just after breakfast, as he had promised. Lauren insisted she had business elsewhere on the coast in the morning, so they checked out and loaded the luggage into Lauren's car. Olivia blissfully spent the morning walking on the beach with Javier, interrupted by diversions for gelato or coffee. Lauren returned to join them for lunch, then drove Olivia back to her parents' farm.

Olivia tried to practise hearing thought voices over the next few weeks, but without the background sound of the waves, she had little success; except that she occasionally heard Javier's voice saying her name, usually just before he phoned her or sent a thought message. That was cute and non-threatening, so she ceased to worry that her parents might drag her back to the psychologist's office for suspected schizophrenia.

The Term Begins

A red flash from the weapon and the man in the insect-like armour fell backward to the ground, scorched and lifeless.

Javier touched his phone. It sprang to life and displayed the time. He leaned back from the keyboard and twirled in his chair. "That's me done for tonight."

"Oh, come on! One more game." Elton's fingers were still poised and ready on his keyboard.

"Nope. It's nine." Javier's mouth widened in a smug grin. "Just enough time to shower before I call, and I'll still make your parents' curfew."

Elton faced his friend with eyebrows raised, hopeful. "You can shower in the morning."

"I don't understand how you shower in the mornings." Javier stood to leave Elton's room.

"It wakes me up and leaves me clean and refreshed for the day ahead. I don't understand how you can shower at night."

"There's no queue for a start." Javier rested his arms on the back of the gaming chair. It resembled a racing car seat perched on a stand with wheels. "And I'm not traipsing the dirt of the day onto clean sheets. It's why my bed smells better than yours."

Elton's shoulders slumped, deflated. "Does not."

Javier gave him a friendly punch to the arm and made toward the door.

"She really has you under her thumb, doesn't she?"

Javier paused at the door. "I like her, Elton. I mean, I really like her. I don't want to stuff this up." He had finally found a girl who liked him; knew him, and still liked him, weirdness, dysfunctional family and all. He was determined to do everything in his power to make it work.

Elton grinned and waved Javier off. "You lucky bastard."

Javier skirted the living room. A man in shorts and T-shirt was stretched out on the couch as the late news announced itself from the TV. From where he stood, Javier couldn't tell if Elton's father was awake or had dozed off.

The two prison escapees from Goulburn gaol were sighted on a property near Moree in northern New South Wales. They stole a grey utility, rifles, ammunition and a supply of food from the sheep property. The farmer was found with minor injuries. He is receiving counselling and assisting police with their investigations. The public are reminded not to approach these men. Call Crime Stoppers if you have any information that could aid police efforts to return them to custody.

The newsreader appeared solemn despite her bouncy hairdo and floral blouse. Pictures of the stolen vehicle and the two men flashed on the screen. Javier wondered if they were as dastardly as the images and the warnings made them appear but decided he was in no hurry to find out. They were too far away to pose a direct threat to him, or those he cared about, and he was hopeful, given the effort and resources being deployed, that the police would soon have them back in custody.

Javier finally settled in bed and selected some music from his playlist to play in the background. It muffled the sound of his phone conversation enough to provide a modicum of privacy. He sent a thought message and smiled at the positive reply. He pressed her number.

"Hi Javier."

"Hello, Olivia. How was your day?"

"Good and bad. Good because Mum and I relocated to the apartment in town ready for school on Tuesday, bad because I can't see you whenever I want, so it still feels like you're far way."

Javier chuckled. "Reckon we can fix that. I have a car in town now and we have a day before school starts. I've got a preseason soccer match tomorrow morning. How about we do lunch and spend some time at the beach after that? Unless of course you want to spend some time catching up with your friends from school."

"Mel doesn't fly in till tomorrow. She's going to be seriously jet lagged for the first day of school. The rest I can catch up with at school, so count me in."

It warmed Javier inside that Olivia chose to spend time with him at every opportunity and that communication with her was so open and easy. It had to be: the other would sense it quickly if anything of significance was withheld.

They chatted until ten precisely, when a knock on the wall signalled Javier to cut all sound so the household could sleep. It was annoyingly restrictive to be regulated, but he had to admit that from their perspective it was fair.

* * *

Tuesday morning, Javier patiently plied the traffic jams on the school approach and parked his vehicle in the student parking area near the back of the school. He wanted to dash to the bus stops at the front of the school and greet Olivia when she arrived, but this was high school—it was a sea of judgemental eyes.

He made his way to where his buddies were congregated and skilfully evaded interrogation regarding the details of his holiday. They had claimed a prize spot: a long table in the school cafe. Only Year Eleven and Twelve students were allowed to use the café, other years were relegated to the school canteen and playgrounds. All last year, his friends eyed the previous cohort with envy and watched them enjoy the benefits of this table: shelter from sun, wind and rain, panoramic views of the main pathways to and from the school through the floor-to-ceiling windows and an ample supply of coffee, tea and cake.

Javier made some effort to participate in conversation, though he had little to contribute on the topic of European ski fields. Mostly he kept an eye on the path from the bus stops. The school uniform hats and dresses worn by the girls made them look alike. He wondered if he would be able to recognise Olivia even if she did walk by. Then she did, and he did. Perhaps it was the manner of her walk or the colour of the braid that trailed from beneath her wide-brimmed hat— he knew her instantly. He flashed her a *"hello"* thought. She glanced in his direction and smiled. He received a *"hug"* thought and his heart warmed and swelled in his chest. He watched her until she disappeared from view.

Javier turned back to his fellows and re-engaged with the conversation. They paid him no mind. They had known Javier for years and were accustomed to him phasing in and out of conversations even if they had no idea why.

The morning classes were intense. In previous years, the first day of school was a process of easing students into the material. Not in Year Twelve. Each class began with a few moments of emphasis on the importance of study, assessments and keeping up, then the teachers launched directly into the subject material and challenging homework tasks were set. Compared to the casual reverie of the holidays, it felt like hitting a brick wall at speed.

When the bell sounded lunchtime, Javier sent Olivia a *"Where shall I meet you?"* thought. Olivia replied with a thought that told him which room she was in and that her class was running a few minutes overtime. Javier waited patiently outside the door.

When she emerged, he couldn't help but drift directly to her side as she walked toward the café. The seating area he and his friends had used last year was now claimed by the Year Eleven group to which Olivia belonged. He felt the stares and surprise of Olivia's friends and fellow students every step of the way; from the expression on Olivia's face, so did she.

Mel, propped in a corner seat, looked about to doze off— until she saw Olivia and Javier. She sat bolt upright, her expression all surprise and confusion. Javier touched Olivia's waist to guide her toward a seat. He sat close beside her.

Mel's brows furrowed and her expression darkened. "How could you?"

"How could I what?" Olivia said.

"Steal my boyfriend, that's what!"

Javier realised he was caught in the middle. He felt compelled to stay by Olivia's side to afford her protection. At the same time, he might need to step aside and let them "fight it out". He simply froze and tried to appear innocent.

"You're my best friend, Mel. I wouldn't do that to you." Olivia's expression was pained. "He never was your boyfriend."

"Before the holidays he was smiling at me and now he's all over you. How do you explain that?"

Javier thought he could help here. "I wasn't smiling at you, Mel. You were sitting next to Olivia, so…"

"Who asked you?" Mel snapped back at him. As soon as she realised what she had done, she froze and her expression of anger gave way to one of shock. "I'm sorry." She fumbled for words. "I didn't mean…"

Under the close, judging gaze of a circle of gathering students, and the distant gaze of Javier's fellow students at the prime table, Javier took the opportunity to continue. "You were sitting next to Olivia on that day, so I can understand that when I smiled at her, you may have thought I was smiling at you."

Mel pouted. "Hmpf."

"Turns out, Javier's mum owns the farm next to ours and, well…" Olivia looked at the ceiling.

Javier watched as she searched for words, trying not to say anything when there was so much to tell. "Well, the rest is history." Javier took Olivia's hand and gave it a gentle squeeze. As if on cue, they glanced warmly at each other and turned back toward the group.

Mel stormed off, parting the student cluster as she pushed through.

"I'm sorry," Javier said. "I don't want to come between you and your best friend. Do you want to go after her?"

"No." Olivia slid further onto a bench seat at the table and Javier followed. "She's tired from jet lag. I'll give her some time to calm down and rest and I'll try to sort it later."

Olivia's fellow students sequentially squeezed into the remaining seats and a small group stood about the table.

"Would you like some coffee and a brownie?" Javier looked for an escape as the curious mob closed in.

"Yes, thanks." Olivia's expression softened as he slid off in the direction of the counter.

He sent her a thought message of relief. She sent a reply that roughly translated as *you're sooo lucky.* By the time he returned to the table, many of those gathered had dissipated, no doubt because of Olivia's reluctance to provide tantalising details. They ate their cake and coffee in the company of friends before the bell rang to summon them back to class.

He sensed Olivia's ache inside at falling out with her best friend.

Friends

Being estranged from her best friend ate away at Olivia. Mel unintentionally made it worse by transmitting her thoughts and feelings to Olivia, who was now able to detect and decode them and experience the situation from Mel's perspective.

Olivia was initially stabbed by thoughts and feelings of betrayal and hurt. These soon gave rise to anger and thoughts of permanently excising Olivia from her life. All the next day, these thoughts poked into Olivia's mind at irregular intervals. It was very distracting.

On the third school day, when the lunch bell rang, Olivia sent Javier a thought that she would like to join his group of friends at the cafe. Javier replied with curiosity and Olivia responded with the idea that they would discuss it later. When Olivia arrived at the café with her packed lunch, Javier had his schoolbag on the seat beside him. He moved it to the floor to make a place for Olivia to sit.

"Everything OK?" Javier asked, as Olivia slid onto the seat beside him. His face was all pensive concern.

Olivia presumed Javier sensed the thoughts that troubled her. "All good, talk later."

Silent conversations were not going to wash with the school crowd, so Olivia made an effort to join in the group chatter. While her friends mostly discussed teacher behaviour and which students were dating, the Year Twelve cohort were more focussed on the task at hand, getting good grades and what courses and careers they aspired to.

When they had finished eating and drinking, Olivia flashed Javier a thought of taking a stroll around the school oval. Javier gave a subtle nod. Olivia excused herself and headed for the door. Javier soon did the same.

"Are you OK?" Javier asked when he caught up. "Mel's giving you a really hard time, isn't she?"

"Yeah." Olivia sighed upon considering the thought-barrage she was receiving. "And she doesn't even know it." They walked the path around the oval. Cricket try-outs were under way and held the attention of the students sitting on the wooden benches and grassy knolls on the northern side. The warm, still air was smattered with the raps of ball on willow and players shouting to each other.

"How bad is it?"

"Initially she felt hurt."

"Not unexpected."

"Fair call." Olivia stared at the path in front of her as she walked and talked. "Now that has been overlaid with anger."

"Is it bad?" Javier turned from gazing at distant trees to give Olivia a concerned glance.

"Pretty bad."

"I'm sorry to hear it."

Olivia sensed his genuine concern. She wanted to hug him out of gratitude and to seek comfort, but these were school grounds and there were rules.

"I hope you didn't mind me barging in on your friend group back there. I didn't want to sit with my usual group lest it drive Mel away from them when she needed their support."

"That's noble of you."

"I don't feel noble. I feel wretched."

"And doubly tormented because the Universal Language means Mel's feelings get piled on top of yours because she doesn't know she's transmitting and you can't stop receiving now that you're aware." The path led to the shade of a poinciana tree; its branches arched over them, giving an illusion of privacy.

"Exactly." Olivia felt more understood than she could ever remember. "When I first chose to learn the Universal Language, I promised myself that I would never use it to manipulate the thoughts of others, especially my friends."

"Nice to know." Javier grinned and winked at her, then focussed. "But now?"

"But now I'm considering, well…"

"Transmitting something to change Mel's thoughts and feelings?"

"Yeah." Olivia turned to Javier. Her brows were raised and her pleading eyes searched his. "Is that bad? Am I a horrible person? Am I unworthy of the Universal Language?"

Javier took Olivia's hand, stopped and hugged her—a total disregard for the rules—while he cast a meerkat gaze least there be teachers nearby.

Olivia melted into the hug and took comfort. It was over too soon for Olivia's liking and they resumed walking.

"Everyone uses the Universal Language whether they know it or not, whether they are worthy or not. The only difference is that we are aware of it." Javier stopped and turned to face her. "If you're a horrible person, so am I."

Olivia was confused.

"When faced with the same dilemma, I figured I could use the Universal Language to send my friends thoughts, but their mental filters would decide whether or not they adopted them. Since I can't make them do anything that they wouldn't do if they thought of the idea, I…"

"Meddled with their thoughts."

Javier sighed and his shoulders slumped. "Yeah."

"Well, that's food for thought."

"Whose?" Javier raised an eyebrow and grinned.

"Ha!" Olivia laughed out loud.

"Well, that's the most cheerful I've seen you all day."

"Thanks Javier, I needed that."

"You're welcome. Now let's head back to the lockers, it's almost time for the bell."

Javier's logic was sound and he appeared none the worse for the choice he made. So, in response to the volumes of anger and turmoil she received from Mel, Olivia just sent back thoughts of calm and caring. Then she waited.

Olivia also detected the thoughts of teachers and fellow students that were unintentionally broadcast or even aimed directly at her. Now she understood why Javier was always distant and distracted. It was a lot to process.

Lauren was right. The world wasn't composed of those who used the Universal Language and those that didn't. Everyone used it at some level. The world was composed of those who were aware of it and those who weren't. Olivia was now aware and her world would never be the same. Lauren was right on another count. This was not something that could be undone. Olivia realised she could not become unaware again any more than she could unscramble an egg.

* * *

On Thursday morning, Olivia waited at the school drop-off zone and searched out Mel's mother's car and Mel's long, dark hair among the arriving students. Mel saw her first and looked away. Olivia caught up and fell into step beside her. She projected friendship as best she could. "Hello Mel."

No reply.

"I think we need to talk, Mel."

Mel kept walking, not even stopping to look at Olivia. Olivia learned it was nearly impossible to use the Universal

Language and talk at the same time. She chose to go with talking, it was less weird. "Are you up for a beach walk after school?"

Mel walked on, ignoring Olivia.

"Text me," Olivia said and swerved away in the direction of her locker.

Every quiet moment during the day, Olivia recalled the pleasant beach walks they had taken in the past and sent Mel the thought. The hostile thoughts emanating from Mel slowly subsided. Finally, at two o'clock, just as Olivia gave up hope, the text arrived.

Mooloolaba 4:30. Usual spot.

Olivia responded immediately.

* * *

Four in the afternoon was a nice time for a beach walk in the summer. The air was warm, the sunburnt crowds had gone home, shadows of the buildings crept across the sand and the water was still warm enough for a swim. Olivia wore a T-shirt and shorts over swimmers and brought along a small canvas bag containing a light cotton towel. She was prepared for all contingencies—except the looming conversation.

Olivia sat on the bench at their meeting spot and furtively gazed about. Her anxiety blocked all attempts to use the Universal Language, so she made an effort to regulate her breathing and focus. She fixed her gaze on the waves. As she calmed, she was struck by a jumble of anger, relief, resentment and grief. Mel was near.

"Olivia." Mel's voice came from beside her.

Olivia tried to maintain calm. Still breathing slowly, she shifted her gaze from the waves to the source of the voice.

"Cripes, Olivia!" Mel looked shocked. "That's the weird look Javier does that freaks everyone out. What happened to you over the holidays?"

The ice was broken. "It's a long story. Are you up for it?"

"Absolutely."

Olivia led the way down the steps onto the soft sand and they set off toward the beacons. Olivia described all the events of her holiday, starting with the fall from Vanilla. She described being rescued and how Lauren became her new riding partner. Olivia was careful to only describe the events and not mention the Universal Language.

Mel was aghast as Olivia recounted being taken to see a psychologist. "I would have just died if my parents had done that to me."

Mel was so entranced at the story of Olivia's near-drowning and rescue, she couldn't even walk. She just stood in the sand, taking in every detail as waves rippled over her feet. "So, Javier just appeared out of nowhere and rescued you?"

"Yep." Olivia was relieved that Mel's curiosity was dispelling her anger. "If he hadn't, you'd be visiting a cemetery to talk to me and it would be a one-way conversation."

Mel stood in silence as the implications hit home. "I'm sorry I was mean to you this week, Livvie. I had no idea. Why didn't you call and tell me?"

"I tried a few times, but you were always busy with dinners and parties and…"

Mel frowned a moment, then rolled her eyes. "I was, wasn't I?" She looked Olivia in the eye. "I'm sorry I wasn't available when you needed to talk. It might have saved us both some grief."

"I'm sorry that I'm seeing the guy you liked, Mel. I told him that you liked him, but he didn't care. Then I figured…"

"Figured what?" Mel's brows came together in a frown. Was she looking for a reason to be angry again?

"I figured, you're amazing and stunning enough to date any guy you want, but Javier may be the only boyfriend I ever have."

Mel's frown melted. "You're forgiven." She lurched forward and hugged Olivia.

Olivia returned the hug, relieved that they were still friends, but with a twinge of guilt over the secret she could not tell.

Mel finally released her and resumed walking. "You have to tell me every single detail."

Olivia had already told as much as she was comfortable with. "I want to hear about your holiday first."

"Nowhere near as exciting as yours. The trouble started when we arrived in Singapore. My grandparents and my parents started discussing what university I will be attending and what course I will do, as if I wasn't even there."

"Oh, Mel."

"By the end of the holiday, my grandparents were discussing who I would be married off to."

Now it was Olivia's turn to be aghast. "No?"

Mel raised her eyebrows, pursed her lips and slowly nodded in affirmation. "I was secretly hoping that Javier would come to my rescue and we could elope or something." She gazed at the horizon, wistful for a moment before her expression hardened. "I guess I'll have to find someone else to rescue me."

Olivia could relate to meddling parents. "Don't you just hate it when parents try to control your life?"

"Yeah, like they didn't do a good enough job making themselves unhappy, so now they want to have another go at our expense."

"Exactly."

They walked and talked all the way to the beacons and back, then talked some more over gelato. By the time their mothers arrived to collect them, all animosity between them had evaporated and they parted with another hug.

"I missed you, Livvie."

"I missed you too, Mel."

"See you tomorrow." Mel broke away and made for their car.

"Text me if you want," Olivia called after her as she slid into the air-conditioned comfort of her mother's car.

* * *

"Glad to see you two have made up." Sheree pulled the car out from the curb. "Good friends are too precious to give up easily."

Sometimes her mum could be wise, but Olivia wasn't going to admit it. She flashed Javier a thought of reconciliation with Mel and soon received a thought of happy relief. Her distant look and vague smile were soon interrupted by her mother.

"You know those two prison escapees that the police are hunting?"

"Yes." Olivia was pushed from her reverie was. She sighed and tried to focus on what her mother said.

"Apparently, they spent a week working on a farm near Toowoomba."

"So, they've made it to Queensland?"

"Yes, but that's not the worst of it." Sherree glanced at Olivia, her face drawn and tense.

Olivia waited, expectant, for her mother to continue.

"They murdered the farmer and his wife, stole a fresh vehicle and stole more guns and ammunition."

This news made Olivia intensely uneasy. "That means the police know where they are now, right?"

"Nope. They've gone bush again and the police have no idea where they'll show up next."

Olivia reassured herself that Toowoomba was a long way from Kilkivan, but she was worried about her dad, out on the farm and alone much of the time.

"Oh, and Dad said to remind you that the Kilkivan Horse Ride is in eight weeks."

* * *

Olivia and Javier planned their participation in the Kilkivan Horse Ride during lunch hours at school, to the intense fascination of their fellow students. The first thing to organise was a farrier to re-shoe their horses. Olivia wanted their horses to be comfortable and the Ride website recommended that all horses be shod as some of the terrain was harsh for their hooves.

Olivia wanted to do the full-day ride.

"I like the sound of the Black Snake Trail," Mel said. "It sounds so outback, pioneering even."

"It's our first time, Olivia. Perhaps we should start with the half-day ride?" Javier looked earnestly into Olivia's eyes.

Olivia's stomach still tingled when he did that. It dismantled her defences. "Perhaps you're right."

"Wide Bay Creek Ride doesn't sound nearly as exciting." Mel looked over Olivia's shoulder at the screen.

"I'm not after excitement, Mel." Javier glanced at her. "I want a nice safe ride though scenic countryside with no injuries so we can enjoy the party at the end."

Mel was instantly animated. "There's a party at the end?"

"Not just a party but a parade and a party." Olivia brought up the details on the website. "See, all the riders meet up for a grand parade down the main street on the Saturday afternoon followed by a band and fireside celebrations at the showgrounds until late."

"Let me see." Mel turned Olivia's computer so she could see for herself. "Hey, everyone, we should organise to go and watch Olivia and Javier in the parade and go to the party."

While Olivia and Javier filled out forms and paid fees over the next weeks, Mel organised for students to car pool to Kilkivan and attend the parade and party.

On weekends when Javier had soccer matches in town, Olivia rode with Lauren to keep Vanilla fit for the event. Lauren would ride Javier's horse, Max, to keep him in condition too. On the other weekends, when Javier's team had a bye, Olivia and Javier would plan long rides that meandered across both their properties. They packed food to take along and the break stops were carefully selected to be secluded so they could spend time in each other's arms.

Still uneasy, Olivia had taken to monitoring news reports. Someone reported seeing the escaped prisoners in Tenterfield. She was relieved that they were back in NSW and further away. Then a report emerged that they had robbed a food store and petrol station in Mundubbera and their identities were confirmed by CCTV footage. The police declared that the previous sighting could not be confirmed. Olivia checked the maps. They were moving northward on inland routes and would bypass Kilkivan. She felt more at ease and turned her focus back to the Ride.

Guest sister

Daphne was due home for the Easter break. Art needed some parts for the tractor, so he volunteered to fetch her from Gympie North Railway Station. By mid-afternoon, Sheree found chores to do in the kitchen so she could keep an eye on the road to the farm entrance. Olivia settled in a chair on the verandah and set about cleaning and oiling her boots and Vanilla's tack. She tried to quell her excitement for the impending ride.

"They're here!" Sheree's voice carried from the kitchen. Moments later she burst onto the verandah and pulled her boots on. Then she waited, restless, leaning against the railing near the steps. She watched the dust trail approach the farm gate and the ute appear in the house yard.

Olivia affixed the lid of the saddle soap container and put on her own boots, now shiny and smelling of beeswax.

Before Art brought the ute to a stop under the jacaranda tree, Sheree flowed down the steps and strode across the grass toward the vehicle. Olivia followed slowly behind.

"Welcome home Daph." Sheree held her arms open to hug her daughter but was momentarily taken aback by what emerged from the car. Daphne had dyed her shoulder-length hair jet black except for a scarlet streak down one side. Her face was white under a heavy layer of makeup with ample dark eyeshadow and shiny, scarlet lips. Even Olivia didn't recognise her for a moment. Sheree gasped, then moved in for a hug. "Good to have you home."

"Hi Mum." Daphne loosely wrapped her pale arms around her mother. "Enough," she said, after a few short moments, and she pulled away.

Olivia took in the black, pleated skirt that swayed around her calves and the black ankle boots with silver studs. A scarlet, ribbed midriff top completed a gothic look that seemed out of place among the fields, trees, ambling chickens and bright sunshine. Olivia braved the potent musk scent and moved in for a dutiful hug of her own. "Hi Sis." Daphne promptly pulled away from the awkward greeting.

Sheree put her arm around Daphne's shoulder and walked her toward the house. "Come on in. You must be hungry."

Art looked drained and hollow, as if traumatised by the drive home from Gympie. Olivia helped him retrieve Daphne's bags from the back of the ute.

"You two are growing up too fast." Art handed a shoulder bag to Olivia. "What happened to the sweet little girls that used to play games around the farm and loved their dad?"

Olivia swung the bag onto her shoulder. "We play bigger games now, beyond the farm." She watched Art haul a heavy black duffel bag out of the cargo space and turn for the house. "And I still love my dad."

Art found a smile and placed his arm around Olivia's shoulders as they walked toward the house. "Thanks, Livvie."

The screen door clanged shut behind them. Olivia placed the bag on the couch and made for the kitchen. Sheree was in full welcome mode and Daphne stood near the serving bench, cool and indifferent.

"I've baked you a cake." Sheree retrieved the confection from the fridge and placed it on the bench. The chocolate glaze was as shiny as Olivia's freshly oiled boots and it was decorated with piped buttercream flowers. A fine trail of icing spelled out "Welcome home Daphne" and the scent of sweet chocolate wafted through the kitchen.

"I'm off carbs."

Sheree's smile vanished. "What do you mean, you're off carbs?" She placed her hands on the bench on either side of the plate and looked to and fro between the cake and the resolute Daphne. She looked at each as if something was wrong with it.

"It looks amazing, Mum. I'll have some." It pained Olivia to see her mother so deflated.

"Me too!" Art called out as lugged the duffel bag toward the girls' bedroom.

"Wait!" Daphne headed to intercept Art before he got to the door. "Not in there."

"Why not?" Now it was Art's turn to look derailed and confused.

Daphne stopped halfway; the bracelets on her arms jingled as she folded her arms and glanced between both her parents. "Because I'm not a child anymore. I'm entitled to my own room." She pointed toward the stairs. "You can take it to the guest room. I can use that when I'm home."

"Now wait a minute." Sheree stepped out from the kitchen. "You can't just come home and order us around."

"I'm an adult now and if you want me to keep coming home at all, you'd better start treating me like one."

Olivia watched with astonishment as her parents processed the ultimatum ... and caved. Art headed downstairs with the duffel bag. The stairs creaked under his weight.

Sheree still had some gumption left. "You get some sheets and make up the bed yourself. You're not a guest here."

"Seems like it to me," Olivia mumbled.

"What?" Daphne glared at her.

"Nothing." Olivia moved to get plates and cutlery for the cake. "Which bathroom will you be using?"

"The main bathroom of course. I've grown out of sharing an ensuite bathroom with my kid sister." Daphne fired one more glare at Olivia. "I'll be in and out of your room to get my things though."

"Hang on." Olivia braced herself against the kitchen bench. "You get personal space but you still get to invade mine whenever it suits you. How is that fair?"

"It's fair because I'm an adult now and you're ... still a child."

Olivia felt a surge of indignation rise inside her, but she restrained herself and held her tongue. Her parents would take Daphne's side in an argument; they always did. She was outnumbered and outgunned. She took a deep breath and stepped back from the bench. "Mum, the cake looks too good to cut. Would you like to do the honours?"

Sheree moved in to incise the confection with deft precision. She placed luscious wedges onto three plates. A fourth sat empty to the side.

Olivia gazed out the kitchen window and took in the green landscape which helped to calm her. Despite realising that she truly was at the bottom of the household pecking order, she derived wicked satisfaction from knowing that Daphne wouldn't be cramping her style when she spoke with Javier in the evenings. Then she recalled how close she and Daphne had been and how most nights they spent as children felt like having your best friend around for a sleepover. They would talk until they dozed off. Olivia's heart grieved for what was lost.

Anticipation

The Horse Ride was tomorrow.

Javier called Olivia for their evening chat. Back on the farm for the holidays, there was no longer a phone curfew. However, tomorrow would be a big day and Olivia would enjoy it more after a good night's sleep. He was determined not to keep her on the phone too late. "Sorry my mum planned most of the day," Javier said, settling comfortably on his bed.

"That's OK. If she hadn't done it, my mum would have. Besides, they can only plan up till the start of the event, then we're on our own."

"Good point. We only have to survive till then." Javier liked the way Olivia's brain worked.

"I just wish my parents wouldn't worry so much. I'm almost seventeen, pretty much an adult, but they still hover like I'm a kid."

"I don't think you're a kid. I think it's just what parents do these days, worry. Though I must admit, my mum isn't too bad."

"Or maybe she just hides it well?"

"Maybe." Javier adjusted his pillows. "So, you're up to speed on the arrangements for tomorrow?"

"I think so. You and Lauren—I mean your mum—will ride over here in the morning, arriving around seven thirty. We groom and feed the horses, then we load them into our float."

"I think your mum wants to feed us."

"Yeah, I forgot. We have brunch before loading the horses. Then my dad drives the float and us to the showgrounds while our mums follow in our car."

"Excellent. Now, we should get some sleep."

"I'd much rather keep talking to you."

"Me too, but we won't enjoy the day as much if we're both dog tired. Remember, it's an early start."

"OK then, if I must."

"You must. Sleep well, Olivia."

"You too, Javier. I love you."

"I love you too, Olivia."

Javier pressed the button to end the call, then set the alarm for early in the morning. He placed the phone on the bedside charger, pulled up the covers and promptly fell asleep.

* * *

The chiming of the alarm tugged Javier to consciousness. He emerged dishevelled from his room to find his mother fully dressed and eating breakfast at the small table, drenched in morning sunlight.

"Good morning, Javier."

"Morning."

Lauren shook her head with incredulity at how slow he was at getting his act together in the mornings. "The weather looks good for your ride." She tilted her head toward the bright sunlight.

"Uh huh." Javier made for the kitchen, where bacon and eggs, still warm, awaited him in a pan on the stove. "Thanks," he said as he slid them onto a waiting plate. He poured himself a juice and joined his mother. "So, what will you be doing while we're on our ride?"

"Sheree is giving me a lift into town to check out the stalls and festivities, and the parade, of course."

"Of course."

"I've got a few things to do. I'll meet you at the stables."

His mouth full of bacon, Javier raised a fork in acknowledgment.

By the time he arrived at the stables, Lauren had both horses caught and tethered. She hoisted the saddle onto Aztec. "We'll need to work fast if we're not to throw out Sheree's brunch schedule."

That was his mum's way of telling him to hurry up. "Sure." Javier had learned that was the most diplomatic response. He ran a brush quickly over Max's body. Just enough so the saddle would be comfortable. They would do a proper groom at Olivia's place. Javier's hands were chilled by the cool morning air and Max's skin felt warm under his fingers.

When they arrived at the creek crossing, Javier checked his phone. "We're fifteen minutes ahead of schedule, Mum. We needn't have rushed after all."

Lauren closed the gate between the properties. Javier coolly watched Art's tractor arrive at a distant field of green lucerne, ripe for cutting. It set off a flock of galahs and the pink and grey cacophony passed overhead, making for the eucalypts beyond the creek.

"Perhaps not." Lauren gazed toward the McKinnon house and her brows furrowed.

"Is there something wrong?"

"I'm afraid so."

Javier felt a pang of terror. He sensed where it was from. "You sense it too?"

Before Javier could reply, his phone rang and everything changed.

Invaded

Despite Javier's best attempts, Olivia had fallen asleep late. She had dreamt of doing the ride for so many years, and now the day was but one sleep away, she was too excited to sleep. She tossed restlessly, churned over recent events, planned the day ahead and was frustrated that she could not find sleep. Thus tormented, she had no idea what time sleep finally overtook her.

When the alarm finally chimed, she reluctantly dragged herself to consciousness. This was the day of the Ride. All memories of sleep and dreams instantly evaporated. Olivia was wide awake. Awake and excited.

By the time her father emerged, Olivia was already in the kitchen cooking up scrambled eggs and baked beans. She wore the grey cotton T-shirt dress that she used as a nightgown and her feet were cosy in thin slippers.

Dressed in grimy shorts and a fresh work shirt, Art dropped slices of bread into the toaster. "Keen to ride, I see."

Olivia put the kettle on and retrieved four cups from the cupboard. "You're hardly dressed for a day in town, I see."

Art retrieved butter and jam from the fridge. "There's a paddock of lucerne ready to cut."

"But, Dad." Olivia leaned against the kitchen bench, her face drawn in disappointment. "You're supposed to drive the float into town for the ride."

"Don't worry, Possum." The toast popped up and Art flicked it onto a plate before the heat could burn his fingers. "We don't have to leave for town till eleven and I'll be back by ten thirty."

Olivia was all scepticism. She rolled her eyes.

"Really, Possum, I promise." Art began to smear butter onto a piece of toast and the comforting aroma wafted through the room. "Besides, I'd rather miss the chatting and brunching and all that. I'll just leave you ladies to it."

"Javier is not exactly a lady, Dad."

"No, but he might feel like it by the time I get back." Art nudged Olivia's arm. "Can you spare some eggs for your old man before he goes to work in the fields to pay for your education and lifestyle?"

Olivia's concerned expression softened into a smile. "Sure thing, Dad." She slid some eggs onto a plate. "Wouldn't want you dying of starvation out in the fields, toiling to pay for that new ute you've got your eye on."

"Thanks, Possum." Art grinned and sat down to his breakfast.

They were soon joined by Sheree, still in her nightdress and wrapped in a white towelling bathrobe embroidered with the name of a prominent hotel chain. Her hair, held back in a ponytail, was rough and dishevelled from sleep.

Daphne emerged up the stairs moments later sporting black flannelette pyjama pants, Ugg boots and an oversized black T-shirt with a pink skull printed on the front. Her black and scarlet hair was wildly unkempt. "It's a ridiculously early time to be up." She made for the kettle. "But there's no sleeping with all that chit chat going on."

"Morning, dear," Sheree and Art said in unison. They shared a grin over the synchrony.

* * *

Olivia washed her breakfast dishes and stacked them neatly on the rack. Her father drove off in the tractor toward the fields beyond the creek. The colours were surreal in the golden light of early morning. Off in the distance, a dust cloud moved along the road toward their property gate. At its head was a small, white vehicle. Once it passed the neighbour's gate, their farm was the only remaining destination. "Looks like a customer is coming for some hay."

Sheree left her breakfast and came to the window. "That's odd. We weren't expecting any customers today." The white ute passed over the cattle grid and headed toward the house. "I deferred all bookings because of the Ride."

The battered, dusty vehicle pulled up in front of the house yard. Two unkempt men in grimy clothing emerged.

"Oh shit!" The colour drained from Sheree's face. "Quick, hide, both of you."

Olivia stood as if paralysed as the men with long shotguns sauntered toward the house.

Daphne sprang from the table to join them at the window. Her jaw dropped at the sight.

"Now!" Sheree shouted.

Olivia glanced at Daphne. There was terror in her eyes. Olivia pushed her toward the stairs and Daphne maintained the momentum and disappeared to the rooms below. Olivia raced to her bedroom, grabbed her phone from the bedside table and secreted herself in her wardrobe, behind the handful of dresses she possessed. Her heart pounded, her hands trembled and her thoughts raced. She froze there. Who should she call? The police? She didn't know the number of the local police. The emergency number? By the time they connected her, she might be found. By the time police arrived, she and her family might all be dead. She dialled.

"Javier!" she whispered, thinking that a text may have been smarter.

"What's wrong?"

There was worry in his voice. "The escaped criminals. They're here. They've got guns."

"Where are you?" Javier sounded really worried now.

"Hiding in my wardrobe."

"Good. Call triple zero. Stay hidden for as long as you can. We're already on our way."

"OK."

"Try to calm your mind as much as you can so that Mum and I can reach you."

That was a huge ask; her brain and skin tingled with terror. "I'll try."

"I'm here for you, Livvie. Remember I love you. Now hang up and call while you can."

"I love you too." Olivia hung up and pressed 000.

There was a click as the call connected.

"What is your emergency?" The voice was female, detached, bored even.

"The escaped prisoners. They're at my house. They've got guns," Olivia whispered.

"What's your location?" The voice didn't sound bored any more.

"I'm hiding in my wardrobe."

"Good. But where is your house?"

"Oh," Olivia said, feeling foolish, but that somehow brushed through some of the fear. She gave them the address.

"Police are on their way."

A thought pushed itself into Olivia's mind and she gave it voice. "They'll be seen from the house when they arrive. Tell them not to use sirens. I'm worried they might panic and shoot my mum or sister."

"I will." The voice was serious but calm. "How many in the house?"

"Me, my sister and my mum. Dad is out in the fields."

273

There was a crashing sound as the intruders forced their way through the front door. Sheree screamed and the scream was suddenly silenced.

"Hurry! They're in the house." Olivia ended the call. She set her phone to silent, turned it off and stowed it in the pocket of one of her coats. She huddled into a ball and tried to focus on breathing, tried to calm herself, all the while worried that her brave mother might already be dead.

The Cavalry

"We should get Art," Javier's panicked mind struggled for a course of action. He turned Max in that direction.

"No." Lauren held Aztec steady. "He'll be safer where he is."

Javier wanted to protest but the words disappeared. Given the gravity of the situation, his mother was eerily calm and somehow it helped him calm down, at least a little.

Lauren was silent, gazing into the distance, her brows slightly furrowed as if thinking intensely. Finally, her expression softened into one of serious determination. "First call triple zero and let them know what's going on."

Javier was relieved that his mother had a plan and, after seeing how the situation with Charlie and his dad had turned out, he was inclined to trust her. He made the call.

"Hello. My friend called to say that the escaped prisoners were at her house." Javier gave them the address. "OK," Javier said, shaking his head, "I understand." He looked toward as he spoke. "Thank you." He ended the call.

Lauren sat astride Aztec, expectant.

"She said they had already received a call."

"Good girl," Lauren said.

"They have police already on their way."

"And?"

"And they said we should stay well clear of the house and let the police handle it."

"But you can't do that, can you?"

"No." Javier turned Max toward the McKinnon house.

"I didn't think so." Lauren propelled Aztec to catch up with Max as he descended into the creek. The water sploshed around the horses' feet. "Stop on the far bank. We must be careful not to make things worse."

"How could things get worse?" Javier pulled Max up as soon as he cleared the water and turned toward his mother, his brows raised, incredulous.

"Right now, Olivia is still alive. Believe me, it could get worse." Lauren pulled Aztec up beside him. "All tracks to the house are visible from the house, right?"

"Right." Javier could see where this was going. It could help.

"Are there any approaches that could be hidden?"

The house was obscured by the rise of a gentle hill. Javier hadn't paid attention to this before. "If we can't see the house, then they can't see us."

"Very good." Lauren's face pulled into a tense smile. "Lead the way. You know the place best. You're here often enough."

The effort Javier made to spend time with Olivia at her home, with her family, was about to pay off. Javier turned Max to the right and cantered along the base of the rise, past the dam near the front gate. Max's canter was strong and smooth and his breath heaved with every stride.

Lauren followed. Aztec and Max briskly responded to every signal, every touch of boots on their flanks and subtle tension on the reins. They were energised, excited and purposeful. Their strong legs swished through the knee-high grass.

They crossed the road that led from the gate to the house near the dam, at the spot where it was hidden from the house by a tree in the house yard. They trotted up behind the hay shed, dismounted and tied the heaving, sweaty horses to a fence railing. It was time for them to rest.

"Now what?" Javier asked as Lauren surveyed the scene.

Lauren gestured Javier to follow as she clambered between the taut fence wires to the back wall of the hay shed and crept along a row of large, round silage bales, sealed in mint-coloured plastic, that jutted out from the side of the shed. "Now, we have to get them out if we can."

"I'm not letting you go anywhere near the house."

Lauren stopped, her expression questioning.

"Just trying to limit the number people I care about facing gun barrels today." Javier tried to sound strong and in control, but inside he imagined the pain of losing both Olivia and his mum. He'd rather die himself than feel that.

Lauren hugged him.

That was unexpected. It also helped to release tension and settle Javier's thoughts. "I need to get inside the house, somehow."

Lauren wore the expression of a mother desperately wanting to avoid sending her son into danger. It gave way to one of resignation and determination. She finally looked back toward the house and pointed at a side door. "Is that the laundry door?"

"Yes. It's never locked when they're home." Javier surveyed the yard. "If I could get behind the chook pen over there, I could sneak up on the laundry door. It's close by." He frowned and pointed as he spoke. "But I'd be exposed as I moved from here to behind that shrub and on toward the chook pen."

"Ah, but we have the Universal Language at our disposal." Lauren flashed him a wink. "If I can get a fix on the thoughts of the intruders, I can let you know when they aren't watching from the windows."

"While you're doing that, I'll try and calm my thoughts enough so we can communicate."

Lauren turned her gaze toward the house. They both fell silent and began to breathe slowly and deeply. Javier closed his eyes to focus.

Javier calmed his mind. Every time a distracting thought or feeling entered his head, he wordlessly reminded himself he would only be of use to Olivia if he remained calm and, with that, he gently pushed the intruding thoughts away.

Javier opened his eyes. "How did you go?"

Lauren still gazed at the house, now with a calm resolve. "They both have simple, weak minds," Lauren replied. "Not unexpected I suppose." She looked toward Javier. "I may try and use a thought distraction when you get there."

"That could be useful." Javier received a thought that the intruders' attention was focussed on the wall of the kitchen, near the door to the laundry. "Got it," he said, his face gritted with determination. Javier dashed toward the cover of the shrub.

Survival

"Is she dead?" It was a young man's voice.

"Who freakin' cares, son?" This voice was deeper and raspy.

"Don't freakin' call me son. Y'know I hate it. I keep tellin' ya t'call me Damien. I'm not a kid anymore. Besides, the more people we bump off, the longer they're goin' to lock us up when they catch us, Dad."

"Well, they'd better not bloody catch us then and, if y'don't want me to call ya son, don't call me Dad. Me name is Blake. Use it."

Olivia breathed slowly and deliberately to try and calm herself. The wardrobe smelled musty. The intruders' words invaded her focus, but she tried not to let her mind react. She just let them wash past. She would be no use to her sister if she was panicked and distracted. What if her father came back? Would they kill him too? Her gut twanged with panic at the thought. She checked herself and focussed on breathing once more.

"Not dead, just unconscious."

Olivia exhaled in relief.

"Drag 'er over there. I'll hold y'gun."

Slow footsteps moved toward the kitchen.

"Look, they've made us brekkie," Damien said.

"Brekkie for two at the table and dishes from two more on the rack." There was a pause. When the raspy voice resumed it was muffled by a mouth full of food. "There's four of 'em."

"There's this one 'ere," Damien said.

"And one was on the tractor 'eddin' to the paddocks. We'll get 'im later."

"That means there's two more in the 'ouse."

"Lock the doors and search the rooms. We can eat later."

"Maybe when she wakes up, she can cook us some lunch?"

The front door thudded closed and the lock clicked, then the laundry door. Loud footsteps echoed on the wooden stairs. The downstairs door lock clicked. There were sounds of doors opening and closing and things being pushed about downstairs, then a loud scream.

"Shut the 'ell up or I'll blow y'flamin face off!" It was Damien's voice.

The scream silenced. Daphne's downstairs hiding spot had been discovered.

"Found another one, 'idin' in a storeroom."

The loud footsteps plodded up the stairs, but this time there was another irregular, slipping set with them and pitiful sobbing. Olivia reached out with her mind, sensed Daphne's terror and immediately recoiled back, struggling to regain focus. She wouldn't be able to keep calm with that intensity of emotion intruding on her thoughts.

"Put 'er there," Blake's raspy voice said. "Beside the other one."

"Mum!"

"I said shuddup or I'll blow your 'edd off."

"I'll watch these two," said Blake. "You find the other one."

Bangs and thuds echoed as Damian rummaged and opened cupboard and wardrobe doors in her parents' room and the living room. Finally the footsteps came into her room. The sudden rush of light meant her wardrobe door was opened. The stench of stale urine and sweat filled her nostrils. She fought to hold back the panic. Her heart started to race and she tried to rein it in. A gun barrel poked about through the clothes. It poked her; the clothes were shoved aside. She was found.

"Out!" A man with grimy clothes and full beard and moustache pointed his shotgun at her and gestured toward the room. "Out, I said!"

Olivia slowly emerged from her haven.

"I found the other one," he called out to his father. He used his gun to gesture toward the door. "Go!"

Olivia moved slowly out of the doorway and toward the kitchen, determined not to make any sudden moves that could cause them to get trigger happy. She arrived to see her mother lying limp on the floor, blood oozing from a wound on the side of her head. It stained her towelling collar and spread to form a pool on the floor. Daphne sat behind her, against the kitchen wall, staring and paralysed like a kangaroo in headlights.

Olivia slowly sat down beside her sister. She took Daphne's hand. It was cold and clammy. She gave it a gentle squeeze to try and reassure her, but there was no response. Daphne was beyond sobbing, beyond sensing and beyond feeling.

The intruders appeared more relaxed now all the occupants were accounted for. The older one, a man with peppered grey hair, beard and moustache, pointed his gun at them. "If y'move from that spot, I'll friggin' shoot ya."

Olivia nodded, silent.

The intruders helped themselves to all the remaining food on the table and guzzled it down with slurps and soft groans. Next, they moved on to the food still on the stove. They made for the fridge and guzzled down milk. It trickled down into their beards over the food that was already smeared there. All the while they kept their guns close by and watched Olivia out of the corner of their eyes.

Not sensing immediate danger, Olivia calmed herself enough to try and sense their thoughts. From the younger man she detected the pleasure of the treasure trove they had just taken possession of, but there was an undercurrent of anger and resentment. From the older one she sensed the enjoyment of eating and drinking, but little else. It felt like cold, dispassionate, darkness and it sent a shiver up her spine. She stopped trying to reach them and turned her thoughts to Javier.

The instant she reached out, she received a thought of reassurance and relief. She sensed he was nearby. She immediately worried for his safety and lost the connection.

Olivia slowed her breathing and tried to calm herself enough to reconnect.

"Olivia."

The sound of her name in her own head startled her. She glanced at the intruders in case her jolt set them off, but they were too focussed on food to notice. She calmed herself down again, waited and hoped the voice would return.

"Are you injured?"

It was the voice again, a familiar voice. She sent a thought in reply. *"Lauren?"*

"Yes Olivia. Good job staying calm enough to hear me. We're here, Olivia. We'll do what we can to help."

"OK. Mum's hurt." She tried to form the thoughts without words.

She received an image of her mum waking and the thought, *"Try and keep her calm."*

"Yes, Lauren."

Sheree's hand twitched and she groaned softly.

"Mum," Olivia whispered and leaned slowly toward her.

Blake grabbed his gun from beside his leg and raised it toward her.

A pang of fear sliced through Olivia as she looked into the dark core of the barrel. "It's my mum, she's waking up."

"Keep 'er there and keep 'er bloody quiet."

Olivia nodded acknowledgment, leaned over her mother and took her pale, cold hand in hers. "Mum, shhh."

Access

Taking his cues from Lauren, Javier worked his way from the shrub to the chook pen near the rear of the house. The chooks squawked and ran toward him, thinking they would be fed or let out for forage. He hoped the intruders didn't notice. It was a short dash to the steps. He climbed the weathered wooden risers slowly, hoping they didn't squeak and give him away.

Javier crouched on the landing at the laundry door. He avoided thinking about the guns and the imminent danger; it clouded his thoughts. He battled his surging adrenaline to calm down and tried to focus on Olivia. He couldn't concentrate clearly. He hoped she was still alive and wondered if he would feel it if she wasn't. Heart pounding, he carefully reached up for the handle of the screen door and slowly drew it down. It yielded. Javier sighed with relief. The door was unlocked. Slowly, he opened it and quietly fastened it to the latch on the railing so the spring mechanism wouldn't slam it shut with a clang.

There were muffled voices inside. Two male voices and one that sounded like Sheree. The next door was painted timber, with a window cut out in the top half filled with clear glass. Javier was careful to stay crouched below the level of the window. He slowly grasped the round knob and turned. It too yielded. He pushed the door open very slightly and slowly released the latch. He could hear more clearly now. The sound of Olivia's voice melted his heart. She was alive. He would do everything in his power to keep it that way.

Javier crept carefully into the laundry and stayed close to the wall beside the doorway into the kitchen. He calmed himself enough to send Olivia a thought of reassurance before he slowly peered into the doorway. The sight stabbed at his heart. The three women were seated on the floor along the kitchen wall. Daphne was closest to him. She sat, in her pyjamas and slippers, stiff, rigid and deathly pale. Javier figured she must be in some sort of shock. Sheree was also pale but moving. Blood from a wound on the side of her head had crusted and there was a bloodstain on the collar of her robe. Her cream slippers were also stained with smears of blood. Javier deduced it was from the bloody patch on the floor near her feet.

It wrenched his heart to see Olivia, clearly frightened, clutching her mother's hand and trying to be brave. The blurred shadows of two tall figures loomed over them and were outlined on the wall. Javier could see the outlines of two shotgun barrels.

He pulled back and sat against the wall, took a deep breath and tried to decide what to do next. The thought that came to him felt like a warm hug, from the inside. It was from Olivia. He fought back tears and the urge to run out and take her in his arms. He would have to think carefully and be very smart about this if he was ever going to hold her in his arms again.

A thought came. He sensed it was from his mother. "*Wait.*" So he sat, still and silent, and waited.

Ammo

By the time the intruders had finished eating their way through the contents of the fridge, Sheree had regained consciousness and was huddled between her daughters against the kitchen wall.

There was a soft click. It came from the laundry.

The light in the laundry changed. Olivia looked away so she could only see it in the corner of her eye. She didn't want to draw the intruders' attention to it. She sensed the thought, "*I'm here*" and it reassured her. Javier's curly locks and his eyes peeped from the doorway. The pain in his eyes broke her heart. His face disappeared back into the laundry. She sent back the only thought that she really wanted him to know, "*I love you.*"

Damien wiped his beard on a tea towel. "I'm gettin' low on ammo."

Blake wiped his beard on his sleeve and walked toward the women. "Well, where is it?"

Sheree feigned ignorance. "Where is what?"

"Don't bloody mess with me." Blake waved his gun at Sheree. "This is a farm. Ya have guns and ammo. Where are they?"

Sheree cowered. "The guns are in a wall cabinet downstairs."

Olivia took her hand and squeezed it for support. It felt cold and clammy.

Damien stepped forward to stand beside his father. "Where's the bloody ammo?"

"It's in the workshop beside the hay shed. In a locked wall cabinet." Sheree's voice trembled.

Blake pointed his gun at Sheree's face. Now there were two barrels aimed at her. "Bullshit. No one keeps their ammo so far from their gun."

"Only people who don't want to get shot with their own weapons," Olivia said, seeing mother was too intimidated to speak. She was not inclined to mention the couple of shells Art had hidden on top of the laundry cupboard.

"OK, smart arse." Damien redirected his gun to point at her. "Where's the key?"

"Key to the gun cabinet is in the top drawer of the desk in the study. My dad carries the key to the ammunition cabinet with him."

Blake went tense and inhaled deeply, about to explode in frustration.

"Don't worry." Damien indicated in the direction of the farm gate with his gun barrel. "I've still got enough ammo to take him out when he crosses the yard."

Talk of Art being hurt fired up Sheree. "No, you won't. The police are on their way. They'll take you out before my husband gets back."

Blake laughed and pointed his gun back at Sheree. "I 'ope you're wrong, luv. See, if we so much as 'ear a siren, we shoot all three of ya."

"Yeah." Damien sneered at the frightened women. "We don't like witnesses."

A thought popped into her head. Olivia sensed it was from Lauren and gave it voice. "It's not the cops you have to worry about, it's our pet dragon."

"What the 'ell?" Blake's face screwed up in surprise.

"There's no friggin' thing as dragons." Damien pointed his gun at Olivia. "We're not stupid and ya've been readin' too many books."

Sheree stared at Olivia incredulously, as if her daughter had suddenly gone mad.

"Well, there are. We have one and she's very protective of the family." Olivia's foot twitched as she doubled down on the dragon story. Sheree squeezed her hand, hard, raised her eyebrows and shook her head as she tried to stop Olivia talking.

The intruders burst out laughing.

"So, youse think you can 'ave some fun with us, eh?" Blake kicked Olivia's foot. "We like fun, don't we, Damien?"

Damien grinned, exposing yellow, crusted teeth. "Sure do."

"Which one shall we do first?"

Damien nudged Daphne's foot with his gun barrel. She didn't flinch. She just stared blankly into space. "This one doesn't look like she's gonna put up much of a fight. Let's do 'er first."

"Good thinkin', Damien. I reckon this one second." He pointed his gun at Olivia. "And this one last." He focussed on Sheree.

"No!" Sheree cried out. "Leave my daughters alone."

"Or what, bitch?" Blake put the barrel of his gun to her forehead.

Sheree slumped back against the wall. She reached for Daphne, but her hand closed on empty air. Damien dragged a writhing Daphne, by the arm, toward Olivia's bedroom.

"Eeeeowww! Draxa!" Olivia screamed in the most unearthly, high pitch she could manage, giving voice to the thought that arrived in her head.

Both intruders paused.

"What the 'ell was that?" Damien held Daphne's arm in one hand and his gun in the other.

"Summoning the dragon." Spurred by a surge of courage, Olivia glared into Blake's icy grey eyes. "You two are so dead."

Blake and Damien exchanged a worried glance before Blake turned his eyes on Olivia and steeled his expression. "The only dead 'ere are you lot." He turned and glared at Daphne. "If ya put up any sort of fight, I'm gonna blow their brains out." He gestured toward Olivia and Sheree. "Goddit?"

Daphne, still pale with terror, didn't respond. Damien dragged her out of sight.

Bed springs squeaked with the sudden weight of a body tossed upon them. Daphne weakly sobbed "no" over and over. Olivia clung to her mother's arm.

"Argh! What the 'ell was that?" Damien shouted.

"Is she fightin' ya? 'Ow bout I shoot the mudder?" Blake put the barrel of his gun to Sheree's head.

Sheree stiffened in terror. Olivia clung tighter.

"Shit! There 'tis again!" There was fear in Damien's voice now. "It's unda the bed. It's big and it's got scales. I think it's a friggin' dragon!"

"There's no such thing, Damien. You said it yaself. Now get on with it, I wanna go at her." Blake kept the gun pointed at Sheree.

The words came to Olivia. "Told you. Draxa is hungry too. Hasn't eaten for a couple days. You know how that feels."

Blake swivelled the gun at Olivia. "Shut the 'ell up."

"Bloody 'ell! It bit me!" Damien's voice was desperate now.

"If either of ya move an inch, the girl dies," Blake hissed as he edged toward the bedroom.

"Javier's in the laundry. Go." Olivia whispered to Sheree. She shoved her in the direction of the laundry just as Javier's face appeared.

"I'm not leaving you here with them." Sheree sneered in Blake's direction.

This was no time for a debate. She tried to focus on her mother going to the laundry, but it was easier to talk. "One of us has to go first and you're closer. Go!"

Sheree kissed Olivia on the forehead. "I love you."

"I love you too, Mum. Now, go."

Rescue One

Javier sat helpless in the laundry and listened to the banter of the intruders as their stench wafted through to his nostrils. He grimaced in disgust. Olivia said something about a dragon. Was the terror driving her mad? He was torn by Daphne's desperate sobs yet pinned to the spot by a potent, recurring thought from his mother that commanded him to wait. Finally, the raspy voice uttered words that hinted he was leaving the women unguarded. Lauren signalled, "*Now!*"

He peered into the kitchen. The intruder was gone and Olivia pointed in his direction as she tried to convince her mother to go to him. He beckoned twice and sent a thought to Olivia that they should both come.

Sheree kissed Olivia on the forehead and moved toward Javier.

Javier stared at Olivia and tried to will her to come to safety, too. She shook her head. The thought arrived; she would try and save Daphne first. Pain and sadness welled in his chest. Would this be the last time he saw his beloved Olivia alive? She was so brave, but he was afraid that her courage would cost her life and cost him his beloved. Javier grabbed the collar of Sheree's soft robe as she approached and he pulled her into the laundry. Her ashen face was tight with terror and pain and stained with dried blood and tears. He pointed toward the open door and pushed her in that direction.

Once they were on the landing, Javier pointed at the hay shed. Lauren's torso appeared from behind the shed and beckoned to Sheree. "See, Lauren is behind the hay shed. You'll be safe there. Run!"

Sheree's eyes were all terror and desperation.

Javier held her firmly by the shoulders and looked her in the eye. "I'm going back for the girls. No one gets left behind."

Sheree nodded feebly. Javier pointed her in the direction of the steps and Sheree fled toward the hay shed, her robe flapping around her legs.

Two police vehicles appeared in the distance, driving quietly toward the house. Lauren beckoned the vehicles before they reached the house yard. They left the track and drove out of sight behind the hay shed. Lauren turned and opened her arms to receive Sheree, pulled her out of sight. All were once again concealed.

The distant dust clouds from the two vehicles slowly wafted away. Good thing the intruders were too distracted to look out the windows. Javier crept back into the laundry.

* * *

The moment Sheree disappeared into the laundry, Olivia took a deep breath, summoned courage and began to crawl toward the bedroom door.

"There! See it?"

"What the 'ell?" There was fear in Blake's voice now too.

Olivia peered into the doorway. Daphne lay rigid on the bed, her pyjama pants around her clenched knees. Her hair was tousled and tear trails glinted on her cheeks in the rays of morning light piercing the curtains. Damien, his pants fly half-undone and shotgun held tense and ready, slowly edged around to the other side of the bed. Blake stood just inside the doorway, grasping his gun so firmly in both hands that his knuckles were white.

Blake gestured with his gun. "Well, shoot the bloody thing."

"Can't get a clear shot." Damien edged further, his gaze fixed on where he had last seen the creature. "It keeps goin' under the bed, then jumps out and bites. See." Damien took one hand off his gun and lifted the right leg of his pants to reveal puncture wounds over his ankle.

"Shit!" Blake edged toward the bed. "Ya take that side. I'll cover this one. When it comes out, shoot it."

Damien nodded and tightened his grip on the gun.

With the intruders focussed on the dragon, Daphne seemed irrelevant, but not to Olivia. She sent Daphne a thought of calm. Daphne's blubbing settled a little. She imagined what she would do in Daphne's position and sent that too. Much to Olivia's relief, Daphne did exactly that.

Daphne slowly rolled onto her side and pulled up her pants. Both intruders had reached the edge of the bed and were nudging the ends of their barrels under the rim of the comforter.

"There! Did ya see that?" Damien pointed toward the only other door from the room.

"Yeah." Blake glanced at his son. "I seen it."

"It went in there." Damien pointed his gun toward the open door of the walk-in wardrobe and ensuite. "It's quick as a lizard on hot tar."

Both men edged toward the wardrobe door and took position on each side of the opening, guns held up and ready.

"Reckon we got it cornered." Blake looked at his son. The fearful expression on his face mirrored his own.

"Yeah." Damien sounded uncertain, like he wanted to flee.

Olivia sent another thought to Daphne.

With the intruders focussed on the wardrobe, Daphne slid gently down onto the floor. Olivia beckoned from the door and Daphne crawled urgently toward her.

Damien glanced in their direction. His brow furrowed. He aimed the gun at the oblivious Daphne, then raised the barrel to aim directly at Olivia's face. Olivia's blood ran cold and she froze. Damien looked fiercely determined. Olivia closed her eyes and braced for her final moment. Her chest ached for the pain her death would cause Javier. "*I'm sorry,*" she thought and tried to send it to him through a wall of fear and desolation.

The shot rang out.

Olivia waited for the pain, for the end, for anything.

"Shit! Missed it!" Blake's raspy voice cursed.

Olivia opened her eyes. Damien still pointed his gun at her, until Blake flicked it upward with his. Another deafening shot rang out; a hole in the ceiling showered plaster fragments onto the bed.

Blake slapped Damien's cheek. "What are you doin'? Focus on the job or we'll never get the bloody thing."

Damien glared at Olivia and Blake followed his gaze. "Don'ya worry 'bout em. We'll get 'em later."

Damien reluctantly turned his gun back toward the doorway.

Daphne, pale and terrified, had almost reached Olivia.

"We go in now!" Blake pointed his gun toward the dark spaces beneath the hanging clothes.

"Right!" Damien tensed, ready.

Olivia inhaled and the breath was divine in her lungs. She was alive. She pulled Daphne out through the doorway by her shirt. Olivia wrapped her arms tight around her sister, though Daphne, still rigid with fear, didn't return the hug. At least she was alive. "Out through the laundry," Olivia whispered in Daphne's ear during the embrace. Daphne pulled away and crawled in that direction with Olivia following closely behind.

A gunshot sounded from the wardrobe. Confined within walls, it was deafening. Olivia jolted, startled by the shot. Daphne crawled faster.

"Did ya get it?" Damien's voice was shrill now.

"Nah, missed."

"Shit!"

Olivia crawled faster to keep up.

Escape

Javier peered through to the kitchen, Olivia was gone.

"Crap!" he whispered, wishing he had just seen Olivia to safety instead of Sheree, then feeling guilty at the thought.

The shouts from the intruders were so loud and intense that Javier wondered if there really was a dragon in the house, or maybe a very large python? A thought of terror, deep sadness and desolation hit him like a punch. A shot rang out. Shocked and confused, Javier hoped beyond hope that Olivia was safe. Daphne's pale, terrified face appeared around a corner and she crawled into the kitchen. As soon as he caught her eye, he beckoned her to him. To Javier's huge relief, Olivia appeared behind her.

A gunshot rang out and the intruders yelled. The girls crawled faster. He ushered them ahead of him onto the laundry landing and pointed toward the hayshed. Heads in black caps peered out from behind the shed over arms clenching pistols pointed at them. Daphne froze at the sight. Javier sighed; more gun barrels didn't help.

Lauren jumped out from behind the waiting police, saying something. The heads looked at her and the barrels were lowered. Something thrummed—a distant helicopter.

"It's only the police and my mum," Javier whispered to Daphne.

Lauren beckoned to them and Daphne glanced back at Javier.

"Go!" he whispered with urgency. He shoved Daphne toward the steps. She was still tense. Could she find the strength to save herself? Suddenly she relaxed a little and took a deep breath. She glanced back at Olivia and fled down the steps toward Lauren.

"Your turn." Javier pushed Olivia forward.

"Together." Olivia grasped his hand with a ratchet-tight grip.

Her hand was cold and sweaty from fear. No time to wonder if his was the same; he pulled her down the steps and the pair fled toward the hayshed. Lauren grabbed them both in her arms and dragged them to safety.

Loose Ends

The helicopter pulsed louder. Javier scanned the sky in the direction of the noise and made it out coming in from the direction of the farm gate. Another dust cloud appeared on the road, heading toward them. The vehicle preceding it was bigger and more angular than a police car; an armoured personnel carrier, but dark instead of the camouflage colours of army vehicles.

"Is that everyone?" A police officer looked them over. "Senior Sergeant John Farrell" was printed on a blue label with a silver police insignia above the right breast pocket of his black bullet-proof vest. The vest fitted snug over his navy-blue uniform and was punctuated with pockets and devices. He looked like a walking police toolkit. His navy-blue cap was blotchy from sweat and his eyes were hidden behind silver-rimmed, dark sunglasses.

Javier tried to reconcile the sergeant's calm manner with the beads of sweat forming on his brow and temples. The dark colours of his uniform absorbed the heat of the sun and the layers insulated against heat escape. Javier hoped the sweat was from overheating rather than from fear.

"Yes, Sergeant." Lauren gave Olivia and Javier one more squeeze and a huge smile before she released them and moved in the direction of the sergeant.

Sergeant Farrell clicked his gun back into the holster strapped to his right thigh. He held down a button on the side of the black microphone attached below his right shoulder. "SERT team, this is Senior Sergeant Farrell. The hostages are clear of the building. Repeat, the hostages are clear of the building."

Two other male officers, also in navy-blue uniforms and caps, and sporting black vests bearing a bevy of devices, clicked their guns into their holsters and led Javier and Olivia to where Sheree and Daphne were huddled near a female officer.

Sheree alternately hugged Daphne and held her at arm's length, sighing at her forlorn expression and the tearstains on her cheeks. When Olivia was close enough, Sheree reached out and drew her into the next hug, dragging Javier in too.

Huddled close to Daphne, Olivia whispered, "Did he?" She searched her sister's eyes and waited.

Daphne shook her head. All three sighed with relief and hugged tighter.

Another gunshot rang out, followed by muffled yelling.

"What are they doing?" Farrell looked confused in the direction of the house. "Are they shooting each other now?"

"Trying to kill an imaginary dragon," Olivia called out from the safety of Javier's arms. "Oh and they said they're low on ammo, if that helps."

"Nice work," Javier whispered into her ear. He was so relieved that she was safe that he fought back tears. He was awed beyond words by her strength and presence of mind at this moment. He hugged her even tighter.

"Sure does." Sergeant Farrell pressed the button his microphone again. "Both suspects are still in the farmhouse. They are armed and running low on ammunition." His voice was almost drowned out by the roar of the armoured vehicle as it approached. It stopped on the track near them, where it remained stationary and churned up dust. "Cover the exits from the farmhouse from each end of the shed." He waved and two of the officers positioned themselves, one at each end of the shed.

They drew their pistols and peered around the edges of the shed so that they could see all the exits.

"Suspects are isolated and contained," Farrell said into his microphone. The third officer removed her sunglasses and remained with the huddled family, offering words of comfort and reassurance.

"Not that I have any expertise in these situations..." Lauren sidled up to Sergeant Farrell, so she could speak softly. "But wouldn't it be safer for your men if you just let them exhaust their ammo on the imaginary dragon before you moved in?"

Another gunshot rang out.

Farrell glanced at his fellow officers and the armoured vehicle poised to take the house. He glanced in the direction of the helicopter. "Now that everyone is safe, it won't hurt to wait for the helicopter." He pressed the button on his microphone. "Hold position."

The officers, with their guns drawn, acknowledged by tilting their heads in the sergeant's direction.

"Holding position," said a voice emanating from a device on Farrell's vest.

"We told them the ammo was kept in the workshop." Olivia wriggled an arm free from Javier's embrace and pointed in the direction of the metal structure near the hay shed. They might make a break for it when they come out."

Sergeant Farrell waved his hand at Olivia to acknowledge the information. He turned to the female officer assisting the family with a stern and questioning gaze.

"Will you be OK now?" she asked Sheree.

"We'll be fine, dear." Sheree's expression steeled. "Go get the bastards."

The female officer gave Sheree a reassuring smile, tilted her head to acknowledge Sergeant Farrell and donned her sunglasses. She drew her pistol as she crept off and disappeared behind the workshop.

Two more gunshots sounded in the house in rapid succession. The helicopter was getting louder, but there was another noise. Javier made out the top of the tractor coming up the rise from the fields toward the house.

Javier reluctantly released Olivia and stepped toward Sergeant Farrell. "That's their father coming back from the paddock." He pointed in the direction of the tractor.

Before Sergeant Farrell finished informing his team the vehicle was not a threat, Lauren stepped away from the group and waved wildly, beckoning Art to come toward them. Sheree sprang to her feet, went toward Lauren and mirrored her beckoning. The tractor veered from the track before it reached the armoured vehicle and stopped near the police cars. Art emerged from the cabin and jumped to the ground, where he was tackled and hugged by his wife.

"Art! Thank goodness you're safe." Sheree buried her face in his shoulder.

Art put his arms around her, glanced at Olivia and Daphne and looked at Sergeant Farrell, bewildered.

"Your wife can explain." Farrell diverted his attention back to the house.

Javier glanced at his mother. She leaned against a rear wheel of the tractor and gazed in the direction of the house. He knew what that meant. Olivia moved to walk toward her, but Javier held her back. His mother needed to concentrate.

Another gunshot rang out. Everyone turned toward the house. There was yelling, two more gunshots, more yelling. A loud, shrill scream rang out and the front screen door burst open. The intruders, still carrying their guns, ran out onto the verandah so fast that they collided with the railing. After getting their bearings, they made for the workshop.

Sergeant Farrell grabbed the small megaphone that dangled from his belt. "Stop! Drop your weapons! You are surrounded!" He glanced at Olivia and the huddled family. "Stay here!"

They all froze where they were.

Sergeant Farrell joined his colleague at the edge of the hay shed. The helicopter arrived: roaring and stirring up dust in the yard, it hovered over the intruders.

The intruders looked about them, their faces pale and mouths agape. A helicopter roared in the sky, an armoured vehicle was poised at the house yard cattle grid and officers with guns peered from behind the workshop and the hay shed. They looked back at the house and their faces went another shade of pale. They looked at each other and tossed their guns aside.

"Move to your right, away from the guns!" a megaphone from the helicopter rang out.

The intruders obeyed, their clothes and hair buffeted by the helicopter downdraught.

Sergeant Farrell gave the command into his microphone: "Move in!"

The armoured vehicle propelled forward toward the intruders and stopped just short of them. A door opened and a German shepherd dog in a bullet-proof vest burst forth, dragging an officer in black kit and black helmet behind him on a leash. Two other officers promptly emerged from the vehicle and followed their colleagues; both wore black uniforms and dark sunglasses, well-equipped bullet-proof vests and black helmets. They sported guns much more intimidating than pistols; pointed squarely at the two men.

"Drop to the ground!" the leading officer shouted.

The intruders promptly dropped face down in the dust. While one officer kept his gun fixed on them, the other cuffed the duo's hands behind them. On the click of the last cuff, all the remaining officers lowered their weapons and some moved toward the intruders.

The officers roughly dragged the dishevelled men to their feet. The dust now layered over their grimy skin made them look like walking corpses.

"Just get us away from the bloody dragon," Damien yelled as they were led to the waiting police cars. "That thing's deadly!" he called out to Olivia as he was led past. "Where the 'ell did ya get a bloody dragon?"

"A gift from a friend." Olivia chuckled and rested her cheek against Javier's chest.

"What's so funny?" Javier expected her to be more distraught than she was.

"The look on the officers' faces when they got into the cars. Those blokes stink and it's a long drive back to town on a hot day."

"I hope their air-conditioning holds up." He placed a gentle hand on the back of Olivia's neck. She was safe. They were all safe.

The helicopter landed in the field on the far side of the house track. Sergeant Farrell went over and spent some time in discussions with the officers in the helicopter and the armoured vehicle.

Javier noticed Daphne sat huddled and alone against the back wall of the hayshed, her hands over her ears. He flashed a thought to Sheree.

Sheree glanced away from Art. "Daphne!" She dragged Art over. They coaxed Daphne to her feet and enveloped her in a three-way hug. Daphne went limp in their arms and sobbed loudly.

A "*well done*" thought from Lauren popped into Javier's head and warmed his already gushing heart.

The helicopter took off and Farrell walked back toward the family group.

"Are you all OK?" he asked.

"We're alive and uninjured," Sheree replied. "That will do for now." She wiped tears from Daphne's cheeks with her thumb. "Thank you, thank you all."

A dust cloud appeared in the distance, trailing a white vehicle with flashing blue and red lights.

"Looks like the paramedics are finally here," Sergeant Farrell sighed, as if he expected them always to be late. "They can check you're OK and deal with that wound on your head."

"Sure." Sheree used the cuffs of her robe to wipe tears off Art's cheeks and her own.

"I'm going to stay for a while and take some statements while my colleagues secure the crime scene." Sergeant Farrell pulled a tablet device from a pocket on the side of his vest.

"What time is it?" Olivia wriggled and Javier loosened his hold on her.

"Ten forty-five." Replied the sergeant. "Why?"

Olivia's eyes pleaded and tugged at Javier's heart. "We're supposed to be riding in the Kilkivan Horse Ride today," he said. "Olivia has been working toward this day for years. Can we leave the statements until tomorrow?"

Sergeant Farrell shook his head. "Procedure dictates that we get your statements as soon as possible."

"Look," Lauren said in a quiet, matter-of-fact tone. "With the car and the shot-up house, you're going to have your hands full securing and investigating the crime scene."

Sergeant Farrell glanced toward the house and car.

"We've all been through a lot of trauma this morning. I reckon it will be an important part of our recovery to do something more cheerful for the rest of the day." Lauren's expression was earnest. "Besides, I don't think any of us is going to forget what happened and certainly not within the next twenty-four hours."

"Very well then. But I need to know where you'll be staying."

"Staying?" Sheree pulled away, leaving Daphne safe in Art's arms.

"Well, you can't stay here. It's a crime scene. You'll have to wait until forensics is done with the place. Could take a couple of days." Sergeant Farrell seemed oblivious to the distress this news caused. "By the sound of those gunshots, I reckon the house will need some repairs too."

Sheree tensed up.

"You can all stay at our place." Lauren turned to the sergeant. "Can they retrieve some items to tide them over, you know, toiletries, clothes and the like?"

Sergeant Farrell waved down one of the officers clad in navy-blue. "My officers can escort you in to make sure you don't interfere with any evidence."

"OK everyone." Lauren gestured toward the house. "Let's get to it." She delegated tasks.

Sergeant Farrell approached them. "Javier, isn't it?"

"Yes, sir." Javier still held Olivia's hand. After nearly losing her, he was reluctant to let her go.

"What you did, going in there and retrieving the women, was idiotic, foolish and went against all rules and common sense."

Javier was too stunned for words.

"So, I will be personally recommending you for a bravery award." Sergeant Farrell held out his hand.

Javier exhaled in relief and shook the outstretched hand with his free one. "Thank you, sir. I just did what needed doing."

Olivia squeezed his other hand.

Sergeant Farrell looked satisfied and walked off to instruct his officers.

Debrief

Under police supervision, Olivia and her family retrieved personal items from their home. They emerged to find Lauren and Javier had caught Vanilla, groomed all three horses and released Aztec into the house paddock. The police wouldn't allow them to take their phones as they were declared evidence.

Sheree and the women set off for Lauren's house in Sheree's SUV, leaving Javier and Art to hitch the horse float to Art's twin-cab ute, load the horses and tack and set off for the Kilkivan Showgrounds to finalise registration.

It helped that Lauren's house had three bathrooms. Olivia was assigned to Lauren's ensuite. She could barely believe, after everything that had happened, she would still get to participate in the Ride. She showered slowly, letting the warm water wash away the dust. The floral-scented soap and shampoo obliterated all traces of the intruders' foul stench. With every passing moment, it became easier to concentrate on the Ride and push the events of the morning further back in her mind.

Part of her twinged with guilt, tugging her to spend the afternoon comforting her mother and sister and helping them to recover, but most of her wanted to enter the Ride with Javier. Thankfully Lauren's words to Sergeant Farrell had convinced her family the Ride would be therapeutic for them all. Besides, she couldn't think of anyone better than Lauren to tend to the emotional well-being of her family for now.

Olivia emerged into the living room clean and refreshed wearing an aqua shirt embroidered with a white leaf pattern and her newest riding jeans, the pockets embellished with white embroidered swirls. Two long braids bound with aqua bands dangled on her chest. She padded across the tiles in thick cotton socks, a sand-coloured Akubra hat in one hand and her duffel bag in the other. She looked to James, who stood triumphantly behind a scattering of plates bearing biscuits and cakes on the island bench. "Where shall I leave my bag?"

James sprang into action and took the bag from her. "I'll put it in Elise's room for now." He pushed a cup of hot tea in her direction. "Lauren is waiting for you." He tilted his head toward the lone figure out by the pool and scurried off in the direction of Elise's room.

Olivia gratefully sipped the tea and made her way out through the sliding glass doors.

Lauren turned as Olivia approached. "You were heroic today, Olivia. I'm so proud of you."

Olivia leaned on the pool fence, holding her cup between her palms to extract its warmth. "We both know who the real hero was today. Without your intervention with the Universal Language and the dragon ..."

"Without your heroic actions, my interventions would have come to nought. You and Javier were so brave." Her expression warmed and she placed an arm around Olivia's shoulders. "Sometimes it's not about being a hero; it's about skilling up and being part of a heroic team."

Lauren was right. It was the three of them working together and using the Universal Language that saved the day. Javier would get most of the credit, she just got some, and amazing Lauren would get little, if any. Lauren seemed OK with it and Olivia was too—too much attention really wasn't her thing.

"Something's bothering you?" Lauren pulled her hand from Olivia's shoulder back to her cup.

Olivia pulled away. "The police statements. I mean, we have to tell the truth. How do we not mention the Universal Language?"

"We can tell them what we said and what we did and even how we felt, but we don't have to tell them everything we were thinking."

That answer satisfied, but something else also bothered her. "Daphne."

Lauren patiently waited for Olivia to find the words.

"Daphne was always so loud and bossy and she ordered my parents around. I thought of her as the most powerful one. Yet..."

"Rudeness, arrogance and bluster do not indicate power. Worse still, they may mask underlying feelings of inadequacy or powerlessness. As soon as the bluff is called, it all falls away."

"And they are left helpless like Daphne was?"

Lauren sighed, pulled her lips tight. "Yes, I'm afraid so." She gestured for Olivia to enjoy her tea. "Don't worry. With help she can recover to be stronger and more confident than she was before, but without the hubris."

Olivia looked quizzical and sipped from her cup.

"Remember Dr Bell in Gympie?" Before Olivia could reply, Lauren was distracted by movement in the house.

The door opened and Sheree emerged. "May I join in?"

"By all means, Sheree." Lauren smiled graciously. "We were just discussing how we could all benefit from some sessions with Dr Bell over the coming weeks to help us recover. You'll help me persuade Javier to come along, won't you?" Lauren glanced at Olivia with a raised eyebrow and a one-sided smirk.

Olivia saw what Lauren was trying to manoeuvre. "Absolutely." She turned to Sheree. "Mum, I really think we need this, especially Daphne."

Sheree glanced back at the figure wafting into the living room with hollow, empty eyes. Until this morning, that figure was her brash, eldest daughter. "I'll make the appointments first thing Monday."

They went back inside to avail themselves of James's hospitality and comfort Daphne.

* * *

There was single knock at the front door. It opened and a bubbly, laughing Henry cascaded in, soon followed by Charlie. She scanned the sombre assembly. "What's happened?

"I'll fill you in later," James said, as he replaced the empty pot of tea with a fresh one. "Charlie and I are teaming up to cook tonight's dinner," he added, in response to the quizzical looks from his guests.

"James promised to teach me how to make that awesome Thai curry." Charlie pulled a bundle from her bag and held it up triumphantly. "Lemongrass, as requested."

James took a stem, wafted it under his nose and inhaled deeply. "Just divine."

Daphne wandered over to where Henry was pulling some toys out of a box onto the rug. "Do you mind if I stay here till later?"

Lauren gazed at Sheree, who initially frowned. "After this morning ... I'd rather not let you out of my sight." Her expression soon softened. "I'm sure that will be fine. It would be good to have someone keep an eye on Henry while our cooks are making dinner."

Olivia watched all this unfold and saw the tell-tale signs of Lauren using the Universal Language to shape the situation to everyone's advantage. Lauren obviously sensed that Daphne was pleasantly distracted by the company of little children.

The Kilkivan Horse Ride

Kilkivan Showground was a sea of horse floats, SUVs, small trucks and utes. As many as possible were clustered under the grand old gum trees scattered about the grounds. Horses and people in Akubra hats flowed around and between them as muffled voices addressed the crowds over the outdated speaker system.

Lauren stopped her car on the track amid the bustle of riders and their supporters.

Olivia wound down the window and was hit by a burst of warm air bearing the mingled aromas of horse poo, barbequed sausages, diesel and beer. The atmosphere was one of camaraderie and anticipation. Olivia tingled with excitement but wondered how they were going to find Javier and Art in the equestrian crowd. It would have been much easier with mobile phones. She focussed on quelling the excitement and calming her breaths so she could communicate with Javier.

"The first group of riders who set out on Friday morning for the two-day ride are all well and all on schedule." The friendly male voice over the speaker said. "In a few hours they will join the group that set out this morning for the one-day ride. Registration for the half-day ride has now closed. All participants begin making your way to the starting area."

Had Javier completed registration on time? Would they still be riding? She tried to quell that too.

A soothing thought came from Javier: all was well.

She relaxed and sent out a *"where are you?"* thought. Barely a moment later, she saw in her mind the image of a grand old gum tree leaning to one side at the edge of the equestrian city, with the disconnected ute parked on one side of the horse float and the horses standing calm, tied to the other side. Olivia opened the car door, stood on the step and scanned the horizon for a matching tree.

"Over there!" Olivia pointed to show Lauren the direction, resumed her seat and shut the door.

"They're at the leaning tree," she said, still pointing out the direction.

"I see them." Lauren turned the vehicle about and drove over the grass.

They weren't actually visible from where they were, but Olivia understood what Lauren meant and smiled acknowledgement.

Lauren pulled her car up beside Art's ute and they all tumbled out. Art appeared first from behind the float and looked about for the missing person.

"Daphne has stayed to help with little Henry. They'll join us later," Sheree said as she moved in to hug her husband.

Olivia all but leapt onto Javier when he emerged. "We're in then?"

"Yep," Javier replied and gave Olivia a squishy hug. "You smell like flowers."

Olivia leaned back. "Is that good?"

"It's lovely." Javier drew her even closer to him.

Olivia relaxed in his arms until he loosened his grip and guided her around the float to the waiting horses. They were all tacked up and ready to go, sporting bulging royal blue saddle bags embossed with the logo of the Kilkivan Horse Ride.

Javier applied a large adhesive number to the back of her shirt and a smaller version to the front. They matched the labels he already wore. "You are now officially tagged and ready to ride."

Olivia bounced with delight and kissed him on the cheek. "Thank you."

Javier gestured toward the saddle bags. "One side has a water bottle and the other has some treats from local food businesses for afternoon tea."

"The horses have had lots of practice with saddlebags bearing snacks," Lauren said as she appeared around the float. "They've had lots of practice walking the local terrain too. You've prepared them and yourselves very well."

"I'd feel much better if they had their phones," Art said as he approached the horses with Sheree trailing behind. "If something should happen out there."

"We'll be just fine, Dad." Olivia smiled to reassure him. "Javier, the horses and I will take good care of each other."

Lauren winked in their direction. "Compared to this morning, I'm sure surviving this afternoon will be a snap."

Olivia intercepted a "*Don't worry, I'll take care of them*" thought from Lauren and grinned. She sent back a "*good luck with that*" thought and stifled a giggle.

"What's so funny?" Sheree asked.

"Nothing," Olivia replied. She exchanged a knowing glance with Javier.

"It's time to mount up and head to the starting area," Art said as he positioned a mounting block beside Vanilla.

Lauren insisted on giving each of them, and both horses, a good luck hug. Olivia found it strange that Lauren's hug made her tingle a little.

"Good luck!" Sheree called after them as the pair disappeared into the sea of riders flowing toward the starting area.

* * *

Vanilla and Max stood calm and steadfast at the starting line. Not so some of the other horses. The jingle of keys on one rider's belt agitated another horse. It was about to rear and its young rider was suddenly terrified.

Javier and Olivia exchanged a glance and Olivia sent the thought, "*I'll calm the rider. You take the horse.*"

The pair turned in the direction of the commotion, a few horses away from them. The horse settled and looked their way. Max answered with a reassuring nod and snuffle.

The girl exhaled in relief and patted the horse on the neck. "Good girl."

Olivia and Javier exchanged a "*nice work*" thought and subtle grins that no one in the assembly noticed.

"OK, go!" a voice called out from the front of the mob.

The start was an anticlimax after all Olivia's anticipation, but a horn or gun would have spooked some of the horses. Olivia was comfortable and sensed that the organisers were experienced at this. The mob surged slowly forward like beads pouring from a cup.

Soon the mob spread out. Some of the riders rode single file, and some two or three abreast, along the dirt cattle tracks. A warm breeze wafted over the fields and the smell of the encampment gave way to the scent of eucalyptus. Buzzing, sticky flies began to target anyone not wearing insect repellent. The numbers built up until some of the riders were wearing black-backed shirts, their label numbers completely obscured. They waved the constant onslaught of flies away from their faces.

Olivia leaned back to check Javier's shirt. Not a single fly to be seen, nor any circling his face.

"Have I got any flies on my shirt?" Olivia turned in the saddle to show Javier her back.

"Not a one," he replied.

"That's strange. I didn't use any insect repellent at all and yet they're avoiding me."

"Seems to happen after Mum hugs me." Javier swayed with a relaxed, fluid motion in the saddle. "I always figured it was her cologne."

Olivia recalled that the flies always avoided Lauren on their training rides. She suspected there was more to it but was content to let it slide. The absence of fly-worry only enhanced the blissful joy of the ride and the warm glow she felt riding beside her beloved Javier.

Afternoon tea at the bend of a creek was a welcome relief for the horses and riders alike. Vanilla and Max drank their fill from the creek and munched on the green grass of the embankment. Tethering poles were hammered into the ground, but Olivia and Javier just hooked their reins onto the horses' saddles and sat to eat the treats from the saddle bags as the horses grazed peacefully beside them. Some of the other riders frowned, disapproving, expecting the horses to bolt off at the slightest distraction. Others seemed impressed that the horses were so well trained. Olivia and Javier had simply asked their horse friends to stay close by.

* * *

At around three thirty, the half-day group walked their horses up the hill to join the riders assembling from the other two groups. The large mob of riders milled about slowly, awaiting the call to proceed. Olivia looked down the hill. The main street was completely empty and people, like clusters of ants, moved away from the many stalls in the park and lined the road, held back by bright orange-and-white plastic barricades. Announcements over the speakers were too distant and muffled for Olivia to make out the words. From her recollection of previous years, this was when they reminded the crowd not to clap, shout, whistle, or wave vigorously lest it scare the horses. The announcements took longer than usual. She hoped nothing was wrong.

A man in army uniform riding a majestic bay gelding worked his way around the back of the mob toward the arriving half-day group. He rode up to the group coordinator and exchanged conversation. Olivia tapped Javier's arm and pointed them out. "I wonder what's going on?"

Javier shrugged and watched them closely.

The coordinator pointed at Javier and the man in the army uniform looked in their direction. He gave the coordinator a parting nod and began to ply his horse between the others toward Javier.

"I hope it's nothing sinister," Olivia said.

"I'm not picking up anything negative. Let's see what happens."

Olivia and Javier turned their horses to face the oncoming rider. Short grey hair peeked out from around the rider's hat and glinted in the light. Olivia remembered that retired members of the army light horse units liked to don uniform and participate in this ride, so she assumed he was one of those.

The rider pulled up beside them. "Javier?"

"Yes," Javier replied.

"And Olivia?" he said, turning his attention toward her.

"Yes." It was all terribly serious and formal.

"Follow me." He turned his horse and wove through to the edge of the mob.

Olivia and Javier followed in his wake. The rider led them around to the front of the mob where an officious, rotund man with a lanyard and clipboard was instructing riders.

"Javier and Olivia delivered as requested," the rider announced then turned his horse to join a straight row of similarly dressed military riders at the front of the mob.

"Very good," the official said and made a weak, improvised salute as he soldier moved away, hitting himself in the head with the clipboard. Rubbing the sore spot, he turned toward Javier. "The buggy leads the parade."

He gestured to a small, open, wooden buggy. It was painted red and sat atop big BMX bike wheels, presumably to make the ride more comfortable. The buggy was pulled by two brown ponies, brushed and groomed until their coats shone in the sunlight. The reins were held by a frail, elderly man in a grey cap and beside him, a taller and more solid man sat upright in his grey Akubra hat.

"Usually this is followed by our honourable light-horsemen." He waved his clipboard toward the row of military riders. "But I've received instructions that this year you and your girlfriend are to walk in front of our fine soldiers." His gaze bored into each of them in turn as if trying to make them out. "I don't know what you've done, but it I hope it was worthy of this. Take your positions here." He motioned to a spot directly in front of him.

Javier and Olivia moved their horses into position and exchanged confused glances.

The official strode up beside Javier and raised the clipboard to the side of his face, shielding the view of the other riders. "If I find out you've paid someone to get this spot, I'll be seriously pissed off. This is a position of honour and is not for sale."

Javier and Olivia exchanged a glance and a shrug. The official marched off to organise other riders.

Olivia leaned toward Javier. "There must be some mistake. Can't we just wander back and disappear into the mob of riders back there?"

"That might piss him off even more. Following orders seems to be a big thing at this end of the mob."

Olivia glanced back at the military riders astride tall, shiny bay and chestnut horses. They were clad in short-sleeve khaki summer uniforms with leather pocket bandoliers slung diagonally across their chests. Half their number wore wide, light-grey braces that held their leather-belted trousers uncomfortably high. The brown leather of their boots, chaps and tack reeked of fresh saddle soap. The closest one gave Olivia a stern, affirming nod that wafted the grey emu feathers on his wide-brimmed khaki hat.

Eventually the official returned to the front.

"It's fairly simple," he said. "Just follow behind the buggy all the way to the Showground."

"Yes, sir," Javier said, all formality.

The official checked his watch then slowly raised his clipboard. At four o'clock precisely, he slowly lowered it. "Go, and good luck."

The frail man shook the reins and the ponies stepped forward down Bligh Street hill. Javier and Olivia, side by side, followed behind. Olivia glanced back and saw the mass of moving riders surging behind. Scattered among the white riding helmets that near glowed in the afternoon sunlight were Akubra hats in diverse shades of beige. The riders wore shirts of all colours: white, blues, pinks and greens. Not so many dark ones because they heated up in the sunlight. There were tall, elegant riders on majestic, shiny horses. There were relaxed riders on all manner of farm horses: bay, chestnut and even palomino. There were tiny riders on small ponies riding bravely beside their parents. "Wow!" Olivia exclaimed.

Javier watched her reactions. "So, you're having a good day then?"

"I'm with you, aren't I?" Olivia grinned and immersed herself in the moment.

Slowly the parade of horses made its way down the hill. Hundreds of well-shod hooves clopped along on the road surface. At the base, the buggy crossed Council Street onto the main street, the part of Bligh Street that was also the Wide Bay Highway.

The gathered crowds leered forward over the barriers.

Olivia and Javier stepped onto the main street and a male voice sounded over the speakers. "Behind the buggy is Javier Evans, a local lad. Sergeant Farrell tells me he went into the farmhouse where the McKinnon ladies were being held hostage this morning and got all of them out uninjured." There were gasps from the crowd. "Beside him is Olivia McKinnon." Another round of "oohs" and "ahhs" from the crowd. "Sergeant Farrell has informed me that both escapees are now back in custody thanks to these two." The crowd dutifully refrained from cheering, clapping or waving, but most slowly raised their right hand in salute or mimed applause as Olivia and Javier passed by.

Olivia's cheeks warmed. She glanced at Javier and grinned; she had not seen Javier blush before. Olivia looked behind just as the entire row of solders saluted Javier. She gestured Javier to look and when he did his cheeks went a deeper shade of red.

The frail man in the buggy turned to Javier. "You won't need to pay for drinks tonight, mate." He looked forward, then turned back. "You're old enough to drink right?"

Javier nodded his head to indicate "yes" and tapped his hat. The frail man grinned and turned back to his task.

Olivia surveyed the crowd of smiling, cheering faces. At the front of the crowd, just behind the barrier, a grinning, dribbling toddler sat atop a man's shoulders. Recognition kicked in. It was Henry, his little hands grasping James's forehead. Wayne stood on one side, shoulder to shoulder with James. Charlie, on his other side, mimed a slow, clapping motion. Beside them Art had his arm around Sheree. A white dressing decorated the side of Sheree's forehead. They both beamed with pride. Daphne stood just in front of them. She held the barrier, managing a pensive grin and a tear ran down her cheek. Next was Lauren who just stood there with a warm smile. When Olivia caught her eye, she received a *"well done"* thought that felt like a hug. She turned to point them out to Javier, but he had already seen them. In unison, Olivia and Javier saluted Lauren as they passed.

Olivia spied a mop of curly, auburn hair plying through the crowd toward her mother. Dr Bell waved a business card aloft and Olivia chuckled at Dr Bell's eagerness to offer much-needed counselling services to the family.

Further along, a voice called out. "Olivia!"

Mel was promptly hushed by a group of their school friends. Olivia pointed them out to Javier and gave them a wave.

Miraculously alive, rescued by her beloved Javier from the intruders and the aftermath, she fulfilled her dream ride with the man she loved riding beside her—Olivia would never forget her first Kilkivan Horse Ride. Her heart gushed with warmth and tears of joy overflowed onto her cheeks.

* * *

By the time their families reached them at the showground, Olivia and Javier had brushed the horses down, ready to load into the float, and their tack was stowed. The sun sank low in the sky, the breeze had cooled and delightful aromas wafted from the food stalls.

"That was so awesome!" Daphne said. She hugged her sister and leaned over to give Javier a peck on the cheek. "Thank you," she said as she pulled away. Her demeanour was too mild now to correctly match her dark, streaked hair and harsh, gothic clothes.

Taking turns, each member of their family hugged Javier and Olivia until the duo were breathless.

Olivia turned to Sheree. "We're going to stay for the party. There is a band and food stalls."

"I don't think so." Sheree shook her head, her brow furrowed.

Art glanced at Javier and frowned.

"Mum, I'm not a little kid anymore." Olivia was determined to stand her ground. She braced for a loud argument with her mum, then paused and took a deep breath. She didn't have to be loud and rude to stand up for herself. After the events of the day, Olivia knew in her gut she was brave and capable and had power over her own life. "Look, Mum, Javier and I have shown that we are responsible and perfectly capable of looking after ourselves and each other. Don't worry, I'll be fine."

Sheree and Art stared as if Olivia had been replaced by a total stranger. They looked at each other and Art gently nodded a few times to indicate assent. Sheree sighed, tightened her lips and turned back toward Olivia's expression of confident determination. Olivia sensed they had caved, without another word spoken. A wave of calm confidence welled from deep within her. Her back straightened and her shoulders relaxed back; she felt taller and stronger.

"We could leave one of the cars so Javier can drive them home," Wayne said.

"Great idea," Charlie said, bouncing Henry on her hip.

"Well, that's settled." Lauren gave Javier a hug. "Be home by eleven," she whispered.

Javier sent her an *"I'm an adult now, I can stay out later"* thought.

Lauren sent back, *"Yes, but Olivia isn't and her parents will worry."*

Javier scrunched his mouth and gave a slow nod of acquiescence.

Art pulled out his wallet. "Do you have enough money?"

"Thank you, but we're fine." Javier replied. "Don't worry, I'll take good care of her Mr McKinnon."

Art stepped up to hug Olivia. "Take care, Possum."

"Dad, I'm grown enough not to be called Possum anymore," Olivia said in his ear, mid hug. "It's embarrassing."

Art released his grip and held Olivia at arm's length. "To me you'll always be my Possum ... Livvie." Art winked and walked toward the vehicles.

"Be safe," Sheree said, stepping in to hug Olivia. "And be home by ten thirty," she whispered in Olivia's ear.

The families walked off, debating who would go in which vehicle and negotiating the loading of the horse float.

Javier took Olivia's hand and tugged her behind the tree, its mammoth trunk concealing them from their families. Heavy beats and twangs signalled the band had begun to play on the distant stage and the air reeked of horses, sausages and beer. Javier pulled Olivia toward him, placed his hand around her waist and gently drew her up against him. Olivia wrapped her arms around his neck, felt his warmth against her chest and inhaled the divine scent of him.

"For a moment today, I thought I had lost you," Javier said, his tortured eyes gazing into hers. "The pain was unbearable." He placed his warm, strong hand gently on the back of her neck. "I love you, Olivia, and I don't ever want to lose you."

Olivia felt a surging warmth deep within her at his touch. The warmth then exploded into cascades of joy at his declaration. What was once a hopeless dream was unfolding before and around her. "I love you too, Javier." His face was so close, she could feel his breath on her lips. She placed her hand behind his head, her fingers splayed through his golden hair and she pulled him toward her so he could be in no doubt of her wishes.

His soft, warm lips caressed hers, then pressed with more urgency until their lips parted and their tongues danced together. Olivia drank in the taste of him and pressed herself hard against his chest, yearning to fuse as one with her beloved Javier and never separate.

"Ahem!"

Olivia was totally focussed on Javier and barely heard.

"Ah ... Olivia."

Her name caught her attention, still she didn't want to pull away. She was blissfully content right where she was.

Javier pulled away from the kiss and looked over Olivia's shoulder. "We have company."

Mel stood, smiling, with her arms folded, eyebrows raised and head tilted. Behind her their friends grinned and giggled among themselves.

"I guess we'll have to finish this later." Javier whispered in Olivia's ear before releasing her just far enough so that he still held one hand.

"Yeah." Olivia sighed and turned to face the interrupter. "Good to see you, Mel."

"Are we going to party or what?" Mel winked at Olivia.

Olivia and Javier stepped forward together and were engulfed by Mel and their friends from school. Javier kept hold of Olivia's hand and kissed it; the warmth of his soft lips sang on her skin. How much joy could one woman take? She wanted to spend years with Javier and find out. The pair and their friends melted joyfully into the crowd. This was their time to dance and sing and celebrate being alive and together at last.

Gardening

Olivia pulled up Vanilla next to the stable. It was a sunny winter's day with wafting puffball clouds and a sapphire sky. A perfect day for a ride. So, when Javier suggested he come by car to collect her so that they could spend the day together, she insisted on riding over to their house instead.

Vanilla snuffled happily as Olivia undid the girth strap, hauled the saddle and blanket off and placed them on a rail. She led Vanilla through to the horse paddock beside the stable, where Max eagerly paced to and fro along the fence line. Once in the paddock, it took a while to calm Vanilla to be still enough to remove the bridle. Not until she sent a *"keep still"* thought did Vanilla put her head down for Olivia to slip the strap over her ears.

Olivia detected a *"sorry"* thought and matched it with a *"you're forgiven"* thought as she wrapped her arms around Vanilla's neck in a warm hug. As she released her grip, Vanilla stepped back. Olivia sensed wild excitement as Vanilla turned and bounded off down the paddock with Max. They threw their heads about and playfully nipped each other on the neck.

Olivia hung the bridle beside the saddle and walked toward the house.

Beside the path lay an extensive vegetable patch ringed by an old-style fence. It seemed to be made of flimsy wood and ancient, painted, arched wire, but anyone looking closely would find the vertical posts had the tell-tale gas bubble depressions of concrete and the wire was new and taut. The arches of the wire sat proud above the top rail to keep chickens out. Chickens didn't like perching on wire. It wobbled and was uncomfortable for their feet. The fence was too tall for them to scale in a single flight.

Olivia passed by the garden as she walked quietly toward the house, her mind calm and clear, taking in the sounds and smells of the farm. A figure kneeled behind a row of bushy capsicum plants. The verdant foliage was punctuated by the bright red of pendulous fruit. A glistening white ponytail trailed behind a wide-brimmed hat. Lauren was intently concentrating on gently separating a punnet of seedlings, oblivious to Olivia's presence.

Ready to make the holes in the soil to plant the seedlings, Lauren reached out for a nearby conical dibbler, crafted from the antler of a feral deer, but it was beyond her reach. Unperturbed, Lauren kept her hand extended and the implement rose off the ground and propelled smoothly into Lauren's hand.

Olivia halted and gasped. Not only was Lauren proficient in the Universal Language, but she was also telekinetic. Was she even human? An alien on earth maybe? Yet she was Javier's mother. Did that mean Javier was only half human?

Lauren froze and frowned. She took a deep breath and held it for a moment before she slowly exhaled and replaced the frown with a deliberate smile. She raised her head. "Hello Olivia. Lovely to see you. Come to visit Javier?"

"Yes," was all Olivia could think to say. She was too surprised by what she had seen to make coherent small talk.

Lauren turned her gaze to the deep blue sky and cotton wool clouds. "Lovely day for it."

Olivia's mind raced. Should she say something? Last time she had mentioned special abilities to Lauren, there was no problem. Lauren had even taught her the Universal Language when she asked to learn. Maybe Lauren could teach her this also?

"I didn't realise you were telekinetic too," Olivia said with the friendliest, most innocuous expression she could muster.

Lauren shrugged it off. "We develop the skills we need when we need them," she replied. "You'll forget all about it soon enough."

Forget that her boyfriend's mother was telekinetic? Not likely. "I don't think so." She shook her head.

"You've watched superhero movies. What happens when the world discovers the superhero's secret identity?"

Olivia assembled the memories until a pattern emerged. "The bad guys target their loved ones." She tensed, anxious as she recalled all the horrible scenes of tormented friends and family in the movies.

"Exactly." Lauren regarded her with a gentle, knowing smile. "So, it will be safer if you forget this: safer for me, safer for Javier and safer for you. By the time you reach the front door, you will have forgotten all about it. You want to feel safe, don't you?"

"Yes, but I won't forget something like this."

"Yes, you will. It's for the best."

The front door opened and Javier appeared.

"Hello Olivia," he called out. He walked to the edge of the verandah and leaned his lithe frame against a carved wooden column to wait for her.

Lauren still wore that same smile. Olivia dipped her head in acknowledgement and Lauren did the same. She walked toward the front door, keen to be close to Javier. She would ask if he knew about his mother's ability. Maybe he could shed some light on it? But what if he didn't know? Would it cause a family rift?

As she approached the verandah, Javier stepped forward, beaming at the sight of her, and wrapped his arms around her waist.

"How was the ride?" Javier planted a welcome kiss on her forehead.

Olivia stood, tense and frowning in his arms.

Javier held her at arm's length and looked into her eyes with great concern. "Is there something wrong?"

Olivia met his gaze. "There's something important I need to ask you." She looked away into the distance before returning her gaze to Javier. "But I can't seem to remember what it was."

Javier released his hold and led her across the verandah. "Don't worry," he said as he opened the screen door. "It'll come back to you later and you can ask me then."

That seemed logical, so Olivia relaxed and followed Javier into the house.

"James has some food ready. I hope you're hungry."

Olivia glanced back. She saw Lauren wave to her and return to her planting task.

Olivia walked toward the kitchen and tried to remember what it was she wanted to ask Javier about, but she could not. By the time she reached the array of pastries James had laid out for them, she had completely forgotten that there was even something she wanted to ask Javier. Olivia relaxed and chatted with Javier about the ride and about school. She lost herself in just being with Javier in this place. Whatever the future would bring, at this moment, her life was safe and wonderful, and she set her mind to live it.

The End

Acknowledgements

Thank you Peter for your help with research and thank you to my dedicated beta readers: Leanne, Rose, Theresa and Gavin. You helped make this book better.

Books by Karin Marchen

Lyric of Vulcon

The Lauren K Chronicles:
Kilkivan Horse Ride; Annum XII
Greetings; Annum XVII

www.ingramcontent.com/pod-product-compliance
Lightning Source LLC
Chambersburg PA
CBHW020328120726
47904CB00002B/329